D0389656

GOD'S EQUAL

Alain Absire

GOD'S EQUAL

Translated by Jon Rothschild

A HELEN AND KURT WOLFF BOOK

HARCOURT BRACE JOVANOVICH, PUBLISHERS

San Diego ✦ *New York* *London*

Copyright © 1987 by Calmann-Lévy
English translation copyright © 1989 by Harcourt Brace Jovanovich, Inc.

All rights reserved. No part of this publication may be reproduced or trans-
mitted in any form or by any means, electronic or mechanical, including
photocopy, recording, or any information storage and retrieval system, without permission in writing from the publisher.

Requests for permission to make copies of any part of the work should be
mailed to: Copyrights and Permissions Department, Harcourt Brace Jovanovich, Publishers, Orlando, Florida 32887.

Library of Congress Cataloging-in-Publication Data

Absire, Alain.
[Egal de Dieu. English]
God's equal / Alain Absire; translated by Jon Rothschild.—1st ed.
p.   cm.
Translation of: L'égal de Dieu.
"A Helen and Kurt Wolff book."
ISBN 0-15-136070-7
1. France–History–Robert II, 996-1031—Fiction.
2. Robert I, Duke of Normandy, ca. 1010-1035—Fiction.
I. Title.
PQ2661.B75E613 1989
843'.914—dc19   88-30058

Designed by Kingsley Parker / Design Oasis

Printed in the United States of America

First United States edition

A B C D E

HBJ

BOOK ONE

In those days of the millennium many wonders appeared in memorial to the Christ. Unaccustomed disturbances troubled the order of the world, as if turmoil in the heavens was no longer testimony to the glory of God but a warning to men that misfortune was about to fall upon them.

So it was that on the third day after the calends of July, in the one thousand and twenty-seventh year after the birth of Our Lord, it became my lot to witness a most startling phenomenon, one that seemed to herald the terrible adventure that I endeavor here to recount.

I was still a mere adolescent. Barely out of childhood, my studies at an end, I had just arrived in Falaise, where I was to learn the arts of war. Everything at the court of Robert the Devil seemed wondrous and magnificent to me, and I waited impatiently to set out at my duke's side to confront some enemy. As an aspiring vassal of Normandy, I yearned only to be dubbed a knight and to return in glory to the castle of my father, lord of Bernay.

On that day, as had already become my custom, I retired after vespers to the library in the square tower. Alerted by the strange dimming of the daylight, I halted on the spiral staircase and looked out through a loophole. What I saw terrified me. The sky was covered with ash. The sun had turned the color of sapphire, its upper part swallowed by a first-quarter moon. Bloodred reflections, quick as sparks, glinted on the black waters of the Ante River and the lakes at the foot of the castle. The normally tranquil landscape was swathed in a thick haze. Fog masked the forest like a sinister veil, the trunks, branches, and leaves of the trees blending in a disturbing, indistinct gloom. The terrified churls had downed their tools and stopped work. They stood motionless in the fields and looked at one another, deathly pale. In the past, they knew, a like marvel had heralded the demise of Pope Benedict, John's predecessor, and foul crimes against law and justice had subsequently been committed throughout the world, in ecclesiastical and earthly domains alike. This spectacle could only mean new misfortune. Never had I seen its like, neither at my father's castle nor at the monastery of Fécamp, whence I had come.

Striving to put aside the fear that gripped my heart, I lingered behind the thick castle walls and watched the earth sink into the blackness of death. I tried to believe that such a phenomenon could have some natural cause, and called to mind the particulars of my astronomy lessons and the movements of the planets, whose paths, as Ascelin had told us, cross as they move. I pictured the heavy wooden sphere he had used to represent the world. I recalled the established order in which the constellations rose and set, and remembered how Ascelin would gaze up at shining stars and have

4

us measure their angles of incidence on the various regions of the earth. I remembered, too, the excellent device from which he hung the animal figures representing the stars in what the Latins called the "vital" circle. I calculated the positions, altitudes, revolutions, and distances of each planet. But my efforts, alas, were in vain: despite the breadth of his learning, never had Ascelin shown us the moon covering the sun.

I waited, fear dwelling within me.

Perhaps the Almighty had plunged the earth into the darkness of hell in the daytime in order to punish men for their transgressions, just as, at the close of the world's first era, He had sent the flood to destroy the disobedient. Was it possible that the light would never return, that life would vanish in this darkness? Who, then, would be the new Noah?

After an interminable time, the dark quarter-moon slowly began to drift aside and a semicircle of blazing light, extremely thin, at last burst out from the top of the sun. Though blinded, I continued to gaze upon the marvel. At first the sky remained black. Then the forest emerged from the baleful mist that had enveloped it. The bloodred reflections faded from the lake waters, a long transparent shaft of gold touched the grass and soil of the fields, a church bell sounded, and many churls, forgetting that it was not yet compline, fell to their knees to pray.

No longer believing that this had been an omen, a warning, I too began to praise the holy name of Christ Our Lord, who, having taken the source of life from us, had now miraculously restored it.

It took me several days to put the strange marvel out of my mind, and even when prayer had removed the sudden darkness from my memory, there remained within me a fear impossible to obliterate. From that day on, I was less happy at Falaise; the splendors of the Norman court, so different from my father's residence of wood, ceased to fill me with wonder. The lessons of Master Savinien, who was teaching me the handling of the sword, and of Master Helgaud, who taught the art of falconry, no longer sufficed to occupy my mind. I ceased to roam the countryside on horseback, and even the time I spent in the library each night began to seem overlong. I was restless, and again felt the craving I had known during my years of study, when, confined within the high walls of the monastery in Fécamp, I yearned to set out on some noble adventure, to serve my duke, sword drawn. I now dreamed day and night of gallop and turmoil, of attack and harsh battle, of vanquished enemies. I saw Robert, alas, only in the evening, at supper. He had ignored me completely for the three weeks I had lived in his castle. My enforced inactivity grieved me. My heart thirsted for assault and conquest, yet I remained unchallenged. I had no inkling of the events I would soon experience, the events I am recording now.

I watched the duke after vespers every night as he took his supper by candlelight, surrounded by relatives, vassals, friends of noble lineage, and the people of his household. Though he sat far from me, in the middle of the long trestle table at the center of the great hall, I did not take my eyes off him. His hair, cut straight across the forehead, and his dark beard, trimmed in the fashion of Burgundy and Aquitaine, lent great nobility to his face, which was surprisingly serious. His golden chair, his coronet inlaid with precious stones, and his long white linen tunic could have been those of a king. Five kitchen servants waited on him; two minstrels and as many musicians performed for him, dancing, leading trained animals, or singing to the glory of his exploits. Often he would turn to Arlette, his consort, who sat beside him. It seemed to me that his gaze came alive and was charged with fire whenever he looked at her.

Each night I marveled at his great wealth and handsome bearing. My boredom was forgotten as I admired the quality of the bread, the abundance of meat, and the liberal flow of wine, which, in his generosity, he offered to all those present, not only his own men but also the poor who had taken shelter in his castle. How many times did I see him cut slices of venison or pork and hold them out to mendicants with his own bejeweled hand! He was said to be harsh to the point of brutality, arrogant, enamored of gambling, hunting, and women, but his exploits had won great power and renown for his house and for the duchy of Normandy. A great lord of war, at the very beginning of his reign he had besieged his archenemy, the count of Bellême, in the latter's impregnable fortress of Domfort. Once reduced to famine, the count was vanquished and overwhelmed, forced to plead for mercy, a donkey's saddle strapped to his back, while his army and vassals watched. And Robert had won his battle against the Breton invaders, compelling their duke to pay homage. Never had he been seen to retreat on the field of battle, and many were the minstrels who roamed from castle to castle singing of his feats. Even today I can recall one of their songs, which I heard in my father's castle in bygone days.

> Robert set out
> with such great fury
> that no knight of Neustria
> was able to follow him.
> Alone, the duke charged the enemy tribe,
> a thousand Breton standards

and fifty lances facing him.
Count Arnoul in alarm
shouted to Robert to stay his steed.
But straight at the foe
the Devil did ride,
and so fiercely did he smite them
that ten lances were splintered
in a single crash.
Robert felt no fear
when he found himself alone,
but brandished the noble sword
of Rollo the Norman,
and cut and thrust
with sweeping strokes,
and slashed mail, and cracked shields
and split iron helmets.
The Bretons fought back in frenzy,
tearing off the duke's helmet
and cutting his forehead.
Long did the battle rage,
and many heard its thunder.
When the knights of Neustria
finally joined the Devil,
he was fighting still, scorning his wound,
and at his feet
more than a hundred lay pierced and slain.

But that summer, alas, his days of glory and greatness seemed over. By day there was no sign of Robert the Magnificent. He lived only for prayer and for Arlette, who had won his heart a year before, when he gazed upon her for the first time from atop the ramparts of Falaise as she, suffused with beauty by the sun, washed her linen in the clear waters of the Ante. He had ceased to dispense his justice, and he allowed poachers to empty his forests of game. Never once did I encounter him in his towers. Never once did I see him set out at a gallop across his lands, his fields and woods. Each dawn found him shut up in his chapel, where he gave thanks to God and devoutly prostrated himself before the statues of the most venerated saints. In the castle court it was said that he sometimes drew blood as he flagellated himself in tribute to the five wounds of Christ Our Savior. Some murmured that this was penance, that it was his way of seeking forgiveness for the imprisonment of his brother Richard, in whose stead he held the throne of Normandy. Master Savinien, whom I assailed with questions, at last told me that the duke had suffered from melancholy, since winter's end, and was spending too much time with Arlette and the child born of their love, William. But when Robert appeared in the evening, proud and magnificent, the living embodiment of divine beauty, my doubts faded and once again I felt certain that I would soon embark on some adventure at his side.

He ate and drank little. Erect in his golden chair, he served the poor in silence. Still, from time to time he would joke with those around him, even burst into great laughter. But the clouds that darkened his countenance swiftly returned. Arlette, seated on a coffer to his left, never spoke, never dared raise her eyes to him. I watched her too. Despite her common birth, her face was noble. A long veil, adorned with a silver fringe, covered and held her hair high on her forehead. Clasped below her slender neck with a valuable jewel, the hair parted slightly as it fell across her tunic embroidered with gold braid. Though she seemed a child beside the duke, her proud and respectful bearing gave her the look of a princess of old.

On the evening of the third Sunday after my arrival in

Falaise, Robert entered the great hall alone, without Arlette. During supper he turned toward the door several times, clearly hoping that she would appear. As I looked upon his sorrowful face that day, I realized to my misfortune that the lady had taken his heart hostage, that she had robbed him of his peace of mind since winter, and that she alone was the cause of his melancholy.

The days passed with dreary sameness. One night, the vision of darkness spreading over the earth returned to me. Jolted from sleep by my fear that diabolical forces had gained ascendance over divine power, I left the oversized bed in which, for the first time in my life, I now slept alone like a person of high birth. I went to the window and looked up at the black sky. As I gazed at the moon, it darkened to a vermilion hue, then paled again, then finally faded away, though there was no cloud to cover it. I watched intently for the first glimmer of dawn, but when it came, it failed to ease my troubled mind. When I left my room between lauds and prime to go to pray, I dreaded the coming sundown, the inevitable return of night decreed by God in His ordering of this world.

After four days' absence, Arlette reappeared at supper in the great hall, but her return changed nothing in the duke's demeanor. In the impatience of my young years (intensified by my desire to depart from Falaise and its gloom), anger at Robert's failure to lead me in a far-off adventure gnawed at my mind. As the days wore on, I became convinced that the Magnificent would never grant me the chance to prove my valor.

A fourth Sunday passed, and yet another, and the summer began to wane. Since I had no desire to make friends, outside of my lessons in weapons I spoke to no one and remained alone. During the day I listened for the bells that tolled the hours of prayer; after supper, as the sun set, I watched the candles melt on the coffer beside my bed, their wax flowing as slowly as the time that refused to pass. Torn between anger and lamentation, I came to miss the life I had lived as a child in my father's castle, and even the two years spent at the abbey school in Fécamp.

At last, on the morning of the fifth Monday after my arrival in Falaise, it was announced that the Magnificent would lead a great hunt in the forest and that he was summoning the men of his domain—barons, knights, and future vassals, the sons of his lords—to join him in pursuit of stag and wild boar. My heart swelled with joy at the news. I called to mind the celebrated hunt at the court of Richard II, which had lasted six weeks. I immediately sought out Gervin, commander of the archers, and requested that he instruct me in the handling of the bow, which I had not yet used on horseback at the gallop.

The castle, so tranquil since my arrival, was now astir. The most stalwart of hunting horses were brought to the central courtyard. Then the dogs were gathered in the second enclosure: more than a hundred pointers, beagles, and bloodhounds, whose barking and fighting caused a constant din. Twenty guards prepared pikes and other weapons and equipment. Fur-lined quivers were filled with long arrows with finely sharpened heads, and the largest bows I had ever seen in my life were set out in rows against the enclosure wall, shielded from sun and rain, in numbers more than sufficient to win a battle.

I slept little during the night before the Wednesday the duke had chosen for the hunt. Long after my exhausted candle had flickered out, I imagined myself standing before a dazzled

Robert and slaying, with a single dagger thrust, an enormous beast. I awoke at dawn to watch the final preparations from my window. In the courtyard below, grooms worked by torchlight, placing bits and bridles on a hundred and fifty blindfolded horses. One would be the duke's, and that one I would have to follow. The grooms draped cloth covers of golden yellow, brown, dark blue, or bright red over the broad croup of each mount. The longer I watched, the lighter the sky became, and the greater was my haste to set out. I dressed before prime, swiftly putting on my tunic and chausses and slipping my dagger into my belt. Highly excited, I waited for the chapel bell to call us to prayer.

A marvelous spectacle greeted us in the courtyard below as we emerged from the chapel, where the monk Granger had said mass. A hundred banners fluttered in the breeze; the bright red colors of Normandy shone on the pennants below the iron points of the lances carried by the equerries. Two gold leopards writhed on the duke's oriflamme: they, at the head of the hunt, were the insignia I would have to keep constantly in view. The bedecked horses, perfectly lined up at the enclosure wall, each tended by a shield bearer, awaited their riders. The dogs, leashed in groups of ten according to breed and size and restrained behind a wooden fence, barked loudly, trembling with impatience. The call of the horns, sharp and strident, rose in the sky. The duke came forward under the eyes of all the people of his household, who were gathered on the tops of the towers and along the castle walkways. He was greeted by a cheer as he descended the stone stairway. Bareheaded, wearing high boots, and, despite the morning chill, dressed only in a fur-trimmed tunic stitched with gold and silver thread, he walked to the most beautiful of the horses. His equerry held out his hands, fingers interlaced, so the duke could mount the tawny beast. The duke righted himself in the saddle, slung his quiver over his shoulder, took his bow and whip, and raised his hand to salute the house of Normandy. A second cheer, even louder than the first, rose from the castle's very foundations. How deeply fixed in my old man's memory is the joy, the exultation, that swept through me at that moment! How different that regal spectacle seemed from my father's modest departures for the hunt! Then Robert the Magnificent blew his horn, and all of us—barons, counts, vassals, ladies of the court, and huntsmen—moved forward to join him.

We crossed the fields at a gallop, accompanied by the barking of the dogs and the call of the horns. My horse, with its broad hindquarters and short legs, seemed heavy and sluggish; even before we reached the forest, I had to use my whip and stirrups to keep up with the duke and his red-and-gold banner. It was a cool and beautiful day. The white light of late summer dazzled me, and I found it hard to see the colors of Normandy as I looked toward the sun still low on the horizon. I did not know that this was the first sign of the failing vision that causes me so much grief today. Crossing the belt of fallow land that separated the forest from the broad fields of grain—rye, oats, and wheat—we entered the forest's edge and thundered down a narrow road through thickets of willows and hazel trees. I whipped my horse in my effort to keep up with the group just behind the duke, but the thorny branch of a shrub cut me under the ear. Onfroy de Coutances seized my tunic, pulled me back, and passed ahead of me. I nearly fell, and had to rein in my mount as it bounded forward. Now hemmed in by a throng of knights intent on pressing ahead through a passage that could accommodate no more than two at a time, I was driven to the rear of the company, where a crowd of hunters obstructed my view of the two gold leopards on the bright red banner twisting in the wind.

We slowed to a walk as we reached the tall trees, and it grew dark around me under the dense foliage. Spurring my mount, I managed to pass the knights and squires immediately ahead of me, but I was able to gain no more than a mile, for Count Guilbert de Tancarville and his four sons, riding five abreast, blocked the path. I listened angrily as the baying of the pack and the blaring of the horns faded into the distance.

Abandoning all prudence, I turned my horse into the undergrowth in an effort to catch up to the leaders of the hunt. I wandered blindly for two miles, turning left and right, ducking under low branches, sometimes stopped by tangles of vegetation, but slowly making my way forward. At last I came to a pine woods. There I halted, listened. Try as I might, I could not hear a horn, nor a dog's barking. Having no idea of where I was and fearing to remain alone in this unknown place, I decided to turn back. But I was unable to find the beech and oak trees that ran alongside the road I had so foolishly abandoned. I was lost. I looked all around, but saw only the disturbing forest, dark and lonely, full of mystery. I looked up at the sun, and when I saw how high it had risen in the sky, I realized with anger that much time had passed and that Robert's hunt was going on without me.

Once again I began to search for the narrow road where I had left Guilbert de Tancarville and his sons. I prayed for God's aid. But the low branches closed around me with their thick leaves. It became impossible to move forward.

I looked up at the treetops, looked east where the sun rises, and west where it sets. The rays of golden light reaching down through the highest leaves were growing dimmer. I remembered the moon swallowing the sun of Falaise and imagined myself wandering through the unspeakable depths of night amid evil creatures. In a panic, I spurred my mount and fled in a mad gallop. Brambles scratched my arms and legs, and a limb struck my forehead. It was a miracle that I remained astride my horse despite the pain, the Almighty undoubtedly coming to my aid for the first time. I did not know, of course, that He would do the same later, toward the end of that day so full of astonishing things. I heard the cry of a beast, and fought down the fear that a wild animal was about to leap out of the copse and fall upon me. I shivered. The treetops were lost in the cold evening mist. How distant now seemed the great adventure that would allow me to prove my daring to Robert the Devil!

And there I stood, bemoaning my fate, weeping in rage, calling for help, shouting like a fool instead of thinking. I was but a child in those days, and had no inkling what future turmoil would be caused by that disorder of mind and deed. After a long while, I thought I heard a distant barking beyond the dark shapes of the trees. I gathered my wits, urged my horse forward. Hope rose within me, for the farther I went, the closer I seemed to be getting to the pack. I came to a broad clearing whose size I found it difficult to estimate in the mist. The sun had set, and the forest was bathed in the half-light of a winter's evening. I had wandered far and wide for most of the day, and the hunt had gone on without me, others accomplishing the feats of which I dreamed. I listened again, but could not hear the dogs. Trembling from the cold, I thought of the soft warmth of the fire that burned in the great hall during supper. As I looked around, I caught a glimpse of a charcoal burner's wooden hut. I dismounted, tethered my horse, and was about to enter that poor refuge, to spend the night protected from wild beasts, when suddenly

I heard the blare of a horn, immediately followed by the muffled barking of the pack. The hunt was still under way! The duke had not returned to his castle, but galloped still, his bow at the ready, tracking the stag, pursuing the boar. Though my hopes of glorious adventure were now forgotten, my heart leaped with joy, for now my solitude and fear would end. I remounted. What happened next took place as fast as a flash of lightning in a stormy sky.

A dark shape loomed before me; in the hazy light of dusk, it seemed of supernatural size. Head lowered, the hell-black beast charged my horse. I grabbed my bow, but as I let go of the reins, my terrified mount reared, my hand shook, and in the excitement I dropped my arrow. I waited for the inevitable impact, but the beast halted ten paces away, as if restrained by some divine force. It raised its enormous head and looked at me. Never in my life had I seen a boar with a body so massive, a pelt so thick, legs so heavy, and tusks so long. Today, as I write these lines with the good sense and judgment granted me by the years, I realize that it was only a beast bigger and stronger than most others, yet in my memory I still see it as a monster. Even now, in my cell, I can see its mud-stained tusks and steaming coat—for I swear that the fur and bristles of the beast, which was exhausted by a run that had begun at the hour of sext, with the sun at its apogee, were steaming—unless it was the mist itself swirling around them.

After a long moment, I took another arrow, set it in place, and stretched my bow with all the strength my young but still trembling arms could muster. The tiny red eyes stared at me. Great was my fear, yet still I hesitated, for I felt that only the hand of God could have halted this beast in its fury. Should I not let it go its way in peace? After all, it was not attacking me. Would killing the animal be a violation of the will of the Almighty? If the game stood still, refusing either to defend itself or to flee, was it right to massacre the thing, one of God's creatures? I heard barking in the forest behind me, suddenly very close. Why had the boar not charged my horse to disembowel it? Why had it not thrown my horse to the ground and wounded me fatally, breaking my bones with its heavy paws, tearing at my belly with the sharp and twisted points of its tusks?

I looked around. In the mist, which cut me off from the rest of the world, the pack might never pick up my scent. The boar moved its heavy head but otherwise stood stock-still. Even now I wonder why God protected me thus that day, for it would have been better had He let me be trampled. My arrow flew of its own accord. Badly aimed, it sank at a slant into the boar's thigh. The beast let out a cry and tried to run—not to attack me, not to charge, as it should have done according to its nature, nor even to evade another shot, but only to flee. The call of a horn rose to the sky, and the barking emerged from the mist. The beast was now turning away, but because of my arrow its leg buckled and it fell on its side, half sitting. Four howling dogs, their muzzles white with foam, fell upon the boar as it struggled to rise, tearing into its belly, biting through its thick coat with demented cruelty. One of the dogs went for its throat and another gripped it behind the ear, teeth sinking into the bristles until blood made them red. The boar fought back. It managed to raise its enormous bulk and with a thrust of a tusk slit the underbelly of the huge bloodhound hanging from its throat. The dog collapsed in a howl of suffering and death, but other slashing teeth closed in, and the beast, caught by the leg, rolled over. The point of my arrow, still buried in its thigh, broke off, and a second dog collapsed, its head smashed. The boar raised its snout, now glistening with blood, and such was its valor that I began to wish that it might escape with its life. Paralyzed by a vision of hell that often returns to my memory even now, I did nothing, though it would have been easy (mad as it may have seemed) to shoot the two dogs and allow the beast to escape. They fought on in a tangle, their coats torn, hair covered with dirt and foam and blood. I soon saw that the duke's animals, though strong, well trained, and furious, could do no more than wound the beast before they themselves were killed.

I heard a whistling, and an arrow, its aim true, sank into the middle of the beast's powerful chest. The boar fell, still under attack by the dogs, which, covered with wounds as they were, refused to let go. Their fangs sank deep into the now defenseless underbelly between the boar's splayed and quivering legs, and red bubbling blood spilled onto the grass and earth.

A shiver cold as snow ran down my back, and the mist filled with the sound of horns, shouts, and barking. Suzanne de Brécy, her tunic covered with mud, galloped past me crying her joy with all the cruelty of a man in the thick of battle. Handlers fell upon the dogs to hold them back. Still motionless on my horse, certain that all the others must be laughing at my indecision and cowardice, I did not dare turn around to see which of the vassals of Normandy had so deftly slain the boar in my stead.

When at last I looked back, I saw the duke himself just five paces behind me. Erect on his tawny horse, his red-and-gold standard planted in the ground, flanked by two shield bearers, he was still holding his bow. He looked at me without a word.

I followed the company back to Falaise, but I kept well apart from the lords and ladies, and especially from the duke, for I had no wish to be conspicuous, lest I be questioned and laughed at. When we arrived at the castle, the entire house of Normandy gathered in the courtyard to marvel at the great number of dead beasts—fallow deer, stags, boar, birds, hares, foxes—that lay on the ground in their own blood. The grooms and kitchen servants began to slit open the bellies and chests to extract hearts, lungs, stomachs, and warm entrails. Meanwhile, I withdrew unobserved to my room, to shield myself from taunts and glances, especially those of Robert. Still wearing my muddy chausses, I stretched out on the bed, tears in my eyes, and prayed to God that the duke, annoyed at my weakness, would not send me back to my father's tower in Bernay, deprived of glory forever. "O Lord," I said, "on this day I forgot the sovereign virtue of prudence taught by the Gospel of John, most sublime of all. Carried away by my excitement, I embarked alone on an uncharted road. I lost the temperance that girds each man in his deeds. Ignoring the sign Thou hadst sent me and scornful of Thy love for all creatures, I wounded and allowed to perish the beast whose attack Thy hand had halted. I am humiliated, shamed in Robert's eyes. It remains only for me to do penance, to fast, to pray that Thou, granting me pardon, might stop the duke from sending me away from Falaise."

I remained on my bed for two full days. My refusal to go out or to eat was, of course, the result of my wounded pride more than of any real desire to repent. (My actions had been those of a youth barely out of childhood, and although they surely did not speak well for me, neither did they warrant such penance. They were serious only in that they foreshadowed my future behavior, but I did not know that then.) The sounds of the feast going on in the great hall in celebration of the duke's hunt—the voices, laughter, song—kept me awake at night, my stomach knotted with hunger. Images of roasted meat, of whole quarters of stag and boar still smoking on Robert's long table, helped me to believe in the value of my sacrifice. Convinced as I was, in my youthful simplicity, that every transgression deserved its punishment and every sacrifice its reward (as if these were articles of commerce between man and his Creator), I came to hope that the severity of my self-imposed penance would allow my prayer to be heard.

At last, at tierce on the third day, a steward came to tell me that the duke wished to speak to me. Legs trembling, I went to the floor where the Magnificent and a part of his household resided. My most painful thought as I mounted the stairway slowly, step by step, was the picture of how angry my father would be, faithful and courageous vassal that he was, when he learned that I was to be expelled from the court of Normandy and would return to Bernay without pride or honor.

Three squires led me to the room. I walked silently into a large vaulted chamber heated by a charcoal-and-wood fire that burned on the tiled floor. The duke, in the half-light at the far end of the room, was lying with his lady on the bed, above which stretched a fabric canopy supported by four golden posts. I immediately noticed the rich tapestries that adorned the entire length of the walls. In colors of brown, blazing red, and reddish gold, covered with Latin inscriptions, they boasted of the Magnificent's feats: on one wall his victory over the count of Bellême, who was shown kneeling before him; on another, his glorious rampage against the Breton knights. The third, at least sixty feet long, depicted his arrival in the far-off court of Byzantium the year before: twelve Negroes bore him on a litter covered with fine silk and regal scarlet damask, and he paid no heed to the greetings of the basileus, who bowed low before him like a vassal. Filled with admiration despite my fear, I stopped to gaze upon these beautiful works.

Robert, in a voice surprisingly soft, told me to approach. He wore no crown, but a collar of precious stones glittered on his chest against his white tunic. Stroking his beard with a hand bedecked with jeweled rings, he watched me come forward. Arlette, holding William, their child, who was less than a year old, did not look at me. I halted opposite Robert, ten paces distant, as required by the respect due a duke of Normandy, the equal of kings. I murmured one last prayer to God: "Now that I have done my penance and deserve Thy pardon, I beseech Thee, O Lord, let Robert not send me away from Falaise and his court forever!" I waited fearfully for the duke to speak, but he was silent for a long while. Could it be, I wondered, that he is still not sure what decision to make, what punishment to inflict upon me? Resigned, not daring to avert my eyes from his gaze, I did not bow my head but forced myself to look back at him like a valorous knight. He did not see my fear. As I will have occasion to note more than once in the course of this testimony, I was capable—even then—of concealing my thoughts and even of deliberately mirroring on my face feelings quite opposite to those that filled my mind. At last, to my astonishment, he smiled at me.

"Odilon de Bernay," he said without anger, "where have you been during the celebration of our hunt? I looked all over for you in the great hall. Why didn't you come, that I might have served you the meat of the boar with my own hand?"

"I was studying, my lord," I answered quickly. "Stace and Virgil, authors whose works I took from your library, are teaching me rhetoric, the art of proper speech, so precious to a future vassal of Normandy, and far better than the *Theoretical Treatise* of Victorinus, master of Saint Jerome."

Robert nodded in satisfaction. He was impressed by my lie, whose temerity and spontaneity had surprised even me. "So you prefer study to a feast," he said softly, smiling again.

"I noticed," he continued in a louder voice, "that during the hunt you single-handedly tracked down and wounded the boar whose trail we had lost after following him so long, since tierce, in fact. Despite your young age, you showed determination, good sense, and skill, virtues you share with your father, Hugues de Bernay, whose loyalty has been dear to me, as it was to Duke Richard before me."

At this, Arlette looked up. I had always been far from her in the great hall, and had never seen her so close. Though my mind was racing with Robert's unexpected words, I still had sufficient judgment to realize how great was her beauty. She wore a delicate chemise with no laces, and her neck and the top of her milk-white breasts were bare. Her long blond hair, held back by a simple thin fillet, fell to her pale shoulders. "Your valor, Odilon de Bernay," said the duke, "merits a reward, a more serious challenge, in which, I have no doubt, you will distinguish yourself no less." His lady, her wide forehead bare, continued to look at me as he spoke. I sank into her sweet, pale blue gaze and felt as though I was standing before a unique being, and thoughts spun in my head.

"I have asked your instructors about you," the duke continued. "They have a high regard for you and report that you are adept, and skilled especially in the use of the sword. Of the bow I need say nothing, for one of your arrows pierced a boar's tough hide. And though you were unable to kill it before I did, do not let that worry you: I know of no young man able to kill a moving beast with a single arrow shot from horseback."

I was unable to take my eyes off the slender lady, and began to understand why she had won Robert's heart without his offering the slightest resistance. William fidgeted in her arms, and the duke fell silent for a moment as he took his son from her. Arlette of the fair neck did not turn away, and

I wondered why she was looking at me that way. Could she see what I hid in my heart? Though her face was serene, expressing only a gentle desire to protect me, as one would protect a child, her beauty seemed a reflection of God's, of God the judge, the source of all truth, He Who likewise watched me and was deceived neither by my lies nor by my silence. I thought of confessing, of telling Robert of my confusion and my cowardice with the boar. I lowered my eyes. "You are here to learn the arts of combat," the duke now said. "Well then, it is my intention to afford you the opportunity you deserve, the chance to become a valiant man of war and a loyal vassal of mine. Is that not your desire, Odilon de Bernay?"

I was about to break my silence and say that I did not merit such great confidence, but then guessed that the Magnificent was at last about to undertake the campaign of which I had dreamed, which might now lead me onto the field of battle. I saw myself as a character in the minstrels' songs or a figure in a tapestry, in the thick of the fray, splattered with the blood of Normandy's enemies, slashing helmets, breaking bones, cutting off heads. My impulse to tell the truth of my misadventure on the hunt vanished.

"Yes, my lord," I answered, thus adding deceit and dissimulation to my past transgressions. "Above all else I wish to serve you and to prove to you my courage and valor."

"Good," said the duke. "Then listen closely. Frisian pirates have returned to the coast. They have burned two villages near Deep.* Worse yet, they massacred my prefect in Arques, Gautier, along with his wife, his sons and daughters, and a number of peasants. Three of our merchant ships have been

* In the seventh and eighth centuries, the Normans called Dieppe by the Anglo-Saxon name Deep, a reference to the depth of the mouth of the Arques River, which allowed oceangoing ships to sail into the city.

looted and destroyed in ambushes on the Varenne and Béthune rivers. The Frisians are killing our subjects and seriously hampering our trade with the lands of the North—trade that, as you must know, is of paramount importance to Neustria. In five days, seventy warriors will set out from Falaise, men-at-arms and knights, to make war against these pirates and vanquish them. It will be a hard campaign, for they are cunning, godless, merciless barbarians who murder even children."

He fell silent and looked directly at me.

"You will be among those sent to fight them, Odilon de Bernay," he said in a louder voice.

In those days tears came easily to my eyes, and they rose now as I listened.

"I will follow you anywhere," I cried with the ardor of my young years. "I will be the best of your men of war! I shall never retreat, however gravely I am wounded!"

"It is not me personally you will serve," Robert said, smiling at my outburst. "I have chosen you to be the squire of the most courageous and best loved of my vassals: Liébaut de Malbray, who, owing me service, just as he served my father, will contribute ten of his knights and will lead the battle. You will assist him in selecting his weapons and mounting his horse. You will bear his shield. And you will fight at his side."

Robert seemed to know the confusion of my thoughts: joy at the idea of the feats I would perform, but also disappointment that I was not accompanying him, the duke of Normandy, but only one of his knights, of whom I knew nothing and whose name I had just heard for the first time. So he told me that he loved Liébaut de Malbray as an intimate friend, that he felt for him an affection such as one would feel for an older brother, and that to serve Liébaut de Malbray was to serve the duke himself.

"Upon your return after the victory, Odilon de Bernay," he added, "should Liébaut de Malbray attest to your valor, you shall swear fealty to me on the Gospel, and by the rite of homage become my knight."

The duke's words turned my life upside down. Every face I chanced upon, every voice I heard, everything I looked at, seemed different.

I did not know whether the joy of the battles to come would wipe away my disappointment at fighting so far from the duke, the sole and true prince-protector of Normandy. Sometimes my mind would burn with visions of the wonderful adventure that awaited me, and then the sunlight falling upon the court would suddenly illuminate the walls, the towers, the castle walkways, and the wooden shelters of the guards and servants with fresh force and clarity. The colors of the world were transformed around me: the gray of the walls was no longer dull, and the filthy blue tunics the peasants wore as they toiled in the fields shone like the azure midsummer sky. I read friendship in every face, even the most serious; every object, even the ancient low-backed chair in my room, seemed beautiful and well made. In these moments of joy, every castle stone, every saint's statue in the chapel, every parchment in the tower library, seemed to belong to a plan, unknown to me, that was connected to the Creator in a new and wonderful way.

But no sooner would I recall the image of the duke, conqueror of the Bretons, depicted in the tapestry, than my ardor would fade. Who was this Liébaut de Malbray, of whose exploits I had never heard the minstrels sing? Had the duke exaggerated his attachment to this unknown knight? And had he perhaps magnified the dangers awaiting us on the coast in order to convince me that he held me in high esteem?

Perhaps he had seen through my miserable behavior during the hunt and really intended to banish me from Falaise, but in a way that would not taint my father (whose wisdom and loyalty he valued) with dishonor? Had I committed the sins of falsehood and dissembling, turning away from God yet again, to no avail? To what penance would I now have to subject myself to atone for them?

In the end, these doubts extinguished the joy of my impending adventure, and after sext, when I was supposed to join Master Savinien for my lessons in handling the sword, I returned instead to my room. There was little light in the cold chamber. The old broken chair, like everything else, had reverted to its former drab appearance. Without thinking, driven by some higher power, I picked up the weapons and armor my father had given me before my departure from Bernay, put on my greaves and hauberk of mail, tied my hood, strapped my belt around my waist, and donned my helmet. Grasping my shield in one hand and my father's sword, with its heavy, jewel-encrusted pommel, in the other, I felt strength rising within me. I stood straight, and the power of the fighters of the North filled my heart, just as it had in my childhood games when I pretended to be Erik the Red, our ancestor, outfitting his *drakkars*, or Rollo, whom Snorri Sturlson called the king of the sea, conqueror of Rouen, Evreux, and Chartres, the first duke of Normandy, a man so tall he could find no horse big enough for him. "I offer you my arm, Liébaut de Malbray!" I cried. "I place it at your service! Do with me what you will, but spare me neither effort nor danger!" I knelt on the floor, bowed my head, and imagined Robert the Devil in the chapel of Falaise dubbing me a knight before his assembled household and vassals. But the vision eluded me and, greatly vexed, I felt my newly recovered fervor vanish.

I did not want to be alone, so I left my armor behind and went down to the courtyard to join Master Savinien. Perhaps he, a loyal follower of the duke for so many years, would know the true reason the Magnificent was sending me to fight the Frisians on the far coast with Liébaut de Malbray. I feared this man Savinien, whose head was shaved not out of penance but because of scabies; he had a low brow, thick bushy gray eyebrows, close-set eyes, small and cruel, a scar on his cheek, the souvenir of an old wound, and a broad and deeply wrinkled face. Without a word he handed me a sword and watched me as a master watches his pupil. I gripped the pommel of the weapon tightly and began to strike the wooden manikin with reckless fury. Was the old warrior aware of my impending departure? I attacked so strongly that some iron links of the manikin's hauberk were shattered and the helmet on its rough-hewn head rolled to the ground, dented and split. Then I stopped, out of breath, my forehead covered with sweat.

"If you fight like that against the Frisians," my teacher muttered in his gruff voice, "you'll be slaughtered in the first battle. You were wild, the swings of your arm too wide. No protective measures. The least skilled enemy would have been able to cut you down ten times before you struck him once. If you intend to fight that way, Odilon, you would do better simply to pray that God grant you life and eternal peace."

So he knew!

"Master," I said, finally daring to speak, "pardon me, but my mind is in great turmoil. Not that I fear the battles that await me. On the contrary, they are a source of joy the like of which I have never felt. And fear not: I will protect my life as I fight, for your lessons are rooted deep in me. But tell me, master, why is our lord sending me to the farthest borders of our duchy, and under the command of a knight of whom no one, not a single minstrel, sings the exploits?"

I saw in his face that my words had angered him deeply.

"You callow fool!" he cried. "Your body has strength, but your head is empty! Assigning you to the service of Liébaut de Malbray was the greatest gift Robert could have granted you: he offers you the example—and may you retain the memory for the rest of your life!—of the most virtuous of all the lords of Neustria. If you have heard no songs of his exploits, it is because your ears are deaf. What did the monks teach you in that school in Fécamp? Do you know nothing of Duke Richard's siege of Auxerre in the year one thousand?"

"No," I murmured. "They taught me the three arts of the trivium, the sciences of arithmetic, music, geometry, and astronomy, as well as medicine, law, and theology. But they said nothing of the battle of Auxerre."

"Pay attention, then," he said, "and you will learn something. It was under the command of Duke Richard, father of our lord the Devil, that we became masters of Auxerre after a bitter siege, and this for the glory of Robert the Pious, king of France, who was then suzerain of Normandy. But you probably don't know that either."

The more he spoke, the greater was his anger and the whiter the scar on his cheek.

"I was there, fighting at Liébaut de Malbray's side. He was a young man then, as was I. It was our first war, and the most beautiful we have ever fought."

"But nearly thirty years have passed since then, and you are almost an old man," I interrupted impatiently. "Is he as old as you?"

"Do you mean that age diminishes the valor of a knight, the skill of a swordsman?"

"No, of course not, but the years can rob the arm of strength and the heart of passion."

"Does my arm lack strength?" Savinien threatened, red-faced. "Would you like to test its strength, arrogant youth?"

"Master," I replied in a low voice, frightened, "I did not mean to question your valor, and well do I know the strength of your arm. It is just that I was surprised to learn that Liébaut de Malbray is no longer young."

"I am older than he," answered Savinien, placated by my fear, "but few years separate us."

He looked at me for a long moment. It was disappointment more than anger that I now read on his brow.

"You judge people and things without knowing them, Odilon," he said. "I saw Liébaut de Malbray fight the Bretons at the Devil's side, and they all fled before him. He was the first to enter Auxerre, smashing through a heavy postern with an axe and penetrating the city alone, in advance of the knights of Neustria. He rushed blindly through a hail of arrows and fought like a lion, ignoring the shaft lodged in his side, which was pulled out in the very heat of battle. Sometimes even now it causes him pain. In those days he was only a squire, just as you are. But so great were his feats that Richard had him swear fealty immediately, dubbing him a knight in the hospital of Auxerre, while barbers and nuns cleaned and dressed his still-bleeding wound. Since then he has performed many other feats worthy of song. Like our Neustrian ancestors and our fathers of the North, Liébaut de Malbray is generous, a lover of justice, a defender of the poor. He is kind to all. His mind is well balanced despite his wrath in battle, and, unlike you, he will entertain no thought unless convinced that it is good. So stop asking schoolboy questions, Odilon, and think like a future vassal of Normandy. Be thankful you are to accompany such a lord. Try to learn wisdom and goodness from his example. Convince him of your valor, and he will give you the chance I know you are waiting for."

I woke up early the next morning, shortly after matins. Savinien's words, though stern, had rekindled my yearning for adventure. My swordmaster had spoken so passionately of his former companion, the conqueror of Auxerre, that even though I still felt some regret that I would not be accompanying the duke himself, Liébaut de Malbray now seemed a true lord of war, and I eagerly awaited his arrival in Falaise two days hence. I hoped that his body would be free of the signs of age that furrowed the face of Savinien, only a few years his elder. A warmth burned in my breast, and once again the world seemed brighter. Even before dawn, I had no doubt that the rising sun would sparkle. All I needed to complete my joy was to recover the sense of my own virtue and nobility, which had been obliterated by my sins of foolishness, recklessness, confusion, and falsehood. I prayed to the Almighty. "I thank Thee, O God, Who has forgiven my sins, sparing me the dishonor I deserved, and now brings to fruition my dream of glory. Bestow upon me Thy mercy and kindness, lead me on the good road to perilous adventure, guide me, help me to believe in my own courage and valor, so that fear neither cloud my judgment nor paralyze my arm. Protect me against myself, against my errors as well as against my enemies, for the glory and honor of my name and of my father's." Having said my prayer, I dressed. Then, as I awaited the dawn, a sudden desire came over me, to do something to restore my faith in myself.

At this point in my account, truth compels me to note that, like all God's human creatures, I was not solely a repository of evil, for there were also times when goodness filled my heart, ruled my mind, and guided my actions. Such was the case that night, when I had the courage to combat, and finally to overcome, the fear and shame that had plagued my mind since the unhappy day of the hunt.

So it was that while the sky was but faintly lit by the moon's pale glimmer amid clouds swept along by breaths of wind, I went down to the courtyard and took a horse. Armed only with a dagger, without waiting for the hour of lauds to herald the first light of day, I who had so feared the darkness of Falaise set out in the black of night. I forded the Ante at a gallop, thoroughly spattering myself, then crossed ponds so dark they seemed bottomless. I rode through a countryside filled with mysterious shadows and reached the edge of the forest. There, in a pure act of will, I set out on the narrow road of the hunt.

Heart pounding, I plunged into invisible places heavy with menace, seeking to prove my courage to myself. I slowed to a walk, lest thorny branches scratch my face. Without looking back, guiding myself by the pale shimmer that showed through the clouds now and then, I urged my horse toward the tall trees, the thick foliage, the gnarled and twisted branches.

Defying my fear of hidden beasts, witches, demonic forces, and the impure spirits that turned into man-eating wolves by night, I forced myself to leave the road of the hunt, just as I had done three days before, and turned into the undergrowth. Once again I covered two miles, murmuring prayers to the Almighty that He protect me from the dangers that surrounded me. Often I raised my eyes, and through the gaps in the branches I glimpsed the moon, a mysterious shape that moved amid drifting clouds. Fear, the greatest I had ever known, made me sweat despite the biting cold of the wind in my face. A hundred times I felt a consuming desire to turn back, and a hundred times I drove that desire from me, and ignored the cracking, the strange sounds, the howls of hidden beasts. For a long time I wandered blindly. An animal's half-human shriek made my blood run cold. I gripped my horse's bridle with one hand and took out my dagger with the other, but by the grace of God I did not lose my head, and though I dreaded some terrifying encounter, I refused to turn back. Then faint streaks of violet light began to drift down through the leaves that covered my path, and I knew that God had protected me, that day was finally dawning. I had kept my head in the hellish night, and now I had but one desire: to find the boar's clearing. "Then and only then," I whispered to myself, "will I be sure that I am courageous enough, that I am enough the master of my own mind, to fight the barbarians with Liébaut de Malbray."

I did not know which direction to take. Several times I crossed a stream that I had not encountered during the hunt. Daylight slowly penetrated the forest, and hunger, a sign of the passing hours, soon gnawed at my stomach. As I cast about for the place I remembered so well, I finally recognized the broad stretch of pines where I had lost my way three days before. Convinced that I was now on the right track, I urged my horse to the right, but when I came upon a pond and another road, I realized that I was lost again.

But despite my weariness I persisted, and finally chanced upon the clearing. A great feeling of pride swept over me. This time there was no mist, and I could see the distant copse and the tall trees. I rushed forward as if into battle. With sweeping strokes of my arm, I mimed visions of war. Now rearing back, now veering to the side, turning in all directions, I slew more than twenty Frisians and saw their blood-soaked heads roll on the grass. Deep in the fray, ten paces from the charcoal burner's hut, howling with fury as the Devil did in the fight against the Bretons, I disemboweled thirty of the enemy, leaving them to perish on the field of battle, their bones broken. Finally, exhausted, I decided that I had won.

I remembered following the company after the death of the boar, and I easily made it back to the castle by vespers. Covered with dust, I hurried to my room, and there, unable to control my impatience, I picked up the sword my father had given me and spoke to it as though it was one of God's creatures: "You will strike the Almighty's enemies who are massacring Christians and burning churches on the far coast. Together we shall conquer. At the side of the lord Liébaut de Malbray we shall punish the Magnificent's adversaries, we shall destroy them."

Liébaut de Malbray arrived in Falaise at sext. I had climbed to the top of the donjon at dawn to await his arrival, and I saw him from afar as a cold sun shone high in the sky. He crossed the fields and forded the Ante at a gallop, ahead of the ten men of war who followed in his wake. I recognized him even though I had never met him: dressed in his hauberk, he sat straight in the saddle, his black horse throwing up dust around him. I could sense his tall stature, the strength of his legs, the breadth of his chest, the power of his arms, arms that could deal great blows to the enemies of Normandy. He rode to the gate and entered the outer, then the inner, court-yard, where the duke came out to greet him. He dismounted. His helmet, with its iron nose guard, still concealed his face, which I was eager to see. He approached Robert as a vassal does his lord, but was so big that he towered over the Devil, who was himself not small. He bent his knee, but the duke immediately bade him rise, took him in his arms, and held him close, as one holds a dear friend. They spoke for a moment, neither releasing the other.

Then Liébaut de Malbray finally uncovered his face. He had a gray beard, and the hair on his head was cut short. Though no longer young, he did not look like an old man, as Master Savinien did. Despite the distance that separated us, his face seemed noble to me. The duke smiled as he listened, and everyone saw he was happy to see Liébaut again.

Together they went into the castle, and I had to wait until supper (with what impatience!) to get a closer look at my future master. I was the first to arrive in the great hall. I took my place at the long table and watched the preparations for the meal: the kitchen servants spit-roasted the game, the vassal knights and barons arrived one after the other and sat down on coffers before their bowls and still-empty goblets. A minstrel came forward to sing, bread was cut and wine was brought, but the duke's and Liébaut de Malbray's seats remained unoccupied. An uneasiness came over me, one I could not understand. Today it is easy to call it a foreboding.

At last, after what seemed an endless wait, Robert, Arlette, and Liébaut entered the great hall, and from that moment on I did not take my eyes off my new lord. As I have written, Liébaut de Malbray was not a young man, and at first I thought him marked by time more deeply than I had realized when watching his arrival from atop the donjon. His hair was as gray as his beard, deep creases ran across his brow, and two furrows went from his nose to the corners of his mouth. Though his face was not unlike that of certain saints whose stone-carved images stood in churches, I was disappointed as I beheld him beside Robert. He could have been the duke's father.

They served him wine and a piece of meat on bread. He began to eat languidly, still talking to Robert and to Vilgard de Chambois. I was reassured to see that his teeth, unlike Master Savinien's, were not black, that the curl of his lower lip suggested some cruelty, and that his square jaw and slightly protruding chin left no doubt as to his strength of will. Although his warrior's features were satisfyingly harsh, his smile seemed too genial—and I saw it often enough that night. His long hooked nose gave him the profile of a bird of prey, yet his dark blue gaze gave his face a glimmer of kindness that spoke of a purity of soul more usual in a lady of great beauty than in a man of war. Power and amiability—those were his two faces, and at the time I felt that they struggled against each other. I admired his proud bearing, his broad chest, his uncommon size, but I did not like the slowness with which he ate, nor the gentility with which he addressed those around him. I did not realize then that those graceful gestures and that smile were merely proof of the extent to which Liébaut de Malbray was the master of his own mind and body.

Unlike Robert and the other vassals, he drank but one goblet of wine. Several times he made the duke's household laugh, but from my remote position I could not hear what he had said to amuse the knights and barons. How well I remember that meal! Was this the conqueror of Auxerre? I yearned for him to look at me and dispel my doubts. When I think of Liébaut de Malbray today, it is his face that evening that first comes to mind, golden in the light of the torches; it is those broad shoulders and chest that I see again under his gray fur-trimmed tunic clasped in front by leather buckles. It is painful to remember him leaning over Arlette's soft shoulder and fair neck to whisper some friendly word in her ear. That gesture, repeated three or four times, now seems to me a sign, a portent, of the evils to come.

Tonight, as I sit here writing, Liébaut de Malbray is present in my cell, seated across from me behind the duke's long table in the great hall. He smiles, strong and upright. Slowly he brings a piece of roasted meat to his mouth. His hand, free of rings or jewels, is large, made to wield the heaviest of swords, to cut down the enemies of Normandy. At this moment his dark blue eyes rest upon me. Their fragile, tender glint contradicts the severity of his features. Does Liébaut de Malbray, who knew me young, proud, reckless, and foolhardy, recognize me now as I recount our story by flickering candlelight? Can he see me now with my shaven skull and bowed back, my face lined by old age, my half-blind eyes forcing me to lean so close over my parchment that I practically lie atop my worktable? And if he does see me, what does he think of me, after more than forty years?

Liébaut de Malbray spent the entire day with the duke, and to my astonishment it was not he but Vilgard de Chambois who took charge of the preparations for our departure. Try as I might to attract his attention during supper, which was the only time I saw him, he ignored me completely. Even when he spoke to the vassals of Normandy and the ladies and people of Falaise from his place behind the table, his eyes never met mine. It was as if he was unaware that I was to be his squire. Was he contemptuous of a mere shield bearer? My unease, my torment mounted. I was angry at my father for not having made sure, before sending me to the court, that I would serve only the Magnificent, and none other.

On the day before our departure, however, to my surprise, Liébaut de Malbray came to speak to me, joining me as I practiced with the sword one last time under Master Savinien, his former companion. Dealing blows to the wooden manikin, I did not see him approach. "You are skilled, Odilon de Bernay," he said to me softly, almost in a whisper. "I have been watching you. You have strength and strike with vigor. This pleases me, for I need a squire such as you to accompany me into the heart of the fiercest fighting."

I did not know how to respond. He stood three paces from me, and his great height and bird-of-prey profile were so impressive that I felt like a mere child beside him. But then he smiled, and I could not help feeling, as I had felt in the great hall, that his gaze was too genial for a warrior as proud and impassioned as the Devil. And his beard seemed too gray. "Watching you," he went on, "I recognize the precious teachings of Savinien, whom I would dearly love to have taken with me to fight the enemy on the far coast."

"You know I am too old," my master said, "to follow you in such an adventure."

"You are the best among us," Liébaut replied. "No knight of Falaise has greater strength and skill than you."

"I have no confidence in my arm any more," the old man answered. "The sword seems heavy to me these days."

"Come, I am nearly as old as you," said one of Liébaut's men, who stood slightly to the rear, a giant who followed him everywhere like a shadow. He was a Viking like those of my childhood visions: florid skin, long blond hair, a full beard, a long dagger thrust into his belt. One eye was permanently closed by a sword stroke so violent that it had caved in his brow and left a scar across the side of his face. "If I didn't know who you are," the man said with a burst of laughter, "I would say you were afraid of the Frisians."

"I'm not as strong as I once was," Savinien said, his voice trembling with anger, "but strong enough to stuff those words down your throat."

"Calm yourself, my friend," Liébaut said quickly and smoothly. "Neither Bernon nor I think you a coward. On the contrary, all Normans know of your valor, and no one has forgotten your many exploits. My faithful Bernon, like me, is simply grieved not to have you at our side in our coming fight. He believes that victory would be more certain were you in our company, and he speaks rashly, spurred by the regret that you will not be among us."

Savinien nodded, but I could see that his pride was hurt. Liébaut took him by the arm and held him close. "In our hearts you will be with us," he told his old friend. "And you will be with us in the valuable lessons you have given this boy. His exploits will be yours as well, and he, like us, will be in your debt. Odilon de Bernay," he said to me, "will you not do honor to your swordmaster, the best in all Normandy?"

"Yes, my lord," I answered, lowering my eyes.

"We leave tomorrow before dawn," Liébaut said in a tone that reminded me of my father. "You will carry my weapons and my shield. Be ready at matins. Sleep well, and pray God give you strength, for winter approaches and the road to the far coast will be long and hard."

"Who goes with us?" I asked without raising my head.

"Vilgard de Chambois, Séguin de Brécy, and sixty men of war besides my own, who are commanded by my faithful friend Bernon. Our army will be the most fearsome in Normandy," he added, but too softly, I thought, and with insufficient determination. "The enemy who threatens the duke's trade and the inhabitants of Arques will be destroyed before next summer."

He fell silent, and I decided to look up at him, that he might not take me for what I really was, a dissembler. He stared at me. His blue eyes seemed to see that in my heart I judged him ill. "You shall stand at my side, Odilon de Bernay," he said, his voice protective, "at all times and in all things. I do not know you, but Robert has spoken of you, of your superb tracking of the boar. I am delighted that it will be my duty to teach you the harsh craft of war."

I could not sleep that night, not because of the adventure

on which I would embark before first light, but because of Liébaut de Malbray's kind words. I could not get them out of my mind. My new master, like the duke before him, was deceived about my worth, though I had tried to atone for my transgression and to prove my courage to myself. The Almighty would not look kindly upon this lie. The thought of my departure brought me no joy. Gloomily I looked at the equipment spread around my bed: my well-lined greaves, my sturdy hauberk with its hood of close-linked mail, my belt, my helmet with its nose guard, my chausses with leather straps, my oval shield, my sword. There would be no glorious combat, no violent fray, no honor, no exploit worthy of being sung, for my lord was too old, his eyes too kind, his voice too soft. "Why, O God," I murmured, "can't the Devil lead this expedition himself? Then everything would be wonderful."

In the middle of the night, finding no rest, I went to the window and looked out at the black sky.

Before long, I saw two stars fighting each other under the sign of Leo. The smaller, coming from the west, pursued the larger, brighter, and more beautiful, which came from the east, and tried to stop it from approaching. It fought furiously, flailing its mane of sparks. The larger star turned in a wide circle and spun around, spewing streaks of fire. Then it fell upon the smaller, casting it into the distance toward the dark regions whence it had come.

It was then, as I was about to go off to war in the retinue of a knight too gentle, that I feared the Falaise night once more.

BOOK TWO

I have neglected my testimony for several days now, and though tonight I lean over my parchment anew, my four candles have already burned so low that I know I will not write for long. The nocturn bells soon will sound, and we monks of Jumièges will don our coarse floor-length cowls and smooth our goatskin blankets back over our straw mattresses. We will slip on our night shoes, draw our hoods over our shaven heads, and form our procession through the abbey's dark corridors to the latrines. Then, in the absolute silence of our meditation, we will file past the tombs of the sons of Clovis, the Stricken Ones, who, chastened for having risen up against their father during his long pilgrimage to the Holy Land, ended their pain-racked days in Jumièges. Crossing the Basilica of Our Lady, its construction nearly complete—with its lantern tower said to be more than three hundred feet high, the tallest of all the abbeys of Normandy—we will repair to the chancel of our church on the far side of the chapter house. Taking our allotted places, we will bow low and then straighten, performing the *ante et retro* greeting.

Then we will sing the fifteen psalms, among them the hymn composed by Saint Ambrose, and read passages from the Old and New Testaments and from the writings of the scholars and church fathers. Only after all this has been done will we return to our cells to go back to sleep.

The flames of my candles will surely be spent by then, the time for writing past. Such will be my just penance for this night too, and I will take up my story again tomorrow night.

On this winter's night in the seventieth year of the second millennium, one thousand and thirty-seven years after the Passion of Christ Our Lord, I return to the testimony I have undertaken so as to warn all men, in writing, of the moral pit into which they can fall, as I did.

There is one, and only one, reason for the silence I have maintained for many nights now, and that is the astonishing pleasure that came over me as I wrote my account of my own transgressions. For I have found that, despite the physical discomfort I feel as I sit hunched before this parchment, my writing, which breaks a silence of more than forty years, far from constituting a penance, has instead aroused an unforgivable pride in the depths of my heart.

Indeed, the further my account carries me from the customs of these times—in which men are content merely to sing the exploits of their heroes—the more strongly does my mind nurture the hope of producing a work of beauty.

If I have kept away from this parchment, refusing to add a single word to it for several nights, it is because every sentence I write becomes a source of pride—and thus leads me in the direction opposite to the goal I seek, which is to sink, through the shame of my past, into the most complete, the most silent humility. Can it be that there is joy in the act of giving new life, by writing, to even the cruelest of memories? Can the mere joining of words into phrases become a source of satisfaction and delight? I had no idea that such a pleasure existed. What value will my penance, my testimony, have, if it causes me not pain but self-contentment?

Yet I must go on.

Fortunately, this new sin I now commit in the sight of God causes me fresh torment and thus becomes an unexpected form of castigation. As of dawn tomorrow I will punish myself by once again donning the hair shirt I wore during my first five years in Jumièges, after my withdrawal from the world. Once again I will mortify my flesh through fasting. Until I complete my testimony, I shall refuse to receive the Eucharist, instrument of salvation, for did not Christ Our Lord say: "He who eats of my flesh and drinks of my blood shall have eternal life and resurrection"? For a time, then, I shall deny myself the gift of the most Holy Body of Jesus, which I no longer merit. I shall refuse that grain of holiness in daily life, for it is forbidden to him who feeds upon it unworthily.

Such will be the just expiation of my pride, which even in my penitence makes me a slave to arrogance and places a thick shield before my heart.

We set out on the Wanbert road before daybreak. The duke himself came to salute our departure. In the courtyard of his castle he held Liébaut de Malbray close one last time. "May God protect you," he told his friend, wishing him a safe journey and victory in battle.

"In three days I will send you a message telling you of our arrival in Arques," my new lord assured him.

Robert nodded. "I will pray for you," he promised. "Come back to us quickly, that we may celebrate your glorious return."

Master Savinien approached me as the warriors of Falaise, dressed in their hauberks, embraced their wives and children. "Be sensible in all your deeds, Odilon," he advised me, placing his heavy hands on my shoulders. "Don't let your fervor run away with you. Think before you act. If you act wisely, you will become a worthy knight, and be the pride of Normandy." I thought I saw a tear in his eye as he spoke. Today I realize that the old man had grown to love me despite his severity. The monk Granger, custodian of our souls during the war we would wage, blessed us all, Crucifix in hand, in the name of Christ Jesus, whose true image he brandished. The gates were opened, and as I took my place behind Liébaut de Malbray, whose lance and shield of silver, azure, and sable I carried strapped to my saddle, I saw to my surprise that Suzanne de Brécy, dressed in men's clothing, was coming with her husband, Séguin, and that Draco, her dwarf, a juggler and half-magician whose evil powers and wickedness I feared, was unfortunately accompanying her. It was Bernon Hildetand, not Liébaut, who rode in front as the seventy-one men of war, my lord and I among them, filed out of the inner courtyard. Despite my uncertainty and the memory of the two battling stars, I felt proud and noble riding through the gate of the outer enclosure behind the red-and-gold colors of Normandy.

Pondering Master Savinien's words of advice, I looked at the broad straight back of Liébaut de Malbray three paces ahead of me, and though I was disappointed that he was not yet at the head of his men, I resolved not to be quick to condemn him. "Protect me, O Christ," I murmured, "Thou Who dost live and reign in the centuries of centuries, that by Thy grace we may return conquerors after destroying those who deny Thee and sow evil and death on the far coast. Guide me in Thy mercy and kindness so that, delivering Normandy from its enemies, I may earn the glory I so ardently desire." Setting a brisk pace, our hauberks clinking and our weapons clattering, we crossed the Ante, skirted the forest, and amid joyful shouts of eagerness to fight the barbarians set out into the vast countryside, accompanied by two kitchen servants, a lady, a priest, and a dwarf dressed in fiery red.

The day dawned gray and cold. I remained close to Liébaut de Malbray and was sorry to see him still in the midst of his army instead of at its head. Séguin de Brécy and Vilgard de Chambois rode up to Liébaut, each in turn, and he told them both that we would reach Wanbert before sext. Soon we left the broad plains of the Falaise region for more hilly pastures. We arrived at the outskirts of Dive between tierce and sext and there were greeted by Lesceline, the wife of Richard's brother William and thus the aunt of the Magnificent. She lived in the community of Benedictine nuns she had founded after her husband's death. We halted at the monastery and took our first meal of the journey.

Liébaut, who carried a message from the duke, withdrew with Lesceline, and we remained in the guest hall, its walls painted with scenes from the Gospel of John: Jesus walking on water, the healing of the blind child, the resurrection of Lazarus, Christ's triumphant entry into Jerusalem, the Crucifixion, the apparition to Mary Magdalene. We were served salted beans lightly fried in lard. When the dwarf Draco saw that our goblets were filled only with water, he loudly demanded wine, but his howling, which made Suzanne de Brécy laugh until tears came to her eyes, drew no response from the sisters, whose impassive faces seemed to be made of wax. To no avail did he wring his hands and tear his hair.

I stayed apart from the others, sitting on the stairway throughout the entire meal, and noticed that the men of Falaise, far the more numerous, kept their distance from the warriors brought by Liébaut. I saw exchanges of glances between the two groups and heard whispers that seemed charged with distrust. I decided then that there was bad feeling between the men led by Vilgard de Chambois and Séguin de Brécy and those commanded by the giant Viking Bernon Hildetand.

We set out again, making haste. Liébaut, strangely silent, still rode in the middle of his army. We passed through a thick forest, but Bernon easily found his way despite the absence of any marked trail, and soon we were again among rolling verdant hills, urging our horses on. Suzanne de Brécy continued to laugh at the antics of her dwarf, whose mount stuck constantly to hers. Annoyed by her cries of delight at Draco's every nasty trick, I finally asked my lord whether it was wise to have brought the lady and her jester to war with us. "Séguin wanted them to come," he answered. "For the moment, they are having fun, not bothering anyone. When the fighting starts, they'll stay out of the way. In the meantime, their joy pleases the men of Falaise." His tone suggested that he was not happy they were with us. But if he did not want them, I wondered, why had he accepted them in his army? Did he lack the power to say no to Séguin?

Troubled by these questions, I paid no further attention to the peasants who stopped their work to greet us as we got closer to Lisieux, or to the women and children in the villages through which we passed, who clapped their hands as we rode by. I barely noticed the two thieves lying in wait in a deserted spot for some solitary traveler. They fled before us, leaving their clubs and poachers' knives on the roadside as though they belonged to someone else.

Twice Vilgard de Chambois approached Liébaut to ask anxiously if he really thought that we could reach Rouen the next day and Arques after only three days' journey. Liébaut assured him both times that it was possible to cover such a distance in so short a time; indeed, it was necessary to do so, for every hour that passed on the far coast without us threatened fresh massacres. How astonished I was to hear my lord, though he rode in the middle of his army, suddenly speak with such resolve! I thought that I would never understand this man, who seemed sometimes so self-effacing before his men and sometimes so proud and determined. I looked at him for a long while, at his eagle's profile, his great height, his broad Norman chest. Toward evening, as we prepared to cross the Touques River, he turned to me and said, in that gentle manner that so displeased me, "Here we are in Lisieux. How do you feel, Odilon? I trust this first day on the road was not too rough for you."

"No, my lord," I said. "We have encountered no difficulty, and I am not the least bit tired. Were it up to me," I added pointedly, "I would continue until nightfall. Then we would be sure to arrive in Arques in two days."

"We all need rest," Liébaut answered, without a trace of the anger I had foolishly hoped to hear in his voice. "To reach Rouen tomorrow, we will have to leave at dawn, for the city is far and the route arduous."

We stopped at the episcopal residence of Bishop Herbert, who was expecting us, having been informed of our coming by a messenger from the duke. The old man greeted us with many a smile and much kindness. Even before we had removed our helmets and slaked our thirst, our swords still at our sides, he led us to the site of the church whose construction he was directing. Half of its façade and a massive steeple already rose over Lisieux's great square. Behind stood the walls of two naves, separated by three broad brick arches set obliquely against one another like ears of corn, as well as numerous sturdy pillars arranged in the form of the mysterious *T*, the still-imperfect image of the Cross, that appeared to Ezekiel. Finally he took us into the underground crypt consecrated to Our Lady, filled with long vaults and closed on the eastern side by vaulted apses. "It will take another ten years to complete," the bishop said. "I will be long dead by then, but someone else will finish it for me."

"It is a wonderful piece of work," said Liébaut. "You can be very proud of it."

"It is my entire life's work," answered Herbert, his voice trembling.

I did not sleep alongside my lord that night, nor did I look after his equipment or his bedclothes and pillows, as my squire's duties required. Invited by the bishop to sleep in the episcopal quarters, he disappeared with his host immediately after the meal without saying a word to me. He was served by the monks in my stead and did not reappear that evening. Unhappy that he had not asked me to follow him, I had trouble falling asleep among the men of our army, despite my weariness. Lying in the darkness of the dormitory on a straw mattress near Bernon Hildetand, who snored loudly from matins until we awoke at lauds, I fretted over Liébaut's humility and self-effacement, over the presence among us of Suzanne de Brécy and her wicked dwarf, and over the hostility between the men of Falaise and of Malbray, having seen more evidence of it that very evening in the refectory. That is what I was like in those days: tormented constantly by things weighty and by things inconsequential, incapable of distinguishing between real dangers and those born of my own mind.

We left the next day before dawn, as Liébaut had said we would. I had not had enough rest. Upon our rising I was irritated to see one of the bishop's monks, in my place, helping my lord don his tunic and hauberk. Liébaut had not demanded that his own squire dress him. Yet had he not told me in the Falaise courtyard, in Master Savinien's presence, that I would be at his side "at every instant and for all things"? With anger in my heart I set out behind him on the road to Rouen. To make our departure even more unpleasant, it was raining heavily. Our horses' hooves sank into the mud; the horses carrying our baggage, seven in number, with packs tied one on top of the other along their flanks, were unable to keep up. It was then that Liébaut gave his first order: that the coffers and sacks be redistributed so the beasts of burden would carry loads no heavier than those borne by the knights' steeds. We were thus able to quicken our pace, and my anger was forgotten as I followed Liébaut, who, streaming with water, galloped from one end of the army to the other, encouraging, urging, commanding everyone, even Suzanne de Brécy, wrapped in a woolen blanket, to move faster.

In Bayeul, only four leagues from my father's tower, Bernon told us to dismount and connect our horses with rope in order to ford the Calonne River, which was swollen by the rains. One by one we entered the icy waist-deep water and crossed to the other bank. I wondered whether my lord's command to redistribute the horses' loads would remain an outburst with no sequel. Remaining close to him all morning, as required by the service he seemed to consider of such little consequence, I often saw him lift his arm and press his hand to his side, as if to soothe a pain. I recalled Savinien's words about the arrow lodged in his chest during the siege of Auxerre and removed in the heat of the battle. My swordmaster, then, had not lied about the exploits of this lord. "But the past, alas, is gone," I murmured. "Liébaut de Malbray is no longer the glorious knight of yesteryear, but a man near old age. And we have set out not to conquer Auxerre but to fight barbarian murderers."

We moved forward with difficulty, and I had the satisfaction of hearing Liébaut reject the entreaties of Vilgard de Chambois and Séguin de Brécy that we stop at the church of Saint-Martin to rest and eat. "We must be in Rouen tonight," he said. We rode in silence. Even Draco, looking grotesque in the rain, had stopped joking; huddled in his saddle, shivering and miserable, he kept quiet, his deformed head drooping forward on his chest. Soaked to the skin, our faces spattered with mud, we pressed on through the forest of Saint-Peter. In Brionne, Liébaut conceived an idea that enabled us to cross the Risle without much difficulty. He had shields placed over the holes in the bridge there, and as Bernon with the God-given strength of his bare hands stooped over and pulled together several dangerously separated planks, Liébaut himself led our horses across. I noted that Vilgard de Chambois and Séguin de Brécy left the command of the crossing to my lord and the giant Viking. It occurred to me then that whereas Bernon was surely the foremost of our warriors, Liébaut de Malbray became, as of that day, their leader and protector. In my heart I felt the beginning of warm joy.

The rain fell relentlessly. We came to resemble a band of beggars with our filthy wet clothes and sad red faces. The road between the Risle and the Seine was so long and difficult that we did not reach Rouen until well after compline, as black night covered the land of Normandy. Half dead from cold and weariness, we crossed the dark moat and passed through fortified gates illuminated here and there by a few torches sheltered from the downpour. We rode through the sleeping town, its narrow streets accustomed at that hour only to roaming dogs, who, shivering, their muddy coats plastered to their bodies, seemed to lack the strength to flee before us. My mount plodded ahead. I followed Liébaut like a blind man, my teeth chattering, but he kept his head high and remained steady on his horse. At last we reached the fortified castle built by Duke Richard I, the Fearless. There, gathered around the fire in the great hall, we drank wine in silence and ate the hot vegetables, cheese, and honey cakes they served us. The monk Granger said a long prayer thanking God for having allowed us finally to reach the city in which we were to rest, and Liébaut congratulated us all for the determination we had shown that day.

Without further ado, we took dry woolen blankets from our coffers and retired to seek some brief repose before lauds. As our warriors left to bed down in the chilly dormitories of the men-at-arms of Rouen, Séguin de Brécy and his wife, Vilgard de Chambois, Bernon, and Liébaut and I were offered large bedrooms heated by fires. I was so tired that I felt no real delight when my lord asked me to follow him. As was my duty, I ignored the discomfort of my own cold and sodden clothing and helped him remove his hauberk and greaves, both heavy from the rain. Alone with him for the first time, I looked upon his nakedness and, as if my benumbed mind was coming back to life, soon found myself admiring the firmness of his chest, the breadth of his shoulders, the strength of his arms. "Dry me, Odilon," he said. "I am cold."

I picked up a thick cloth and began to rub his broad back, his hard belly, his long legs. How can I explain today what I felt then? It was as if a burning force, his force, entered into me as I stood so close to him. Despite the cold that made me shiver, a warmth I had never known before swept over me, a warmth so overwhelming, it set me ablaze like a dry twig licked by a flame. How can I describe it now, forty-three years later, without abasing the memory? It is sad to realize how inadequate words can be, despite their power! I was so frail beside him! And yet, near his flesh, it was as though I too had suddenly become one of Normandy's most manly lords, without performing a single feat. His skin reddened as I rubbed it with zeal. When I touched the wound that deeply scored his side, I had a sudden vision of him at Auxerre, when, not much older than I, he broke through a gate with his axe and entered the besieged city alone.

I could not resist asking, "Why, my lord, do you not march at the head of your army?"

"There is no need," he answered. "Bernon holds that place for me. My time to lead my men of war will come."

He was silent for a moment and then, as I continued to rub his chest with all my might, he took my arm and stayed it. "You warm me better than the fire does," he said, smiling. "I thank you. You will be a good squire, Odilon. Robert did well to place you in my service." The flame that burned within me turned my face crimson under his penetrating gaze. I stepped back and once again lowered my eyes, so that he would not be able to read my thoughts. "Your legs are shaking, Odilon," he said. "Remove your hauberk and your wet clothes, put them near the fire with mine, wrap yourself in my blanket, and come and lie in our bed. An even harsher day awaits us tomorrow."

So great was my weariness and so deep the warmth within me that I fell asleep immediately in the wide bed, wrapped in the thick blanket beside my lord. No dream or vision troubled my sleep, and my memory of that night is one of absolute confidence and repose.

I opened my eyes the next morning because someone was shaking me awake, and when I looked up through the haze in which I floated, I saw Liébaut de Malbray's face leaning over me. "Let us go, my squire," he said in a voice that seemed to come from far off. "We must go now." I struggled up on my pillow. My lord stepped back, smiling. He was already dressed in his hauberk, and his sword hung from his belt.

"Why didn't you wake me earlier?" I cried. "I should have helped you dress!"

"Don't worry," he said with a laugh. "I managed. But if you don't get out of this bed right now, it is I who will have to fetch your greaves for you and tie the straps of your chausses. It is almost lauds, Odilon. Time is pressing. It has been raining all night, and the road to Arques will be difficult. We cannot delay."

I dressed and joined the men in the courtyard as fast as I could. They were tying up the baggage, once again distributing the load evenly on all the horses. It was still raining and, despite the Latin prayers the monk Granger intoned as we trudged through the dark streets, we were soaked even before we reached Rouen's moat.

The journey was more taxing than the day before, for the wind was stronger, hurling sheets of icy water into our faces. We leaned forward, heads on our chests, necks hunched into our shoulders in misery, following Bernon single file like a long procession of blind men. Was this the proud army of Normandy? Shortly before daybreak we entered a wood of incredible size. I don't know by what miracle or what science Bernon managed not to lose his way on a narrow path that, surrounded by thick foliage, seemed to wind in all directions. At dawn we climbed slippery hills that caused several of our horses to fall. Among those who fell was Draco. To my great pleasure, he rolled in the mud squealing like a stuck pig. Then we crossed broad plains and went through many villages, in whose streets no one, not a single woman or child, came out to watch us pass. Liébaut still rode in the middle of his sorrowful army, but through the trials I endured under the roiling sky, the image of his powerful naked back, his broad chest, and his red skin as I rubbed it in the room in the castle of Richard the Fearless stayed with me and gave my heart new strength. On this day, as before, he rejected the entreaties of many of his warriors and refused to stop at sext. Ignoring both the complaints of the men of Falaise and the fatigue of the horses, who stumbled more and more often now, he ordered us to keep moving.

Despite the slowness of our progress, Liébaut's determination—and Bernon's unfailing sense of direction, which always seemed to tell him where we were—enabled us to cover eleven leagues, and we reached the Varenne River before evenfall. But there the treacherous rain-swollen current forced us to halt. "We'll never get across," Vilgard de Chambois shouted. "No one can ford this river."

Liébaut looked at the gray water strewn with stones and mud, then turned to Bernon. "Is there a bridge farther on?" he asked.

"Yes," the giant said. "About half a league from here, just at the entrance to Bois-Robert."

"Let us go," my lord said. But, realizing how upset his men were, he now rode to the head of the army to take command himself. "Perhaps," I thought hopefully, "he has decided that the time to lead his men has finally come."

Rain poured from the sky, and there was thunder. Some of the men muttered, accusing Liébaut of arrogance. Then the exhausted mount of one of the Falaise warriors, weakened by cold and hunger, collapsed under its rider and died as if struck by a bolt of lightning. But Liébaut urged us on, leading us along that raging torrent of a river. I loved to see him like this. Séguin de Brécy had to take his lady onto his own mount, for she was no longer able to withstand the storm. Had he finally realized how foolish it had been to bring her along on this adventure? Granger began to speak to God in Latin, asking that He come to our aid.

When we reached the bridge, we saw with despair that part of it had collapsed and could no longer support the weight of our army. We stopped in our tracks. Night was near, and fear rose within us. "Take the ropes holding our baggage," Liébaut suddenly shouted, "and tie them end to end. Run them through the planks of the bridge and anchor them to the largest trees." When that was done, Bernon, at a gesture from my lord, walked courageously over the tottering bridge, which ten times nearly gave way under him. When he got to the other bank, he strung two other ropes through the loose planks, just as we had done on our side, then tied them around the trunks of the largest trees there. It was raining so hard that I could barely see him as he carried out this perilous task. Yet I knew at that moment that he was the most valiant among us, and that Liébaut had shown great wisdom in entrusting the leadership of our army to him.

"Now wrap the ropes around the nearest posts," my lord ordered, "and pull, all together, until they break!" It was done. The foundations gave way, the bridge fell, and I watched in admiration as it hit the water and floated like a raft, bobbing in the turbulent current but held firmly in place by the four ropes tied to the trees on the banks. The men of Falaise, followed by those of Malbray, had only to cross in single file, holding their horses tightly by the bridles as each carried one of our coffers or sacks. Liébaut, at whose side I doggedly remained, stood on the bank and yelled to the warriors not to separate, but to walk across slowly, and above all not to let go of their mounts. Thorfin alone was felled, by a gust of wind, but though the sack he was carrying was lost to the swirling current, he managed to recover his frightened horse and lead it to Bernon on the opposite bank. Liébaut and I were the last to cross, walking over the shifting floor, over the river that threatened to sweep us away at any moment.

As I was about to set foot on land, a particularly strong sheet of rain nearly cast me into the water. Liébaut grabbed me by the arm and quickly righted me. Though this was no great feat, it was then that I felt that I need fear nothing as long as I remained at his side.

It was night when we entered Arques. It seemed that the rain would never end. No man-at-arms stood guard, and no one stopped us as we crossed the half-destroyed enceinte of wood and hard-packed earth. Bernon had taken the lead again, and we rode in silence down a narrow street bordered by wooden houses covered with thatch and grass. No torch burned in any of the homes, and many dwellings, in varying states of ruin, lay open and abandoned. As we passed the church, one side of which was in ashes, I began to wonder if indeed anyone was here, for there was no sign of life, not even a stray dog. As if in answer to my question, I heard a soft tinkling to the right, a sound like bells. It was a string of amulets in shapes depicting both the hammer of Thor, Viking god of war, and the Cross of Our Christ: proof that men still lived in this place. Hanging from the branches of a tree, the amulets swayed in the wind, knocking against one another.

We started the climb to the tower at the crest of the high promontory of Arques. Here too an entire length of palisade and enceinte had been destroyed. The peasants were defenseless against the Frisians, just as we had feared. When we reached the outskirts of the castle, Bernon let out a curse. The moat, filled with earth and uprooted trees, no longer isolated and defended the stronghold; there was no secure area. Burned-out floors, shattered roofs, and broken walls were all that remained of the stables, the barn, the bakery, the kitchen and its hearth, and the houses of the men-at-arms and the retinue of Gautier—the foresters, marshals, tenants, and domestic servants. All that was left of the tower itself was the ground-floor storeroom and half of the next floor. The other floors, reserved for the lord and his children and servants, and the castle walkway and the roof were gone: charred wooden posts stood naked against the sky. No one could live in or defend this spot.

Many of our men, seeing the wretched state of the place which we would have to hold all winter long, began to complain and lament their fate. We dismounted. A strange dread in my heart, I was the third to enter the remains of what had been the tower, following Liébaut and Vilgard de Chambois. We walked on a carpet of ash and could still smell the fire that had reduced the floor to charcoal. At first I was surprised that the whole castle had not burned in the attack, that some walls still stood, but then I realized that the besieged Gautier must have had time to extinguish the blaze before being so cruelly slaughtered along with his children and the people of his household. We found only empty grain coffers. Though the stairway was half destroyed, Liébaut took a resin torch and climbed to the great hall. I followed him, pretending to be unconcerned that the blackened steps might give way at any moment.

On the upper floor, which was open to the sky and soaked by the rain, we found only a broken armchair, two trestles, and the overturned wooden frame of a bed that had fallen from the room above along with pieces of the floor on which it had stood. I wondered who had removed the bodies of the defenders, of Gautier and his children, and who had carried off their swords and other weapons. The Frisians or survivors in the village? I waited for Liébaut to speak, but he remained silent, as did Vilgard de Chambois, who was frightened by what he saw. Finally my lord knelt, and in the rain, which fortunately had now lessened, he prayed to God in a voice loud enough for everyone to hear:

Lord, be praised
for having protected us
and for leading us safely here.
Glory to Thee, great God,
Master of all succor,
who embraces and enters all places,
preserving the army
that fights in Thy name.
Glory to Thee, God of power,
Master of wind and flowing water,
of rains and storms,
who has willed that we reach
this far-off place unharmed.
Glory to Thee for eternity!
And may Thy mercy never cease
to protect us from danger,
but may it stay with us
until the cruel barbarians
who profane Thy blessed name,
who destroy Thy holy churches,
perish in this place
by our hand and our glorious swords!

Our army stood in silence. My lord rose, removed his helmet, stood at the top of the stairway, and told the warriors gathered in the storeroom below to post six guards, wrap themselves in their blankets of wool, take shelter from the rain, and go to sleep. "At dawn," he added, "we will begin to rebuild this tower and its surrounding defenses, and to clear the moat. We will bring strength and security back to this village, which has suffered too much."

After dividing the cheese and the few loaves of now soggy bread that we carried with us in our baggage, all of us, the men of Falaise and of Malbray alike, huddled together for warmth under what remained of the ceiling. It took me a long time to fall asleep. Lying next to my lord, pressed against him as he was pressed against me, I spent an amazing night. Though I knew that the Frisians might launch a sudden attack, I felt no fear. It would have been easy for our enemies to slaughter us that night, for we would have been unable to defend ourselves, numbed by the cold and the rain and exhausted as we were. Yet peace and confidence filled my heart.

Liébaut fell asleep before me: soon I could hear his regular breathing and feel his breath on my face. We were wrapped in the same blanket, our chests touching under our wet clothes. The image of his powerful back and naked belly turning red as I rubbed them in our room in Rouen came to my mind. This memory alone was sufficient to drive away fear of the enemy. I understood now why he led his army as he did, and I admired his wisdom, which had enabled us to cross the river and had brought us safely to Arques. The true virtue of the conqueror of Auxerre, his nobility, lay not merely in strong arms and broad shoulders; it lay most of all in his self-control, which allowed him to act only when necessary. Like a child seeking protection, I clung to him more closely as he slept in that devastated tower, clung to him until I could feel his hard belly against mine, and his chest against my lips and on my face. I felt his strength pass into me, just as it had in our room in Rouen, and I was sure that if I held myself against him like this often enough, by the time our war was over I would be like him.

Soon it stopped raining, and as I lay there with my lord in the ashes of spent fires, looking up at the black sky through the gaping hole in the ceiling, I told myself that I had loved this day, despite its trials, more than all the others of my life.

We awoke at dawn, having passed the night free of attack. Liébaut woke up before me and roused me from my slumber. When I opened my eyes and saw him standing there, I regretted for a moment that my deep serenity had been broken. The memory of that night remains sweet.

From the hilltop we were on at the foot of the ruined tower, we looked out at the valley that stretched beyond the port of Arques to the high cliffs of the coast and the sweep of the endless sea. Behind us we could see thick forest and the three rivers over which we ruled: the Varenne, the Béthune, and the Eaulne. They flowed together and poured into the wide gray water at Deep. The grandeur of the countryside seemed to us a true mirror of divine power, the very image of the infinite richness of creation. We prayed. Unhappily, in the daylight, more clearly than at night, we could see the extent of destruction in the village and the port and how badly Gautier's defenses had crumbled, completely breached in many spots. The rebuilding of which Liébaut had spoken the night before seemed impossible.

Because the rain had stopped, we could take off our wet clothes and put on the dry linen shirts, thick breeches, and long tunics we had brought in our coffers. Bernon divided the little bread and cheese that remained. Liébaut, ignoring the hunger we still felt after this brief meal, ordered us into the forest to hew and chop wood. "The palisade around the castle must be repaired before nightfall," he said, silencing the complaints of some of the men of Falaise, "and we will do that whatever the cost. We cannot remain here unprotected."

Bernon led sixty warriors armed with knives and axes into the forest, while Liébaut and I went down to the village, accompanied by Draco the dwarf, who could not refrain from screwing up his already ugly face, and Suzanne de Brécy, who refused to stay in the tower with her wicked jester-magician as her only protection. As we walked through the streets looking for villagers, I noticed strange figures carved into the bare trunks of the bark-stripped trees between the abandoned dwellings. When I asked my lord about one of them, which depicted a knight mounted on an eight-legged horse, he explained that this was a representation of Odin, the greatest of the Viking gods, and his magic horse, Sleipnir, born of the union of a stallion and the giant Loki, who had both masculine and feminine forms. "Like many villagers who live far from the cities and monasteries," my lord added, "the people of Arques remain attached to the beliefs of our ancestors. They pray to our Christ, but also invoke the dark and bloodthirsty gods brought from the North by Harold the Dane, by Oger and Ragnard. In their minds they confuse the triad of Odin, Thor, and Fria with the three persons of the most Holy Trinity. They defer to the practices of religion, but they retain their own beliefs."

We had almost reached the enceinte outside the village when we saw, coming toward us, a group of men dressed in breeches and thick hooded cowls similar to monks' robes. They looked threatening, for they were holding tools of the field, spades and hoes, and brandishing them like weapons. They halted about twenty paces away, and from that distance the oldest of them, a man with a rugged face, a white beard, and long hair parted in the middle of his skull, called out in a voice of command that we were to stay where we were and come no closer. "What do you want here?" he asked in bad Norman mixed with Germanic and some unknown or distorted words. "Be on your way! There is nothing for you here."

"We are knights of Robert the Magnificent, duke of Normandy," Liébaut replied proudly, "and we come in friendship, to bring your village back to life, to rebuild your church, your defenses, and your tower, and to protect you from the Frisian enemy. We come to combat and destroy him, that the land may recover its joy and wealth."

"Go!" the old man shouted. "We have been at peace in Arques, at peace since Gautier lost his life fighting the pirates of the North, just as you wish to do. We have made an alliance with Ubbo, their chief, who holds two of our sons hostage, and we have promised to do nothing against him. We live in harmony now and will rebuild Arques without you. Go back and tell that to your Duke Robert, who did nothing to save Lord Gautier in his time."

Liébaut, surprised by this reply, was silent for a moment. I saw him frown, and thought that the churl's speech had caused him anger. "Who are you? What is your name?" he finally asked the man softly, with a smile on his face. Observing his great skill and self-control, now more than ever I regretted having judged him so harshly.

"I am Thorer," the man said, "chief of the peasants of Arques. You must go! If you stay, Ubbo, who has not attacked us since Gautier's death, will kill our two children. You cannot defeat his army, the cruelest and most fearsome we have ever seen. He will kill you, and kill us as well for having broken our agreement. You must go!" And he turned to his companions, all of whom nodded in approval of his words.

"The Frisians interfere with Normandy's trade," my lord answered. "They burn churches, plunder monasteries, and slaughter priests, men-at-arms, and peasants such as you. We must restore peace in this land, from Deep to Bois-Robert. Be advised, Thorer, that our warriors are the strongest and the most valiant in Normandy, and that victory will be theirs. But I understand your fears—they are holding two of your children. Come and join us tonight behind the palisade being rebuilt at the foot of the castle even as we speak. We will guarantee you aid and protection. Tomorrow, Sunday, our priest, the monk Granger, will celebrate the Eucharist in your church. If you prefer, come then and receive the body of Our Christ. Together we will talk, for I understand your fears and mean to save the lives of your two children."

As he finished speaking, Liébaut raised his hand in a gesture of friendship, turned without another word, and led us toward the port at the other end of the village.

After sext the men of Falaise, commanded by Vilgard de Chambois, began clearing the moat, removing the earth and uprooted trees, while the men of Malbray, under Bernon's command, undertook the more arduous task of cutting up the great logs that had been brought from the forest that morning and sinking them deeply into the ground in a close pattern as part of the castle defenses. Meanwhile, Liébaut took me with him through the countryside. Alone on our mounts, we followed the Varenne to where it emptied into the sea. I saw that my lord was uneasy, disturbed by the unexpected problem of the two child hostages. I left him in silence, as he no doubt contemplated some clever ruse by which to deceive the enemy and get the children back. Clearly, he feared that the peasants of Arques might make an alliance with Ubbo against us. I saw how seriously he took the danger in which the Frisians' tactic had placed us (and the days that followed, alas, proved that he was not mistaken). I followed without a word, feeling for him.

Beyond the port of Arques, near the former Bridge of Arches, we came upon the gutted remains of a sixty-foot Norman ship, half sunk in the river, its mainmast broken, its sail shredded, its decking smashed, and its oars and massive rudder shattered. But even so greatly damaged, the carved prow and stern were beautiful. We went aboard, and discovered the bodies of merchants and sailors floating in the water, stripped of their weapons, their faces swollen and gray, hideous as devils. Eyes bulged wide open to the empty sky, slashed chests and throats gaped like gigantic mouths filled with white foam and clumps of black blood. I had never seen men massacred this way.

At first it was not fear I felt, for my mind and tongue were unaccustomed to such thoughts. I recalled how, long ago in Bernay, as a young child in my father's tower I watched the bloody corpse of a stag while the entrails were torn out in glistening, warm brown lumps. Now, intense disgust froze my limbs, crushing my stomach and my breath under an enormous weight. I threw myself against Liébaut and hid my eyes against his chest. He put his hands on my head and slowly stroked my hair.

"Don't be afraid, Odilon," he said in a gentle voice that I can hear even now. "Look at what the men we must fight have done, and harden your heart. Let this give you the strength to destroy God's enemies, to vanquish them when your time comes, to break their bones with your sword. Cast mercy from your heart and let violent hatred in, for the glory of Robert and Our Lord Almighty."

How long did I stand there shedding my childish tears upon him? I could not pull myself away, and in the end he had to take me by the shoulders and hold me up. "Forgive me," I said, "I'm ashamed to act like this in front of you."

"There is no shame," he answered, "in weeping at such suffering."

I have no clear memory of what happened during the rest of that day, until evening. I could not forgive myself for having shown such weakness in my lord's presence. What sort of whimpering warrior was I? After leaving the ship, we followed the old Roman road that runs along the sea on the tall cliffs. At Deep, where the coast breaks suddenly, we crossed empty fisheries. We walked along the wooden docks of the deserted port, and despite the wind we stood there for a moment watching the shifting expanse of sea as it cast its white waves against the flat rocks. We saw no vessel, as though out of fear none dared ply the waters of the far coast. Liébaut said that the Frisians would soon return and that we had to prepare ourselves for battle, but in my anger against myself I listened not so much to his words as to the cries of the wide-winged birds who flew low above us, their every call sinking into me like a knife wound. Humiliated and confused, I fought back new tears. Why did I always have to strip myself of pride? Why did my reason always have to be in disorder? The perfect line traced in the distance where the sky met the green sea blurred before my eyes, and I lowered my head to conceal my turmoil. But my lord understood and drew me to him. Though he spoke no words to soothe me, his warmth and confidence entered me, just as they had during the night I spent beside him wrapped in the woolen blanket. Once more I felt the firmness of his chest, the hardness of his belly, and the calm of his breath, and in the end I told myself that I had committed no crime, for indeed there was no shame in weeping at death and suffering.

The blaze had brought down an entire row of arches in the church, and it was among their scattered remains, which covered nearly a quarter of the holy site, that we gathered on the first Sunday of our adventure to attend Mass and celebrate the Eucharist. The godly Granger had hastily supervised the construction of a portable altar to hold the golden Crucifix he had brought from Falaise. The gleaming Cross now bathed us in the light of faith. Ten paces from our priest, before God, in a high stone niche in which some mosaics and baked clay statues had been placed, the carved wooden figures of the four evangelists stood, two by two. The faces of John, Luke, Mark, and Matthew were turned toward the depiction of the immaculate Lamb placed between them. Glorious angels, their wings spread, formed an ensemble near the arch of Solomon, behind the old half-burned altar. A candelabrum with seven branches, certainly of no monetary value, since it had been left in place, stood in a chapel to the side; it symbolized the seven gifts of grace. Against the wall was a beautiful statue of God's valiant knight Gabriel felling a demon with his lance—just as my lord would strike dead the devil Ubbo. The more I looked at the disheveled monster, the more I found that its spindly neck, rough and furrowed brow, pinched nostrils, swollen lips, receding chin, bristling hair, dog's teeth, and humped back made it resemble Draco, whom I feared and detested and who, in the midst of our prayer to the Almighty, emitted his awful, shrill laugh from time to time in the back of the church.

The pyramid-shaped stone reliquary had been broken, the precious holy contents looted by the Frisians. All that remained were the words carved in the stone: "Here lie a piece of the staff and the belt of the Precursor of Christ Our Lord." These could only have been relics belonging to John the Baptist. The enormity of the crime committed by those who had seized them so treacherously, who had perhaps destroyed them, surpassed my understanding. From my place near my lord, among the men of war, I could see from the force of his prayer how deep was his faith in Our God. Recalling then the warm friendship he had shown me the day before, when

I had behaved so shamefully with my tears, and recalling also the second night I had spent coiled with him under the blanket in the ashes of the tower, I saw how pleased I was by everything about him, how completely my earlier doubts had disappeared. How happy I was to serve him! How I admired, respected, loved him!

We shared the body of Our Christ. When the Mass and its magnificent mystery were over and we were filled with the instrument of our salvation, protected from all harm and from all danger of falling from grace, we returned to the tower. In front of our palisade, rebuilt by Bernon and the men of Malbray, who had toiled well into the night, we found Thorer and more than fifty peasants of Arques—men, women, and children. They awaited us armed with their farming tools.

Liébaut, pleased that the peasants had come, invited them to cross the wooden bridge we had put up across the moat, which was now cleared of the earth and trees that had filled it, so that they might hold their talk within our enclosure. Thorer, his face impassive, declared that he prefered to remain outside. "See how much we have accomplished since yesterday?" Liébaut said, pretending not to have heard Thorer's blunt refusal. "And look: though today is Sunday, we are already rebuilding the walls and floor of the storeroom at the bottom of the tower." The peasants stood in silence.

I looked at them closely, one by one. Most of the men wore dirty tunics and coarse cowls and had beards and long hair. Some had knives hanging from their belts, bits of rope for tying thatch, and flints. Their faces were slack and uncouth, expressing only menace or discord. The women, about a dozen of them, stood by their husbands and wore wooden clogs and shabby dresses that fell to mid-calf; the older ones had wrapped scarves around their heads to conceal their foreheads and hair. Two of the women held babies in their arms. They stood with eyes downcast, and I saw fear, more than anger, in their faces. My lord, flanked by Vilgard de Chambois, Séguin de Brécy, and Bernon, began to speak kindly to them, hoping that agreement could be reached now that they had gathered here. Standing behind him, as I always did, I listened in silence to what he said.

"I realize," he began, "that we must free your two children. That is the first thing we must do, for those innocents must no longer be held hostage. We will undertake no hostile act until they have been returned to the village. I am convinced that the barbarians have not departed for their own lands. They are hiding somewhere on the coast, at the foot of the cliffs near Deep, for they have not yet looted enough ships to return to the North. I will find them, and the next time that Norman merchants sail up the Varenne, I will take advantage of Ubbo's attack to free your sons from their imprisonment."

"Do you think yourself so valiant," Thorer blurted in the angry voice he seemed never to abandon, "that you can defeat them alone, and on their own ships?"

"I will not be alone," Liébaut replied. "Normandy's strongest knight will go with me"—he pointed to Bernon—"as well as two of my men of war and my squire. The five of us together will free your children and bring them back while the rest of our army defends the merchants on the Varenne and holds off the enemy."

"You will fail and be killed," shouted a peasant barely older than I, who stood beside a red-haired woman, also very young.

That was the first time I saw and heard Ivar. At the time, I did not know that this angry youth was Thorer's son; nor could I know of the role he was to play in our terrible adventure. Yet I realized immediately, instinctively, that he was unlike the other peasants of Arques and that, if we were not careful, his pride might be a greater danger to us than the Frisian foe. How right I was! Would that our paths had never crossed, his and mine, so disordered were our minds, so uncontrolled our thoughts and deeds! But how could we have changed the course of our destinies, Ivar and I, and averted our meeting on that autumn Sunday forty-three years ago?

"I will wait for a Norman ship to sail into Deep," Liébaut continued, "and as soon as the Frisians attack, I will lead an assault on their defenseless ship. I will not fail. But when that melee is over and your children are once again among you, you will have to remain at our side for your own protection."

"Do you really know anything about them?" another peasant, with a thick black beard, asked sharply. "Do you know how cruel they are? Do you really hope to defeat them through a mere trick?"

"I will be satisfied simply to bring your children back. Once that is done, and the merchants have cleared the port, we will break off the battle and retreat behind this moat and these palisades. Our army's role will be to divert Ubbo and to repulse his attack, no more. The battle will not last beyond that. I will need the entire winter to vanquish this enemy, whom I know far better than you think."

"And what if you cause our children to be slaughtered?" exclaimed Thorer, his black teeth showing.

"Their blood will be on your hands!" a woman shouted.

"And God will curse you!" shrieked another.

"And we will kill you with our own hands!"

"Leave! Leave us in peace!"

"Yes, or you will die like Gautier!"

A child began to cry, and a tumult of Germanic words filled the air.

"Suppose we refuse to stand with you behind your palisades and, instead, warn Ubbo, whom we have promised not to oppose?" Ivar asked, silencing the others. "What then?"

"Then it is you who will be slaughtered," replied Séguin de Brécy, his voice dripping with scorn.

Liébaut cast a look of reproach at the chief of the men of Falaise. "Alas," he said gravely, "my friend Séguin de Brécy speaks the truth. You must seek protection behind our moat and our palisades. Together we will rebuild your village, and soon, once we have restored the outer defenses of Arques, you will be able to return to your homes to sleep in peace. In the meantime, stay here with us, under the protection of our swords and our arrows."

They all stood silent, but in their faces I read anger, antagonism, and even, it seemed to me, treachery. I was deeply troubled, and decided to speak to my lord about this, to warn him.

"Within ten days," Liébaut continued, "your children will be here with you. You have my word on it. But you must understand that I will not leave this place until Ubbo is destroyed. I will wage this war to its conclusion whatever you decide to do."

Our encounter with the people of Arques filled me with anxiety. I kept silent as the men of Falaise and of Malbray, divided by mistrust and envy, gathered around the fire and ate their first real meal since our departure. Though I was hungry, I did not touch the soup and warm bread the kitchen servants had prepared, nor the few pieces of spit-roasted game with herbs. I was almost unable to swallow, and made do with some griddlecake. It was the angry face of Ivar—of whom, I repeat, I knew nothing—more than of Thorer that I could not get out of my mind that evening. And Ivar's threat to betray Liébaut. Even as I watched and admired my lord, who, though it was Sunday, cheerfully helped with the repair of the guards' wooden huts and the storeroom at the bottom of the tower, I knew no rest. It was as though some premonition of the tragedies to come had entered my heart and dispelled the confidence I had felt that morning. Liébaut himself, apparently unconcerned, told jokes that moved his own men, as well as Vilgard de Chambois and Séguin de Brécy, to laughter. But the hard knot in my stomach stayed for the rest of the day. As I waited to be able to speak to my lord that night, I felt the same kind of dread that had come over me in the duke's tower when Falaise was plunged into unnatural darkness in broad daylight.

I told Liébaut of my fears as soon as we were curled up in the woolen blanket. Speaking softly, so that those around us would not hear, I confided to him how disturbed I was by the animosity of the people of Arques. He listened and said that he was well aware of the dangers we faced. He repeated what he had said to Thorer outside our rebuilt palisade just after mass: that he had come to restore peace to the far coast and to defend Normandy's gravely threatened trade. That no amount of anger or resentment from anyone would prevent him from waging—and winning—this battle for the glory of Robert the Magnificent. "It is about the people here that I am concerned," he said. "If they reject our protection, they will be slaughtered, and we will be powerless to save them."

"What if they warn Ubbo that you intend to free the two children?" I asked. "What then?"

"They will not do that," Liébaut murmured, "for they know that then they would make enemies of us as well as of the Frisians. No, they will shrink from such peril."

"Did you notice the man barely older than I? The one who was so angry at us?"

"Yes, I saw him." He sighed.

The silence of the bitter-cold night fell over us. And, though more than ever I needed my lord's strength to enter me in that moment of doubt, I dared not move closer and cling to him. Then another thought was added to those already troubling my mind. As I looked at the patch of sky above us, now reduced to a mere sliver, I realized that by the morrow the tower storeroom would be entirely rebuilt and the roof above our heads restored. Once we were properly sheltered, we would no longer sleep together under the same blanket. I would be deprived of the heat of his chest, which warmed me more than did the fire, of the sweetness of his breath on my brow, which soothed my doubts better than could any words, and of the firmness of his belly, which, pressed against mine, gave me courage more surely than could the most powerful thirst for glory. I realized then how necessary this new closeness had become for me in just a few nights, and how indispensable it would be until at last I acquired the manhood I so cruelly lacked. An impulse to ask Liébaut about the nights to come swept over me, so strongly that it was hard for me to breathe. Fortunately, I restrained myself (with what I took to be God's aid), and for once managed not to appear ridiculous by talking like a schoolboy who cannot find confidence within himself, unaided.

I slept badly that night, the fifth since our departure from Falaise, the third spent in the ruined tower of Arques curled up in a blanket with the conqueror of Auxerre, who slept peacefully. I found no rest, torn as I was between joy that my lord had shown affection for me and fear that I would now find myself alone—on the eve of an adventure that had once filled me with fervor but now terrified me. Thus tormented, as I often was without reason in those days, I began to pray to God that Liébaut de Malbray's warmth and strength would not be taken from me, that I would be able to bring them into my heart for good.

At daybreak my lord and I set out in search of the Frisian ships. He led me through the countryside, across cultivated fields and wet valleys, forests and muddy marshes, to the cliffs beyond Deep. Convinced that our enemies had stopped farther to the north, on a course that would later lead them back to Frisia, Liébaut decided to urge our mounts along the high white walls toward the coasts of France instead of going down to the mouth of the Saâne. I spent the first hours of that day wondering about the nights to come instead of scouring the sea below us for the barbarians.

Liébaut, though perfectly erect in the saddle and proud in his armor as we rode on, occasionally raised his arm and pressed his hand to the wound he had suffered at Auxerre, and I realized that the pain caused by that ancient arrow probably never completely left him. We guided our horses along the sheer cliffs for hours. Despite my torment, which I tried to put out of my mind, I admired those white walls, those towering ramparts bordered by narrow beaches and battered by the waves at their base. The salt wind lashed our faces so sharply, it blurred my eyes and made icy tears run down my cheeks, but I marveled at the grandeur, at the beauty of the impregnable peaks, and the grottoes carved into the rock over thousands of years. But we saw no sign of the enemy.

"They must be here somewhere," Liébaut repeated several times. "They must be, since they have to be able to lie in wait for Norman ships." We went as far as the mouth of the Bresle, marked by a break in the cliff. That was the last place from which it was still possible to see merchant ships coming toward the port of Deep from the open sea. "Let us turn back," my lord said. "From here they could not catch Robert's ships before they sail past Arques, up the Varenne, and into Normandy's well-protected heartland."

We headed back along the same route. Hunger gnawed at my stomach, and too often my thoughts returned to the storeroom ceiling, which the men of Malbray surely had repaired by now. Suddenly, as the sky was darkening, casting a deep gray-green glow over the sea and the foam-topped swollen waves, Liébaut caught sight of a narrow path dug into the cliff and leading down to a beach sixty feet below. Without hesitation he followed it, moving with his usual wisdom and caution. Behind him, I held back my mount with all my strength.

When we reached the bottom, we went at a walk along the narrow pebble-strewn beach wedged between the turbulent sea and the immense wall that now loomed over us. Time and again we were stung by sheets of water hurled in our faces by the wind. Though my lord barely budged under these assaults, I was nearly thrown from the saddle, and only my fear that he would think me a coward kept me from turning back. As vespers drew near and the sky of autumn, season of the Last Judgment, grew ever darker, slowly invaded by the night, we found our path blocked by a section of the high wall that jutted twenty feet out into the waves like a ship's carved prow.

"Look," Liébaut said, "the cliff is hollowed out on the other side and curves up into an overhang. If a ship were hidden there, we would not be able to see it from above, from the road we took this morning." He dismounted to see how dangerous it would be to skirt the wall that prevented us from going on, then came back and told me to wait for him. Despite the cruel cold, he took off his hauberk and greaves and waded bare-chested into the raging sea to walk around the obstacle. The water reached his waist, waves broke on his shoulders and back, and he clung to the rocks. After a few more steps, the water rose to his neck, and twice white foam bubbled over his head. Fortunately, he had not far to go and did not lose his footing. He rounded the wedge of sheer cliff, and I could no longer see him.

I waited on the narrow beach. It seemed to me that he was taking too long to come back, and I began to fear the worst. In my mind's eye I saw him founder, carried off by the hateful waves. Realizing the pain his death would cause me, I prayed to God to save him. I was fairly confident that my lord would not have attempted this action had he considered it too dangerous, but I could not help imagining myself returning alone to the tower of Arques to tell Bernon and our warriors that Liébaut de Malbray had lost his life. I could see myself at night without him, wrapped alone in his woolen blanket, weeping and reliving over and over the memory of the night in Rouen when I rubbed his chest and shoulders.

As more time passed, I saw what an ordeal this adventure could become without the one I served to guide me and offer me the example of his manliness. I told myself that I depended on him too much, that my emotions should not be so immoderate, so extreme, going from doubt and disappointment to equally excessive admiration and affection. But I could not accept the idea that I might have to continue this war, with all its perils, at the side of a knight other than the conqueror of Auxerre. I resolved, whatever happened, to refuse to serve Vilgard de Chambois, in whom I had no confidence, or, worse, Séguin de Brécy, with his timorous wife and her horrible dwarf. If I had to face the enemy without Liébaut, this adventure, once so full of promise and glory, would be too much for me. But these dark fears, perhaps, were the result of my anxiety about the people of Arques. I should be more sensible. If this knight—whom, after all, I barely knew—were to come back alive, I should put some distance between us, for my own protection. But I knew that I would not, could not.

When Liébaut reappeared, streaming with water and clinging to a rock, joy rose in my breast and I thanked God for having protected him. The moment he set foot on the broad flat rocks on the beach, he called to me above the crash of the waves. He had discovered three Frisian ships concealed in a vast hollow carved by the sea between two sections of the cliff. A vision of bloody combat came to me. Here was the chance I so desired to become a knight of Normandy! Forgetting my prudent decision to maintain some distance from Liébaut de Malbray, I leaped from my horse, my heart bursting with joy, and ran to him, to dry his back, to rub his hard belly, to warm his icy naked chest.

My lord continued to share his blanket with me at night even though the storeroom ceiling had been completed by our return. My mind at ease, I told myself that this would last at least until the restoration of the top floor of the tower, with its great hall and bedchamber. I chided myself for having worried needlessly.

The next day, Liébaut told everyone that we had found the enemy. He posted four guards on the coast and in the port of Deep to watch for the appearance of any Norman ship, and he informed the men of Malbray and Falaise that they were to be ready to come to the aid of the first merchants to sail up the Varenne. With Bernon, two of his most valiant men, and me, he worked out a simple plan, which, taking account of the Frisian position in the hollow of the cliff, would enable us to free the children without excessive risk. To my great joy, he told me that I would follow him onto the barbarian ship to snatch the hostages from their fate.

We labored five days on a second palisade of sharpened stakes and hard-packed earth at the base of the hill on which our tower stood. For five days, from dawn to dusk, the men of Malbray, led by Bernon, chopped down and cut up hundreds of trees, while those of the men of Falaise who were not working on the second palisade, under the command of Vilgard de Chambois, placed roofs of grass and thatch on the twenty huts erected behind the moat and between the two enceintes. In these the warriors and the peasants would be quartered. There was great excitement in the village and in our camp as we awaited the battle. Elated by a fever that now seemed to grip us all, I forgot my fear that Ivar might betray Liébaut and I enjoyed what I now consider some of my life's most beautiful moments. Even Séguin de Brécy's men, always so quick to complain, ceased for a time to bemoan their fate, and by the middle of the week they had begun the next floor of the tower and the stairway that would eventually lead to the great hall.

Bernon set up straw dummies in the courtyard, and the archers were soon training at long distance. A millstone was installed near the well so that everyone, myself included, could sharpen his sword. Only the peasants of Arques remained aloof from the preparations for war. Not once did Thorer come to visit Liébaut to discuss his people's protection. In the storeroom, now under lock and key, we put weapons and armor as well as ever more stocks of food: vegetables, game, apples, chestnuts, beechnuts, from which we extracted oil, and entire quarters of pork, salted for preservation. The oven was fired constantly, providing us all the bread and griddlecakes we desired. We made litters of dry leaves, so that Liébaut and I, wrapped in our blanket, were now able to sleep without awakening in the morning with too much back pain. Our supply of wood, already large, grew steadily, which enabled us to keep many fires burning, so that we were less cold, especially at night. My enthusiasm returned, and I began to train with the sword again, as I had in Falaise. My arm felt stronger than ever, and despite the sneers of Draco, who spent more and more time taunting me, I continued until nightfall to strike at the straw enemies posted in the courtyard, pretending they were Frisian barbarians.

At dawn on Thursday Liébaut ordered those who knew the art of the forge to begin making heavy projectiles and iron reinforcements. He had two catapults built in a single day, between lauds and vespers. Mounted on large wooden wheels, they were placed atop the inner rampart. He organized our defense magnificently, and on the evening of the tenth day after our arrival in Arques, when he planted eleven banners bearing Normandy's red-and-gold colors in our new stronghold, the feeling that no one could defeat us swept over me.

At dawn on Saturday, winter having frozen the earth during the night, a number of the peasants of Arques—all of whom had until now remained outside our defenses, not approaching us—crossed the moat and the outer palisade. Firmly holding a churl whose face was bruised, they asked to see Lord Liébaut de Malbray. Standing in the midst of the group of at least twenty men and women was the red-haired girl I had seen with Ivar on Sunday morning after our monk had said mass. The peasants were escorted to the largest of our huts, where Liébaut now stayed. They told him that they had come seeking justice, then threw the churl at my lord's feet. The man was accused of theft. Having no one to defend him, it seemed, he tearfully protested that he was innocent. As I looked at the angry faces around him, however, I saw that in fact he had a friend, that the red-haired woman was on his side and wished him set free.

"He stole twelve chickens from me," shouted one of the peasants, the angriest. "And money, too. He entered my house at night while I slept, and took ten deniers, but my dog bit him. This villain, alas, killed the poor animal with a blow of his staff and fled. But I found him, I caught him. Look, my lord," he added, seizing and twisting the wretch's arm so that Liébaut could see. "The teeth marks in his flesh."

The elbow and hand indeed bore traces of bites. I concluded that the man had done the crime.

"It wasn't me!" the churl cried. "I swear before God, I didn't steal anything!"

My lord looked at the wounds, then at the accuser and the accused. "Who are you?" he asked the first.

"I am called Tyrker," the man said. "I am a tenant, like my father before me."

"Are you aware," Liébaut said, "that if you are a tenant, as you say, then you owe me chickens from your flock, wheat from your fields, honeycombs, even pieces of silver? Are you aware that my moat should have been cleared and my defenses rebuilt by the strength of your arm and the sweat of your brow and not by my warriors? You come to me seeking justice, but do you really accept me as your lord?"

"Yes," the peasant said in a low voice after a moment of silence, his head hanging. "You are the lord of Arques."

Liébaut smiled and nodded, as if amused by Tyrker's embarrassment. He turned to the man at his feet and told him to rise, that he detested speaking to people humiliated, what-

82

ever infamy they may have committed. "And you," he said, "tell me who you are."

"My name is Talvos," the man answered dully. "I am a serf. I live in a hut just outside Arques and I have nothing, not even a wife and children. But I do not take—I swear before God—what does not belong to me."

"He's lying. Don't listen to him," shouted the tenant. A gesture from my lord silenced him.

"Tyrker," Liébaut said, "did you see the face of the man who took your property last night?"

The accuser hesitated, then replied, reluctantly, that he had not. It had been too dark. "But I have often seen him lurking near my house. He's always lying around, and refuses to work. Besides, he's a foreigner, from another village. They must have driven him out."

The red-haired woman's eyes flashed at these words, and the mixture of anger and pain on her face made me wonder what connection she had to this man Talvos. The answer was not long in coming.

"And you, Talvos," asked my lord, who, I felt, had already made his decision, "do you have any witness, one who can testify that you were at home last night?"

"No. I live alone. My sister, Mathilde, now lives at Thorer's and serves him," the accused replied, gesturing at the girl. "She is soon to become the wife of Ivar, our leader's elder son."

Liébaut turned to the red-haired woman, barely older than I, and their eyes met.

He looked at her intently, as if seeking the truth in her face, which was as smooth and beautiful as a child's. I saw entreaty, supplication, in the peasant girl's green eyes. Then she blushed and lowered her head, just as I so often did, to escape that blue gaze that entered so deeply. My lord, now unsmiling, stared at her for a long moment, as if the decision he would make were inscribed on her brow. "Why is not Ivar here with you to defend your brother, to whom he will soon be related by marriage?" he finally asked her.

"Forgive him, my lord," the girl answered in a voice so soft we had to lean forward to hear, "but he did not want to come into your castle today."

"And why is that?" Liébaut asked.

"He fears the wrath of the Frisians."

"And you, who are here, do not fear it?"

"My lord," she said, not raising her eyes, "I fear it more than anything. But the accused man is my brother."

"You believe him innocent?"

The girl nodded. "He is my brother," she murmured simply.

From his grave expression I could tell that the courage and humility of this girl Mathilde, as she stood alone among the people demanding the punishment of Talvos, greatly impressed Liébaut. Everyone, in silence, awaited his decision. He was thoughtful for what seemed an interminable time, his eyes fixed upon the motionless girl in her distress. When his gaze met mine, I saw a deep and unusual agitation.

He sighed, as though the decision he had seemed only too happy to make, minutes before, now weighed upon him.

At last he turned to the man whose property had been stolen.

"Do you have any evidence against Talvos apart from these bites on his arm?" he asked.

The tenant, after much hesitation, answered that he did not.

"Did any of your family see Talvos enter your house?"

"No," the man said. "No one saw him. But it had to be him."

Liébaut regarded the people gathered around him. "Know, all of you, that I shall show no mercy to him who commits transgressions in my land of Arques," he said in a ringing voice. "I shall stop at no punishment, I shall not hesitate to have gallows built, because the peril we face is too great for us to tolerate any crime, however minor. Yet I cannot now decree that Talvos be punished, for I judge him not guilty of the crime of which you have accused him." Had I not known my lord, not known his great self-mastery and wisdom, I might have thought that he had lost his reason when I heard those words and looked at the distressed faces of the peasants. "Go in peace, then, all of you," he continued, now in that gentle tone I had taken for weakness at the beginning of our adventure. "The evidence you have brought me, Tyrker, is unsound."

"But you can see the bites on his arm as well as I can," the tenant shouted. "They are the marks of my dog's teeth."

"No," Liébaut answered, his face somber, "they are not your dog's, for they are already hard-scabbed and therefore made not as recently as last night, as any man of science would tell you."

"Then who took what belonged to me?"

"I do not know, but if you find him, I will punish him and grant you justice."

"It was him. I know it!" Tyrker screamed.

"Talvos is not guilty. Such is my decision!" Liébaut said in a voice whose severity astonished me. He rose. "I have things to do. I will hear no more of this matter."

Instead of rushing to her brother, taking him in her arms, and clasping him to her breast, the red-haired woman, eyes fixed upon the new lord and master of Arques, did not move. As for Tyrker, the burning look he flashed at Liébaut as he left told me that my lord had made another enemy.

My master was grim for the rest of the day. I had not been close enough to the marks on Talvos's arm to judge for myself how old they were, and I had little knowledge of medicine in any case. Admiring Liébaut for the good sense and courage with which he had pronounced his verdict, I believed that he had made his decision on the evidence. Today, however, in view of the events that followed, I am not so sure that Liébaut, in his heart of hearts, really thought Talvos innocent.

At dawn the next day, two of our lookouts posted in Deep galloped back to announce the approach of a Norman ship, and for a time, on the threshold of my first battle, I forgot both Talvos and Mathilde, his red-haired sister.

As most of our warriors prepared to hold off the Frisians on the Varenne River, my lord, Bernon, two knights of Malbray, and I, with a guard for the horses, headed for the coast. On arriving we were delighted to find that the sea, far from raging as it had on the day we discovered the enemy ships concealed in the recess of the cliff, was calm, barely stirred by a few waves. This was necessary if, once having freed the hostages, we were to make it back around the prow-shaped cliff without being slaughtered.

I followed Liébaut down the path in the side of the high white wall, descending steeply to the narrow beach. My hands began to tremble, so powerful was the mixture of fear and joy within me at the approach of this first battle. As I held my mount's rein, I could not resist fingering my father's sword, which hung from my belt, and I turned my long wooden shield, kept in place by its shoulder strap, to the front, as though to protect myself from an unexpected blow. My lord, two paces ahead of me, had insisted on carrying his equipment himself. He looked like a fearsome giant in his iron helmet and neck protector of mail. His hauberk, slit on either side to enable him to mount his horse, covered him almost completely. He was like Thor, the Viking god of strength, son of Odin the hurler of thunder and lightning. As I looked at him, his strength penetrating my heart, I placed my confidence in him now more than ever. He seemed invincible in his war lord's pride and grandeur. How well I remember you, Liébaut de Malbray, tall in your saddle as you crossed the narrow beach of the far coast! May those who read this testimony be able to picture your beauty at that moment!

We stopped at the section of cliff jutting into the sea and there dismounted. Something my father used to say when I was a schoolboy back in our home in Bernay suddenly came to mind: that the Normans' strength in combat was their skill on horseback. I drove the thought from my mind, lest the fear that had already shamed me strike my chest again with its thudding blows. We followed Bernon into the icy water without removing our hauberks, helmets, or shields, leaving the guard behind to tend our mounts until our return. Slowly, only slightly buffeted by the gentle waves—and may God be praised again today for that!—we skirted the high wall in silence, careful to keep close to the rocks. We found, as Liébaut had foreseen, that most of the Frisians, confident of their hiding place, had gone off to loot and slaughter the Norman merchants, leaving behind only one of their three ships. Its sail was furled around the mainmast and its oars were withdrawn. We saw only four barbarians: they were directly in front of the half-deck, and had their backs to us, facing Deep. We halted for a moment, swords drawn and shields in hand, but saw no other enemies.

"Protect us, Almighty Lord," I whispered. "Let the two children be here and let us snatch them from their fate without coming to harm." Though my task was simple—to follow Liébaut and protect him from attack from the rear—I found it hard to breathe, hard to stand on my weak legs when my lord, separating from Bernon and the other two warriors as planned, began his noiseless advance toward the enemy vessel. Chest-deep in sea water, I still believed, in my confusion, that it was shameful to dread wounds and death before a battle, as though fear and courage were adversaries and never went together, as they did for me that day.

While we approached the ship, the others, farther away, made for the stern. As we had agreed, Liébaut and I waited until Bernon and the two men of Malbray had climbed aboard and launched their surprise attack before climbing aboard ourselves. We rushed to the stern. I saw the dangling, half-severed arm of one Frisian, and cries of rage and pain and the clashing of swords filled my ears. Suddenly two of the enemy, who looked even bigger and stronger than our giant Viking, loomed before us, blocking our way. Liébaut swung his mace faster than a falcon swooping on its prey, and I heard the crack of a skull. Before I could turn, a third enemy threw himself upon me, howling like a demon. I saw a hate-twisted mouth and a huge red face thickly bearded, and a mighty blade flashed and struck my shield a stunning blow. Off balance, I almost fell, but I forgot fear and danger and hurled myself forward. Ducking under the man who desired my death, I slashed at his leg with all the strength my arm could muster. My father's sword bit deep, and I saw blood spurt. The man fell to one knee with a cry and swung his weapon in an arc so powerful that I felt the breath of death on my face. But the Frisian missed and, carried by the motion of his sword, collapsed on his side.

What happened next took place so fast, I do not know what I did, and it is difficult for me to describe it now. I saw the point, then the entire blade, of the weapon I had sharpened so often on the millstone in the courtyard in Arques. Wielded by an arm that seemed to fight more swiftly than I, it struck the man's chest and sank in. His eyes clouded in terror as I stood breathless, holding my sword in his body. Pink foam appeared on his lips. A formless moan rose from the back of his throat, then his head sagged and fell back. Time froze. "He's dead!" shouted Liébaut, who had just felled his second enemy. "Come, hurry!" I pulled my weapon from the chest—the sword now was red with blood—in a nerveless motion that seemed to belong to someone else, and I numbly followed my lord, empty of fear and joy alike.

Under the deck, we found the two children of Arques tied together with thick rope. Liébaut freed them with a sword stroke, and we took them with us to the center of the ship, now strewn with enemy dead. There we saw Bernon and our other two warriors in hand-to-hand struggle with five more Frisians. Liébaut, carrying the terrified children in his arms, called to our men to break off the fight and return with us to the beach beyond the cliff. To our misfortune—for otherwise the rest of our adventure might have been different—he pushed me from the ship into the sea, thus preventing me from protecting him. Our two warriors joined me, but before Bernon could rush to his side, a wounded Frisian threw himself upon my master, who, passing the children to us, could not possibly defend himself. I screamed to him to jump, but he ignored me. As he raised his arm to hand us the second hostage, he received a sword thrust in almost the exact spot where the arrow at Auxerre had pierced him. He fell more than leaped into the water, and as we fled, pursued by the shouts of the Frisians, I could see the wound bleeding heavily under his slashed hauberk.

———

We returned to Arques as quickly as we could. Despite the wound he had just suffered, Liébaut kept control of his horse the entire way, and the bleeding seemed not to sap his strength. I had no faith whatever in the remedies of Nicolas, the physician Suzanne de Brécy had brought with her from Falaise, and therefore refused to consider the possibility that the wound could threaten Liébaut's life if it went untended. As we approached Deep, galloping along the crest of the cliff, we saw the two enemy ships in the sea below; they were returning from their attack on the Norman ship to their hiding place in the hollow of the rock. "The battle is over," shouted Bernon, pointing at the sea. "May God have smiled upon us!"

As we drew nearer to our tower, one of the Falaise lookouts told us that the Frisians, taken by surprise, had been unable to sustain the fight on the Varenne with Vilgard de Chambois's men and had broken off the battle and fled, allowing the merchants to continue on their way. Six of their men had been killed by our arrows. "Now our war has truly begun," I said to myself. "Henceforth we will know no peace. The barbarians will seek to avenge the ambush we prepared for them. Now more than ever we need Liébaut de Malbray to lead us. No wound must be allowed to remove him from the fight." Bernon, as if echoing these thoughts, said that only the total destruction of one of the two armies would end this war now.

The peasants of Arques, in their fear of the barbarians, had gathered at the foot of the hill in the castle courtyard, between our two palisades. My lord, who had the good sense to strap his shield to his side so that no one could see his wound, handed the two children to their tearful parents, who rushed to embrace them. "I promised you I would bring them back," he said. "Here they are!" Some of the peasants surrounded his horse and touched him, crying out their joy and their confidence, and even Thorer had to offer thanks and praise Liébaut's courage. I noticed, however, that some of the peasants stood apart, their faces impassive, and Ivar, with Tyrker at his side, asked loudly where he and his family were supposed to sleep now to escape the wrath of the Frisians.

"The huts we built at the foot of our tower, behind the outer palisade, are for you," Bernon replied. "You can take shelter in them until we have rebuilt the enceinte around your village. If you are wise, you will move in tonight and stay there."

When Liébaut dismounted, we gathered close around him so that no one would see the wound he had suffered. The four of us—Bernon, the two men of Malbray, and I—pushing aside the men and women who tried to take his hand and kiss it, accompanied him up the hill to the storeroom inside our second line of defense. Though he was still losing blood, my lord wanted to hear about the battle on the banks of the Varenne before lying down and having his wound tended, and he sent me to summon the commander of the men of Falaise. Vilgard de Chambois, who was made to swear that he would say nothing of the wound, confirmed that he had repulsed the enemy, who had been surprised by the counterattack, and that his archers had killed six barbarians on the decks of their ships, while only two of our men had been wounded. Liébaut, despite his pain, praised Vilgard (which did not please me), declaring that he considered him a true lord of war, worthy of the love of our duke, Robert the Magnificent.

Thus I was not able to rejoice in the feat I had just accomplished by killing my first enemy, or in the successful return of the two children, or even in the victory our Norman army won on the Varenne. As soon as we climbed to the upper floor of the barely completed tower, my beloved master collapsed, exhausted, on his bed of grass and straw. With great difficulty Bernon and I relieved him of his armor, his hauberk, and his bloodstained tunic. Since the floor and the walls were of wood, we could light no fire to warm him, so we covered him with many blankets. Soon he was shivering with fever. Bernon refused to call Nicolas, the physician from Falaise. He looked carefully at the wound, from which blood continued to seep. Finally, he said that if the cut did not close by vespers, he would have to burn it to prevent corruption from entering Liébaut's limbs and spreading through his body.

As the music of the songs and dances of the feast celebrating our victory rose from the courtyard and the huts below, Liébaut fell asleep, sinking into a deep slumber despite the pain. Left alone with him, I wiped his face, neck, and chest, which were drenched from the fever. My eyes filled with tears. I begged him to recover as I pressed pieces of cloth to the wound to stop the flow of blood, which now began to spread through the straw beneath him. Then I lay alongside him under the blankets, to warm him. He groaned, and I wrapped my arms around his icy belly. I do not know how long we lay like that.

What Liébaut had said to me about death the night before, seeing my fear on the eve of this first battle, rang in my mind as I huddled near him, my chest against his, our breath mingling. He said that death was not a sundering, that we must not fear it but live in expectation of it, for it was our way to God, the beginning of the road that led souls free of sin to Him. I looked at his eagle's profile, his noble face now so pale. I told myself that I had never known so handsome a knight, so beautiful a man. Even today, cut off from the world in the isolation of my cell in the abbey of Jumièges, that beauty, when I recall it, stirs me to the depths of my being.

It would, in truth, have been far better had Liébaut de Malbray's age erased his beauty instead of enhancing it.

After vespers, as daylight faded, I left the bed of grass and straw on which I had lain so long—and was surprised to see Bernon escorting Mathilde, the red-haired woman, to my master's side. "Liébaut," the giant Viking whispered in my lord's ear to wake him, "this girl knows of the injury you suffered and says she has a medicine that will heal the wound. She asked me to bring her to you, so she could persuade you to use her remedy. Do you wish to hear her, or would you prefer that I burn the wound now?"

Liébaut opened his eyes. He shook his head as if to clear it, then struggled up, bracing himself on one arm. He looked at the young woman, who held in her hand a few half-crushed leaves, a hen's egg, and some material of animal origin. He recognized her and smiled faintly. "I need to be on my feet tomorrow," he said slowly. "The barbarians may attack, and it is I who must lead the battle. If Bernon burns my wound, the pain will make me even weaker than I am tonight, and it will be days before I can fight again. Can you promise me, woman, that with your unguents I will be on my feet at dawn tomorrow?"

"My medicine will close the wound," Mathilde answered, timid in the tower of the new lord of Arques. "But you will have to be moderate in your actions if it is not to reopen."

My master, breathing with difficulty, looked at her carefully, just as he had before pronouncing judgment on Talvos. A sudden thought darkened his brow. "Who told you of the wound?" he asked sharply. "Do they know in the village?"

"No one knows," the woman replied, "neither warriors nor peasants. I alone in the castle courtyard saw your drawn face when you gave the two children back to their parents, saw you hide your wound behind your shield."

Liébaut seemed reassured by her words, and turned to his faithful friend Bernon for advice. Bernon shrugged. In his view, it was better to burn the wound with a blade reddened in the fire. "We have no time to lose," he added. "The corruption sinks deeper into you with every passing hour." My lord nodded. Still hesitant, he looked at me.

"And you, Odilon," he said, addressing me as he would the wisest of his men, "what do you think?"

Honored that my master would question me thus, I took care, before answering, to observe the young woman as she stood holding her medicine. "I would not like to cause you to err through my own lack of judgment," I then said, "but this woman seems very sure of her peasant remedy. There are such women in my father's lands around Bernay, and their simple medicines are more effective in healing corruption than the nostrums of many men of science. The men of science, in accordance with their theories of the four humors, prescribe fasting that saps the strength, administer purgatives that empty and desiccate the bowels, and recommend thick potions of honey and crushed fruit that bring on convulsions and colic, uselessly inflaming the stomach. If she tries to cure you and fails, if the fever remains and your wound does not close, will there not be time to burn it in the morning?"

"That is by no means certain," Bernon said. "With such a delay, you risk remaining on this straw for days on end, a prisoner of your pain, weak and mindless—if you heal at all."

Liébaut heaved a deep sigh. His mind was clouded by fever, and for the first time since the beginning of our adventure, he seemed not to know what decision to make. "Has your medicine healed others?" he asked the girl as blood began to leak from his side again, seeping through the cloth I had placed on the wound.

"Yes, my lord," she said, her voice louder now. "I learned it from my mother, and I myself have seen it close the deepest wounds."

My master asked her to come nearer. "Night is falling, and it is suddenly hard for me to see your face." Their eyes met when she reached his bedside; it seemed to me that he was seeking the truth in her eyes. "Are you a sorceress?" he whispered.

"No. All I know is this very old medicine."

"I believe I can trust you, Mathilde," Liébaut said softly after a moment of silence. "Since you claim to have the power to cure me, do so, that I might stand at the head of my warriors tomorrow."

I expected Bernon to protest, to insist that the wound be burned immediately, but he said nothing, only stood impassive on the other side of the room, his arms crossed on his giant's chest. The torch he had lit for us cast glints on his long blond hair, his beard, his face as red as that of the Frisian I had killed, and his permanently closed eye. I did not yet know him well enough to realize that he never disputed Liébaut's decisions once they were made. He too loved Liébaut, but his love was different from mine, for though he was no older than the master of Malbray, he protected him as one might a son or younger brother.

My lord tried to move to turn the wound to the red-haired woman, but his face twisted in pain, and I had to help him. I removed the cloth I had placed on the wound; it was soaked with blood, and pieces stuck to his raw flesh. Mathilde knelt beside him and gently wiped the outer edges of the wound, slowly coating them with animal fat and egg white. Gradually she neared the mark left by the arrow of Auxerre and caressed the raw, gaping edges of the slit made by the treacherous sword stroke. I watched her, my eyes fixed on her agile, supple fingers. Though I did not know it at the time, I realize now that I was disturbed by the sight of that soft white hand touching my master's firm flesh, as though it trespassed on a place reserved for me alone.

My lord flinched often, tensing and gripping the blanket from the sharp pain, but his courage was great and not once did he moan or complain. For a long time, Mathilde applied the peasant medicine to his wound. Then, in the silence of the room, she took the various yellowed autumn leaves she had brought with her and delicately set them over the wound, one by one, in three layers. When that was done, she asked my lord to sit up, so that she could tightly wrap his chest with strips of cloth.

"You must sleep now," she said. "If you rest this night, tomorrow you will be able to stand and command your men. And if you are careful, in three days you will be able to take up your weapons again and wield your sword without much pain."

Liébaut lay back on the woolen blanket. As the woman made to leave, he took her by the arm and stayed her. "Why are you doing this?" he asked. "Are you not afraid that the man who is soon to be your husband will chide you for it?"

"You saved my brother," she answered, her eyes lowered.

"Look at me," Liébaut said after a moment of silence. "Why do you always turn away like that?"

"You are the lord of Arques," she murmured.

"So I am," he said. "And I have come to deliver your people from the peril that threatens them. But you must not fear me. Raise your eyes. Do not bow your head before me like a thieving serf before his master."

She stood straight, obeying him as one must obey a lord. They looked at each other for a long moment without uttering a word. She seemed a child next to him.

From that day on, our adventure assumed a different face.

BOOK THREE

spirit of penance, of self-mortification, that caused me to reject the glory of a life at arms that was offered me? I was still a young man when I abandoned the world, spurning forever the temptations of the flesh, the natural gratification of which never seemed to me to be the devil's work—an admission at variance with the monastic spirit that should be mine. Knowing that my soul was lost, did I not renounce the pleasures of the world and retire to the order of Jumièges with the sole aim of redeeming myself in my own eyes?

I have spent thousands of days of silence in a community of men solely dedicated, under the guidance of their abbot, to achieving salvation through prayer and supplication, and through the love of God that binds them. I have sacrificed my hair, which was handsome and thick, and fourteen times a year I shave my beard, symbol of power, chanting psalms under the cloister's arches. Thousands of times, in accordance with the rules, I have awakened in the middle of the night to recite the service, to read the Bible and pious works until lauds. I, once a knight of Neustria, rise every day at dawn—except Sundays and solemn holidays—and study, copy, and annotate liturgical writings. Every morning, winter and summer alike, I wash my face in cold water and soak my clothes to keep them clean. At sext I sit down to meager meals of fruits and vegetables, having the right to no more than a pound of bread and a pint of water a day. I to whom the lands of Bernay were due now own nothing more than two tunics and two cowls. Until vespers each night, I toil in the scriptorium, and there have ruined my eyes. Not a day goes by that I do not sing compline, and until they gave me my own room because of my advanced age, I spent every night in the monastery's icy dormitory, on a wooden bed frame. Respecting the vow of silence, I use signs instead of words, and I have not touched a woman in forty-four years.

Twice, out of what I believed was humility, I refused the coveted post of precentor, which they wanted to confer upon me because of the apparent holiness of my life, and despite my strong desire—indeed, because of it—I have not become a grand master of the liturgy, nor librarian and conservator of the gospels, epistles, and psalters. So great has been my thirst for penance that I have declined to keep the account book for the monks of Jumièges. I would not be a master of ceremonies or a director of processions, and not once have I presided at the blessing of beans or fresh bread, or even of first wines. Firmly resolved to remain the most lowly of our monks, I have never joined the parties welcoming honored guests to our abbey.

Thus has my long life passed, and my vigor and beauty as a young knight of Normandy are long gone. My gaunt face is furrowed by deep lines, my teeth have turned black, my chest has withered. Pain bows my back, and every winter I suffer a wasting fever that tears at my throat and fills my lungs with thick phlegm. Saint Fiacre's disease has claimed me, and I cannot evacuate without agony. My hands, once strong and broad, now are deformed, my fingers so stiff that it is hard for me to write. Failing vision—the worst of all these evils—clouds my world. All this I welcome, not for the salvation of my soul, which I know is lost, but in the love of God to abase myself through penance, to humble myself. And now I find that my humility, won with so much pain, is arrogance.

Today my mind is illuminated by this testimony, which I continue in the very image of my long penance, that is, in both suffering and satisfaction. Let he who reads my words know that in the end I feel no remorse, for I am too old for that, my demise too near. Let him come to know me fully and judge me as I am, in my repentance and in my pride.

May God allow me to complete my work and through it

As Mathilde had promised, Liébaut's fever abated by dawn, and as I changed the cloth on his wound, I was amazed to see that the edges of the gash had knitted together, leaving in his flesh only a long line just under the scar left by the arrow of Auxerre. As I touched the closed, dry line with my fingertips, I was not sure whom to thank more, God Almighty or the red-haired peasant woman. I helped my master don his linen shirt, his breeches, and his tunic with its fur-trimmed leather buckles, and I could not resist telling him of the joy that filled my heart, joy at seeing him on his feet again, freed of the corruption that had gnawed at him the night before, drenching him with sweat, choking the breath in his throat, sinking his mind in a thick haze. He rested his hand on my shoulder in a sign of affection and told me that he was in my debt for this cure, since I had overcome his hesitation by advising him to accept the woman's medicine.

The Frisians did not attack that day, as we had feared. Liébaut, though at times strangely pensive, was strong enough to direct the construction of the great hall and the walkway around the top of the tower, as the people of Arques, gathered at the foot of the hill between our two palisades, looked on. Bernon's warriors managed to put the roof on the donjon before evenfall, a true feat. To my great surprise—for I had never seen this done before—Liébaut ordered ox skins placed over the thatch-and-grass roof, to protect the castle from the firebrands our attackers would undoubtedly hurl in an attempt to set it ablaze. At dusk the red-and-gold colors of Normandy fluttered proudly from the top of the tower. My lord posted four lookouts on the walkway, one facing east where the sun rose, a second west where it set, a third in the direction of None, and the last toward Septentrion. From the peak of the tower it was now possible to survey the countryside from the forest of Arques to the coast, and to see from the port of Deep well up the Varenne, into which flowed the waters of the Béthune and the Eaulne. "They will not easily oust us from this position," Séguin de Brécy proudly announced; though, as usual, he had done nothing useful since dawn, being more occupied with his wife, Suzanne, than with the construction of our defenses.

A bitter cold now settled over the village, so my lord had large fires lit throughout the camp, for warriors and peasants alike to warm themselves. He worried too much, I felt, about the people of Arques, for though they remained fearfully gathered under our protection, they had done nothing whatever to help us. When the work was finished, on our eleventh night on the far coast, I saw from his face how weary Liébaut was.

"You need rest, my lord," I said, "or your wound will reopen, and the fever will sap your strength again."

"Your advice is good as always, Odilon," he replied. "I know it is unwise for me to remain on my feet. But Séguin and Suzanne de Brécy await me in the newly completed great hall tonight, to share the game their men killed in the forest this morning, foolishly ignoring the danger. It is most important for me to show no sign of weakness now, and it would be a sign of weakness were I to decline this invitation and go to bed instead."

As night fell, the important people of Falaise and Malbray gathered by candlelight at the invitation of Séguin and Suzanne de Brécy. Seated at trestle tables on the top floor of our tower, served by the kitchen servants, and accompanied by Draco's intolerable antics and by the fortunately more clement notes of the flute and the monochord, we ate the roasted meat of the rabbits and stags of Arques and drank the peasants' bitter wine. During the meal, my lord was thoughtful, distant. He did not respond when Séguin de Brécy angrily complained that the warriors of Malbray were, as he put it, too arrogant and vainglorious in their treatment of the men of Falaise. I had never seen my lord so indifferent to those around him. Was this reticence, this silence due to a returning fever? Before we had finished the griddlecakes, Liébaut announced—to the great satisfaction of Bernon, whose face was flushed with anger as he restrained himself under Séguin de Brécy's repeated attacks—that everyone should now retire, for we had a difficult day ahead of us. Ignoring Suzanne de Brécy's protests and Draco's shrieks as he rolled on the floor battling with a puppy over a scrap of meat and bone, he told the monk Granger to say a final prayer before the clearing of the table.

And they obeyed, for when my lord raised his voice, no one dared challenge him.

With the candles extinguished, everyone left, and my lord and I retired to his room on the floor below. He was silent as I performed my duty as his squire, helping him remove his tunic and linen shirt. When I bared his chest, I saw that bright blood had soaked through the cloth I had wrapped around him that morning. "The wound has reopened," I said, my voice full of fear. "You need fresh medicine."

He looked at his side. "Yet I have no pain or fever," he murmured.

"Should I fetch Bernon?" I asked, not sure what to do.

"No. It's nothing," he said. "Don't alarm him for such a small matter."

"But, my lord," I insisted, "if the corruption returns, you will be unable to remain at the head of your men, and someone else will take command of our army, to Normandy's misfortune."

He sighed.

What would happen, I asked, if Séguin de Brécy were to lead his warriors in his stead? "Did you hear how he attacked the men of Malbray tonight?" I blurted. "Did you see how his words upset your faithful friend Bernon?"

"I know. I feared that this might happen. But you should know that if anything happens to me, the leader of our army will be Vilgard de Chambois, not the lord of Brécy."

He sat down on the bed of grass and straw, put his hands to his brow, and thought awhile. Then he looked up and said that although he felt no pain, I should go at once and fetch Mathilde, the red-haired woman. "Even if I need no further medicine," he said, "I must thank her for what she did. Yesterday, because of the fever, I did not express my gratitude properly, and have regretted that all day."

He stopped me as I turned to carry out his order. "Be careful, Odilon," he said. "It is late, and none of the people now with her know that she came to me. Tell Thorer and his son that I am summoning her to discuss the accusation of theft against her brother, Talvos. Answer no questions, and be sure to tell them that I will send her back very soon."

I hastened down the tower stairway, descended the hill,

and crossed the inner palisade. It had begun to rain, and the peasants, most of them now gathered in the courtyard, were putting out their fires and entering the huts that had been built for them. I asked several churls where the woman was, but none could tell me, so I had to ask instead where Thorer was, and his son Ivar, whom I feared as much as I did Ubbo the Frisian. Finally I found myself in the hut of the chief of the people of Arques. It was so dark inside, the air so smoky from the fire that burned between two flat stones lying on the hard-packed earth, that at first I was unable to recognize anyone among the men and women sitting with their animals on beds of straw. The woman my lord needed was sitting between Thorer and her future husband.

"Liébaut de Malbray, master of Arques, wishes to speak to you. I will take you to him," I said, without further explanation. She raised astonished eyes to me.

"What does he want with her at this hour?" said Ivar, his voice shaking with rage. "Who is he to order a woman, a woman who will soon be mine, to visit him at night?"

"The lord of Arques," I replied, indignant, "wishes to speak with her again about the accusation against her brother, Talvos."

"The lord of Arques has already given his decision. What more does he want to know?" Ivar went on. "Does he doubt the wisdom of his verdict?"

"I am only his squire," I said, remembering Liébaut's instructions, "and know nothing more. Come"—I turned to Mathilde—"he will not keep you long."

The girl, after some hesitation, rose to follow me, but Ivar took her by the wrist and stopped her. "Isn't it enough that he has broken our agreement with Ubbo and is about to loose war and pain among us again?" he said. "Must he also send for our women in the middle of the night?"

Seeing that I would get nowhere with Ivar, I addressed

Thorer, a wiser man, who sat watching us without a word. "You, who are the chief of this village, persuade your son here not to oppose the will of the lord of Arques, who— need I remind you?—has restored your defenses and at the risk of his own life brought your two children back. Liébaut de Malbray, conqueror of Auxerre, frees you from an alliance with treacherous barbarians," I added, seeing that the old man was lost in thought. "He will protect you, for he is the most valiant lord in Normandy. You yourself, Thorer, cannot deny his valor, for everyone witnessed your delight in his feat yesterday. Moreover, he has not exercised his power over you by dispatching one of his warriors to bring Mathilde, but has sent me, Odilon de Bernay, his squire, who comes to you unarmed. It is not an order he gives, but a request he makes." I went on to say, raising my voice in the silence, that Liébaut de Malbray was no enemy of the people of Arques but their friend and champion—by the will of God Almighty and of Robert the Magnificent, duke of Normandy.

At that, Thorer slowly nodded. "Let her go," he said to his son. "Now that we are here behind his walls, there is no point in opposing Liébaut de Malbray's will." Ivar spat out a Germanic insult whose meaning escaped me, then released the girl's wrist, flashing me a look of hatred. An old woman draped a woolen blanket around Mathilde's shoulders, and without another word I left the hut with my charge.

I took her back to the tower in the rain, which now fell heavily. In the middle of the deserted courtyard, among the closed huts, I told her the truth: she had to treat my lord again, for his wound had reopened.

"But I know only one medicine," she said. "If he has moved too much since dawn, I will be able to do nothing for him. I warned him. I thought him wiser."

"He had to complete our defenses," I replied, annoyed by her hasty judgment of my master.

I turned to look at her as we crossed the inner palisade and started up the hill. She was small compared with me, though her shoulders were sturdy enough. Wrapped in the blanket, she held herself erect as she walked, despite the trepidation she must have felt. I thought I saw a kind of fire in her eyes, pride, even, though she was young and a peasant.

Entering the room, we found Liébaut with his chest bare; he had removed the strips of cloth. The lips of his wound were separated slightly and reddened by a thread of blood. Mathilde stood motionless in the doorway.

"I would like to express my gratitude better than I did yesterday," he said, approaching her. "Thanks to you, the fever abated, my strength returned, and I was able to complete the construction of the tower and walkway. Because of your medicine, no one has learned of my wound, and for that I am in your debt." He looked at her, a simple peasant girl shabbily dressed, rather pitiable with the drenched blanket on her shoulders and her hair plastered to her brow by the rain. To my surprise, Mathilde raised her head unbidden and looked at him. "What reward would you have for what you have done?" my lord asked gently.

"I want nothing," she said. "Only that you save our village and our lives, since you have decided to stay in this place and make war."

"Like the others, you regret that I have come." Liébaut sighed.

"We fear," she said, "because we have already suffered so much. All we want now is peace."

"And you think I bring only war?"

"You know you bring war," she murmured, staring back into the blue eyes that were fixed upon her.

I expected my lord to reply that war was necessary if the peace which everyone in Arques desired was to be restored, but he said nothing, and the woman finally lowered her eyes before him.

"Where do you come from?" he asked finally. "Tyrker called your brother a foreigner."

"We came here from Saint-Martin more than a year ago," she said.

"Why did you leave your village? Wasn't Talvos a serf there?"

"He was," she said, almost in a whisper, "but he had to leave."

"Or flee," my lord added, thoughtful. "I will not ask what crime he committed. I know that if I asked, you would tell me. You are truthful. So many people seek to conceal their thoughts and deeds, attempt to deceive me, as though I could not distinguish lies from truth. I am glad, woman, that you are not like them."

She looked up at my master, and he smiled at her.

"I repeat," he said. "Do not hide what you desire for yourself or your family, for I shall grant it."

Instead of responding to this offer, Mathilde reached forward and touched his wound. "I will replace the cloth," she said. "But you must move carefully for two full days, or the corruption will return and stay with you for a long time."

Without another word, my master went and sat on his bed of straw. Mathilde leaned over him, wiped the raw cut and, eyes lowered as Liébaut continued to stare at her, rewrapped the torn strips of cloth, one by one, around the wound.

The Frisians attacked at dawn on Thursday. Our army was taken completely by surprise. Fog, which seemed to transport the entire countryside into the clouds, covered the church and the village of Arques at the foot of the hill, and our lookouts on the tower walkway did not see the enemy ships slip into the port of Deep and turn up the Varenne. Their horns sounded the alarm just after we had awakened, as we were kneeling and reciting the prayers of prime. Liébaut, wearing only his linen shirt, rushed out before I could even move. As if the horns were the signal the Frisians had awaited to launch their attack, the dull thud of countless leather drums began to shake the ground. I ran out to the walkway, where Liébaut was shouting commands, ordering the catapults to be loaded and sending the archers to the palisades and the bearers of pikes and lances to the outer rampart.

What I saw below made my blood freeze: two hundred menacing shadows gray in the fog, their faces and arms invisible as they advanced ponderously, still shapeless, moving toward us to the rhythm of their drums of war. I forgot my dreams of honor and glory and had a sudden urge to flee, to run to our room and cower there until the fighting was over, or better yet to sink into the ground and hide like a man dead and buried. By the grace of God, just as I was about to turn and run, forever drowning my life in shame, Liébaut ordered me to follow him into the tower and help him don his armor. The force of his voice steadied me. Swiftly I did my duty, pulling on his hauberk, closing the buckles of his greaves, placing his helmet on his head. Then, my hands shaking, I dressed myself in haste to accompany him and protect him in the battle.

When we reemerged on the walkway, our enemies were no more than seventy paces from the outer enceinte, and I could see their entire army as they came out of the fog. There were a hundred wooden shields, round with sharpened points and barbs, and two hundred helmets adorned with gleaming animal horns. Then I saw the barbarians themselves. Covered with fur and iron, armed with hatchets twice the size of woodcutters' tools, bows as big as men, and swords so heavy they had to be held with both hands, they closed in slowly from every direction, as if borne by the smoke of hell. Some, I saw with horror, carried ladders. My fear returned. Liébaut did not order the archers to loose their arrows, but wisely waited for the enemy to come closer, for it was still hard to see them, and we had to make every arrow count.

Through the fog shrouding our tower, as in a dream, I saw Bernon herding the terrified peasants into their huts, the roofs of which we had also covered with ox skins, two days before, slaughtering much livestock for that purpose. For a fleeting instant I saw the monk Granger standing at the foot of the hill, holding a staff with the Cross of Christ Our Lord tied to the top, and blessing our army. Our warriors, in the fog below, suddenly seemed too far from us, too isolated, too weak, almost defenseless, as though they would never be able to stop the barbarians, who were three times their number.

The enemy began to shout with eagerness as they advanced, and my thoughts became jumbled. Was it really I who had killed the Frisian on the ship by the cliff a few days before, or had I dreamed it? Everyone in our castle seemed ready to fight—was it I alone who feared the battle? "The moment has come, Odilon," said Liébaut, and before I could speak he ordered the archers to shoot, for the enemy now was visible enough.

A rain of arrows fell upon the Frisians, and many were gravely wounded. But this did not stop them. Behind their large round shields, they continued their march. "Our moat is too small," Liébaut said in a dull voice. "They'll cross it easily and attack the palisade. Pray God that it is strong enough." As my lord predicted, our bows and crossbows were now useless, for the enemy rushed into the moat, which we had been unable to fill deeply enough, having insufficient water in our well. We hurled heavy stones at them as they waded across, only chest-deep in water, but they ignored the few of their number who fell. Through the veil of fog that was like the vapors of hell, I could make out nearly two hundred of them. They threw their ladders against the slope of our moat and climbed up to attack the outer enceinte.

The knights of Malbray and Falaise, led by Bernon and Vilgard de Chambois, struck with their swords, lances, and pikes. Attackers and defenders merged, mingled along the entire length of the palisade, and the air was filled with shouts and the clash of weapons. Through the fog I saw the barbarians striking our raised drawbridge with great hatchet blows, and I saw that many had fallen on both sides of the rampart, but at that distance could not tell to which army the bodies belonged. When the palisade began to break under the force and number of the attackers, Liébaut hastily descended from the tower. My father's sword in hand, clutching my shield before me and driving all thought from my mind, I followed him on trembling legs.

The bodies of several of our men lay on the ground, their skulls split or throats slashed, and to my horror I had to step over a gaping chest to enter the battle. Blood flowed everywhere. Liébaut, quicker than I, joined Bernon and hurled himself at the Frisians, who, trying to break through the palisade at the raised drawbridge, were advancing fifteen abreast. I went to follow him, but stones were flying around me and one of them struck me on the lip before I could join the fight. My mouth filled with blood, and I was deafened by the screams of hatred, the clashing of weapons, the thudding of drums, the blare of trumpets, and the cries of the wounded. The earth seemed to move beneath me, and Lié-baut looked as though he were a hundred paces away as he stood in the distant fog and swung his mace, bringing it down on an enemy with all his might. Before I could recover my wits, a barbarian charged into the courtyard and fell upon me, aiming his barbed shield at my shoulder. I leaped aside, but because of the pain in my mouth and my dizziness, I fell to one knee. Howling, he took his sword in both hands and swung at my throat. Seeing death before me, I rolled away, moving even farther from the man I was sworn to protect. I bumped into a catapult, lost my shield, and awaited the mortal blow, breathless, powerless, my eyes closed. But, instead, I heard above me a sound like the strangled groan of the enemy I had killed on the ship. I looked and saw Bernon's red sword passing through the body of the man who had been about to end my life. So it was that on that morning, unaware of the true nature of my soul, the giant Viking Bernon Hildetand, dearest friend of my lord Liébaut de Malbray, unfortunately saved my life.

When I regained my feet, I searched for my master and saw that he was far from me, outside our defenses. Well beyond the breached palisade, on the other side of our half-filled moat, he and four other men of Malbray were fighting to drive the barbarians back into Arques. I saw him snap a large pike with a single stroke of his sword. Tears filled my eyes at the sight of such valor in a man whose wound was barely closed, and I promised myself that when peace was restored, I would write a song to immortalize his great feats.

Suddenly a hundred flaming arrows fell around us, but instead of sinking into the roofs and setting them ablaze, the arrows slid off the ox skins, as Liébaut had foreseen, and fell harmlessly to the ground. Now free of fear, forgetting how near death had come, and abandoning even simple caution,

I threw myself into the battle. Despite the pain in my mouth, which made it difficult for me to think, I cut and thrust furiously, hoping to reach my master. But the press of our own warriors, trying to prevent the enemy from entering the castle, stood in my way. I had no choice but to fight in the rear, at Bernon's side, and thus I failed, for the second time, to do my duty to protect the lord of Arques, whom no one else was shielding.

Liébaut continued to move forward, and the farther he went, the more he melted into the fog. When he was no more than a gray shadow recognizable only by his great size, the fear struck me that Ubbo was deliberately luring him from our camp. But—God be praised!—I had underestimated my master's judgment. He went no farther, and I was able to keep his unreal silhouette in view until the battle's end, a silhouette as large and powerful as Thor himself, the invincible god of war.

I fatally wounded two of the enemy on that day of slaughter, but I cared more about my lord than about my own safety. The prayer I addressed to the Almighty during the battle, that He protect Liébaut, was surely heard, for my master, unfailing and magnificent in the face of the greatest peril, swinging now his mace, now his sword, drove the enemy back without suffering a single blow.

It was past tierce, and I was covered with enemy blood, when the Frisian horns finally sounded retreat, since it was now clear that they would not succeed in overrunning our camp. Bernon and I managed to capture two of them, preventing their escape. The barbarians left twenty-eight men, dead or wounded, on the field, on both sides of our palisade, and a great cheer of victory rose from our army. Only Bernon remained silent, uttering no cry of joy. When I asked him why, he told me that the barbarian defeat was deceptive.

"They nearly vanquished us," he said. "They crossed our moat and were on the point of invading our camp. They were unsuccessful in the end only because they did not know our valor, and therefore waged a disorderly attack, using no war machine to open a wider breach in our defenses. They will be back, better armed and with a better plan of battle, and on that day many of us will perish." Finding him too gloomy, I left him and hurried to join Liébaut, who was still outside our palisade, at the site of his exploits. "Your victory is now certain!" I cried, throwing myself into his arms. "Listen to how they praise you! Forgive me for not having done my duty to protect you, but Bernon will tell you how the enemy separated us." I clung to him with all my might until he took me by the shoulders and held me at arms' length.

"Odilon, you're wounded!" he said, seeing the blood that had spilled from my mouth.

"It is nothing, my lord," I said, taking off my helmet. "Just a stone. But I was almost killed, and if Bernon hadn't saved me, you would have had to find another squire."

I saw him smile, though his hood and nose guard hid half his face. "God was with us today," he murmured, holding me close again. "You fought well? With the courage and skill you showed on the Frisian ship when we rescued the hostages?"

"I killed two barbarians," I said proudly, "and captured a prisoner."

"Good, Odilon." How strange, a gentle voice coming from a man in armor that was covered with the blood of his enemies!

"And your wound?" I asked. "It didn't reopen in the battle?"

"No. Do not worry," he said softly, affectionately stroking my hair. "There is no pain at all."

It was one of those moments I wished would never end, for the joy that my lord and I were together again was stronger than life itself, greater than youth or the thrill of love. After that morning of his victory and great feats, I lost all sense of judgment and measure in my admiration of Liébaut de Malbray, forgetting that he was, after all, no more than a man. I came to love him as one should love only a saint.

A fresh clamor rose from our camp, and I turned and saw that the enemy horde, in its retreat, was burning every house in Arques, setting ablaze also the church we had tried to rebuild. Flames leaped up everywhere, even from the meanest hut, turning what once were human habitations into ruins. Through the red-tinged fog we saw three peasants—two men and a woman, who foolishly had remained outside our camp—fleeing their burning home. We watched with horror as the barbarian devils fell upon them and with terrible dagger strokes slit the throats and bellies of the two men. "May God curse you! May you burn in hell forever!" I shouted, though too far away for them to hear. Having butchered the men, they completed their revenge by carrying the woman off with them, back to their ships, where she would surely suffer an unspeakable death.

The flames spread destruction through the village and the surrounding fields. The smoke made the fog even thicker. "It will be a long time, now, before we can rebuild Arques," Liébaut said. "Whether we want to or not, henceforth, and until this war is over, we must keep the peasants with us in the castle."

As we gathered our eight dead and eleven wounded behind the breached palisade, the people of Arques emerged from their huts, huddled together and holding one another—men with eyes wide with fear, women trembling, children crying. When he saw Liébaut comforting Gerbin, who had lost a hand, Thorer walked quickly toward him, followed by Ivar, Tyrker, and many others.

"Look what you have done now, with your rekindling of this war!" the village chief shouted at my lord. "Not only did the Frisians cross the moat, breach your defenses, and nearly slaughter us all, but they have devastated Arques as well, turned our houses to ashes, burned our fields, destroyed our church. Because of your arrogance and vainglory, we now have no place to live."

"So long as this war lasts," Liébaut replied calmly, "you will remain in the shelter of my castle. Tomorrow we will begin erecting new, stronger and higher, defenses around our camp. If need be, we will sustain a long siege with you, for in the storeroom we have provisions to feed everyone until spring. Here, under the protection of my warriors and of Almighty God, you will have nothing to fear."

"And the property we have lost?" Ivar screamed. "How are we to live without houses for shelter, without crops and hay to feed the animals?"

"Once peace is restored," Liébaut said, patient despite his weariness, "I will rebuild your church and your houses. I solemnly swear that I will restore your village before Easter, and protect it with an enclosure. Not only that. I will see that your fields are plowed. I will sow winter and spring wheat, and remain among you through the harvest season. I will wield the sickle myself. I will cut wood for you, enough for a year, and plant gardens around each of your huts so that you do not lack for vegetables. I will make you a mill to crush and grind your grain, and build an oven outside the castle, that you may bake your own bread. As for the church, the warriors of Falaise and Malbray will spare no effort in building a new one, more beautiful than the one you lost. I will fill it with statues of all the saints, and the most precious of Normandy's relics will be brought to it, in the bishop's presence. All this will be done, I swear before God, on my honor as a knight."

I watched the peasants as Liébaut said these words to them. Most listened in humility, as a good tenant listens to his lord. But some fidgeted, scowled, muttered Germanic insults and threats. In anger, I felt that these people should be driven from our camp and left without protection.

"You say fine things, lord of Malbray," replied Thorer, his old face still flushed, "but you forget that to keep these promises you must first vanquish the Frisians, against whom you have so unwisely renewed this war, despite our warning on your arrival here. And already you have forgotten that they nearly defeated you today, that repelling their attack cost you many of your warriors, and that you were unable to prevent the burning of our village and our fields. They will surely return, driven by rage, to take their revenge on us, and you will not be able to protect us then."

"You would do better," my lord said, "to consider how many of the enemy we killed, wounded, and took prisoner today before repulsing and routing their army."

"Because of you we have no houses, no crops!" Ivar shouted.

"Everything will be rebuilt!" roared Bernon, whose anger was mounting.

"No, it won't," Tyrker said, pointing at my lord. "This man speaks like a lunatic, and we will all be killed because of him!"

"That's right!" shouted another peasant. "Just as pride brought down Lucifer, so it will bring down Liébaut de Malbray, and us with him!"

"Your good sense has been warped by grief and fear," said

121

my lord. "Again, a second time, I forgive your outburst, for I understand what you feel. But I will tolerate no discord that might weaken us and benefit our enemy. Be advised, then, that no one is compelled to remain behind these walls, and he who wishes to leave my castle may do so. The bridge will stay lowered until nightfall for those leaving. No one will stop them. But all who remain must stand in accord with us."

"Enough talk!" said Bernon. "We have much to do. We must care for our wounded, rebuild our defenses. As your lord, Liébaut de Malbray, has promised, you will be protected and Arques will be restored. Let those who spurn his protection be gone before this evening, for when night falls, the bridge will be raised and no one else can go."

We left the peasants of Arques standing there, the humble and the discontented alike silenced by the severity of my master, and carried the wounded into Liébaut's room on the second floor of the tower. By torchlight, we laid them on beds of grass and straw, just as we had done for Liébaut when he was wounded on the Frisian ship, and one by one we uncovered the wounds inflicted by sword, hatchet, or pike. Some were cuts, in the leg or shoulder, that seemed of little consequence, but others—in the head, stomach, or chest— were grievous and bled copiously. I began to fear that new losses would be added to those already suffered by our army.

Bernon, my lord, Nicolas, and the monk Granger cleaned each wound with pieces of cloth I moistened for them. The cries of pain from those racked by fever troubled me deeply; it was as though their pain was mine as they twisted on their beds. Often, seeing slashed flesh and crushed bones, I had to close my eyes. Even today I hate the sight of blood. Though my own disease and death hold no terror for me, I dread them when they strike the other monks of Jumièges, my

122

brothers in God. Such is my heart, and I no longer struggle against the turmoil that Liébaut de Malbray did not judge shameful that day in Deep, on the far coast, at the beginning of our adventure. Examining each wound, Bernon and Nicolas in most cases announced that burning would prevent corruption. My lord frowned, became pensive, then suddenly said—as Bernon began heating the blade of his dagger in the fire—that he believed it would be wiser to use, instead, Mathilde and her remedy.

"But do you think that Thorer and Ivar will let her come this time?" I asked, not pleased at the prospect of going back to the hut in which she lived and where her future husband was. He was scarcely older than I, and yet I feared him.

"They must," Liébaut replied in a voice whose resolution surprised me. "We will send three men-at-arms to bring her here with her medicine immediately."

"Will this not stir up the people of Arques against us?" I insisted, at the risk of seeming to contradict my lord.

"The peasants are afraid, they will hold their tongues!" he said with unwonted impatience. "The important thing is not to try to resolve what cannot yet be resolved, but to restore our army to its fighting strength as soon as possible."

Before long, three men of Falaise escorted the red-haired woman into the room. She carried with her the crushed leaves, hen's eggs, and animal fat she needed to prepare her remedy.

Liébaut went to her the moment she appeared. "You must heal these men as you healed me," he whispered in her ear. "I need them. When the enemy returns, every arm will be precious to me."

The woman examined the wounded one by one. "I will not be able to treat them all," she said humbly. "The injuries of some are too great."

"I know your skill, Mathilde," Liébaut said. "Do all you can—for Arques, for the defense of your own people, and for these poor men gripped by pain and fever. And for me as well," he added, lowering his eyes, which was not his custom, "since I will be hard pressed in the coming battle if I am deprived of the strength of so many warriors."

"We told you how fierce the Frisians were," Mathilde said in quiet reproach. "Why did you not listen to us?"

"I must win this war," Liébaut replied, "for Normandy, for Robert, and for you, the people of Arques, who would have been slaughtered sooner or later had my army not come. But now I need you, for you know how to stay corruption and restore vigor." And he took her by the shoulders with affection, just as he had done to me.

"My people will cast me out if I do what you ask," she moaned. "Ivar will refuse to take me as his wife."

"Are they so determined," Liébaut asked, "that we be destroyed?"

Mathilde said nothing as my lord continued to hold her. I watched her, hoping to guess her thoughts, and saw a tear in her eye.

"Perhaps they still hope for a shameful reconciliation with Ubbo," my lord continued, "and mean to betray me by concluding a new alliance with him."

The tear spilled down Mathilde's cheek. My master wiped it away with a finger.

"Have no fear," he said with strong affection. "Nothing will cause you grief, for you will be under the protection of the lord of Arques and his men-at-arms. If you wish, you can stay here in my tower until our enemies are vanquished. Then, when peace is restored, everyone in the village will praise you for the aid you gave us."

The girl lowered her eyes and stood silent, as if fearing the decision she had to make. Her red hair, fallen over her pale face, made it difficult for me to see her expression. She seemed wretched at that moment, in her coarse dress cinched at the waist by a piece of rope, a poor and humble creature huddled before the most noble of war lords, a peasant woman of no importance. Her face barely reached as high as Liébaut's chest. Yet she raised her head and looked up at him without fear.

"I cannot force you to help me," he murmured then. "I understand your torment. Return to your people, if you wish. I will hold you in no reproach."

With a movement of her head she tossed the hair back from her face, and I saw a light in her eyes, that same glint of pride, so strange in a peasant woman, that I remembered seeing several days before, when I led her through the rainy night to treat my lord the second time. She stood motionless for a moment, then handed Liébaut the crushed leaves and animal fat and asked him to come and help her place them on the wounds of his men.

While Bernon and the men of Malbray repaired the palisade, Liébaut stayed with Mathilde. He watched as she mixed the animal fat and egg whites and applied the ointment with her fingertips to the open wounds. I was surprised at this attention, but assumed that he wanted to learn to administer the remedy himself. Mathilde had little trouble treating Foulques, Orderic, Guilbert, and Richard, the first of our wounded men, but things were different when it came to Arnoul, whose side had been pierced by a pike. Under the watchful eyes of Suzanne and Séguin de Brécy, whose second in command Arnoul was, she tried to apply the medicine as she had done for the four other warriors. But the moment she touched the wound, Arnoul screamed and writhed in agony. His face drenched with sweat, the poor man clung to the woolen blanket with what strength he had left and begged to be allowed to end his life in peace, in the presence of our priest Granger, bearer of the Cross of Christ. After trying in vain to treat the wretched man, whose brow already bore the mark of death, Mathilde sadly declared that she could do nothing for him.

"You must burn the wound," said Séguin de Brécy, always quick to tell others what to do, though never undertaking anything himself. "Why use a witch's remedy?"

"The remedy works," Liébaut replied. "It will cure him."

"No. My master is right in what he says, Séguin is right!" exclaimed the dwarf Draco, whose arrival I had not noticed in the dim room illuminated only by a few resin torches on the walls. "When the corruption is burned away, nothing remains of it."

Liébaut, ignoring that shrill outburst, leaned over Arnoul and gently wiped the poor man's face with a piece of cloth. Leaning close, he murmured words of comfort to this warrior who was not even from Malbray. "The medicine will close your wound," he said. "Your fever will abate, your pain disappear, your strength return. In four days you will stand at our side ready to fight again, as you fought this morning, earning the admiration of us all. Fear not, Robert will know of your valor and your exploits, and he will honor you in Falaise."

Soon Arnoul seemed to be at ease. My lord rose and ordered me to fetch a pitcher of strong wine, the kind that carries the mind away so easily.

"I'll go, I'll go!" Draco cried with a grimace so ugly, it made him look like a demon, and scurried out on his spindly legs before I could stop him, thus preventing me from obeying my master.

Without waiting for the dwarf to return, and against the repeated objections of Séguin de Brécy, Liébaut took the animal fat and egg whites from Mathilde, who stood motionless, uncertain what to do. He asked her to stroke Arnoul's hair and brow as he had done. Then he dipped his large fingers into the two materials, mixed them together, knelt beside the ugly wound, and with the greatest care applied the unguent to the lips of the torn flesh. He was so gentle that this time Arnoul lay still, moaning softly like a child. As we looked on in amazement, Liébaut slowly dressed the wound. The ointment spread over the half-dried blood, joining the edges of the flesh together in a kind of clear paste. Draco had still not brought the wine my lord had wanted in order to make Arnoul sleep, so he told Arnoul to breathe deeply, like a boar exhausted and out of breath at the end of a long hunt. In the silence of our room, among the wounded men stretched out side by side, my lord continued to care for this poor warrior with magnificent skill. Need I write, yet again, how I admired such nobility? At that moment, even I, who prided myself on knowing Liébaut de Malbray well, was astonished, for I had thought of him as a glorious god of war, whose strength was so precious to me. Now I realized how great, also, was the goodness of his heart.

Then Draco, the night creature, exhilarated by the effort he had just expended in running through the camp, burst into the room with two pitchers of wine, his clothing in disarray. "Here I am!" he cried, shattering Arnoul's rest and undoing my master's gentleness. "I bring the medicine that cures all ills! Who wants this joyous brew, this blood of Christ sweetly perverted by Satan in the fires of the abyss?"

So loud was his laughter and his beastly howling that Arnoul was gripped by pain again, and Liébaut had to stop applying Mathilde's remedy and hold the man's shoulders.

The loathsome dwarf had already angered me by usurping my place as squire, and now, as he approached the wounded man to give him wine, I flew into a rage and ripped the pitchers from his hands. Then I seized him by his tunic and threw him to the floor as hard as I could. He rolled, arms and legs flailing like those of a broken doll. "Don't touch my dwarf!" shouted Suzanne de Brécy. "He is under my protection!" But I could not control myself and kept on hitting him.

"You will be punished for this," he yelled, his face red with fury. "Heaven's fire will fall upon you and reduce you to ashes!"

I kicked the little monster down the stairs and cried, "Away with you, evil incarnate! Wicked heart!"

"You will be punished for this," he repeated through his tears. "I will see to your punishment."

By the grace of God, before I could rush down the stairs and strike him again, Suzanne de Brécy shouldered past me and went to him. Otherwise, in my madness I might have committed murder, and who knows what harm such an act would have caused Liébaut? But perhaps it would have been better if I had murdered the dwarf and been hanged on the gallows in Arques as punishment.

The lady of Brécy took her dwarf in her arms as one would a child. "My poor Draco," she moaned, "what has this wretch, more evil than Ubbo the Frisian, done to you?" She held his ghastly head, caressed his pointed skull and coarse, wrinkled brow. As the hunchbacked creature continued to moan and wail, she cursed me and swore that before the war was over, she and Draco would revenge themselves on me. Unwilling to hear more, I left them clinging to each other and rejoined my master, my limbs trembling.

Liébaut, still occupied with Arnoul, did not chide me as I

deserved. But as I passed Séguin de Brécy, my stomach still in a knot, he shot me a look of hatred.

Kneeling side by side, Liébaut and Mathilde were covering the wound with dried leaves, Arnoul having been calmed again after Draco's abrupt departure. I watched them place each leaf until the wound was covered by three layers. The girl's hands looked like a child's next to my lord's, which were twice as large. Then they took a long strip of cloth and, under Séguin de Brécy's suspicious, hostile gaze, silently wrapped it around Arnoul. I caught Mathilde's rapid glance at my master as he carefully lifted the wounded warrior so that she could reach around his back with the bandage. For the first time I thought I detected, deep in her green eyes, a glimmer of admiration for this lord who cared so well for a man cruelly pierced by a pike's thrust.

When all the wounded had been treated, Mathilde spoke to Liébaut. "Now you will have no further need of me," she said humbly. "You know my remedy and can apply it better than anyone."

"Thanks to you," my lord acknowledged, "I will be able to tend my men and to restore their strength myself. But I would not have been able to help Arnoul had you not been with me. If he recovers and returns to combat in four days, it is to you that he will owe his good fortune: to the serenity and kindness that passed into me from you."

"To come to the aid of those who suffer is our duty to God," she murmured.

Seeing how solemn she was, Liébaut divined her anxiety and asked her not to return home immediately, but to stay in the tower until nightfall, in the great hall, where she would be able to rest. "Inasmuch as it is impossible for you to remain here," he added, "and because you must return to Thorer and Ivar, I will hand you back to them myself. I will invite them to supper at my table, they and the other tenants of Arques, and will tell them what I commanded you to do and explain how much our army owes you. Fear not, they will listen, for I know the words that will convince them. I must go now, to bury our dead with our monk Granger and to see to the repairing of our defenses with Bernon, most valiant of the knights of Malbray. I leave you now, but wait for me. As soon as my tasks are done, I will come back to you and have a table prepared for your people."

"What if they refuse to come?" she asked.

"They will not refuse."

As I dreaded, my master chose me to deliver his invitation to Thorer and Ivar. "I want them at my table tonight," he told me, when Mathilde had retired to the great hall. "You are skilled, Odilon, you will be able to convince them."

I wanted to protest, to warn him about me, but said nothing, because I could not bear disappointing him, and once again my silence deceived him. I was reluctant to speak, also, because he now referred to my unfortunate behavior with Draco, saying that as far as he was concerned the service I would now perform would erase the memory of that outburst against Suzanne de Brécy's dwarf. "In no way do I hold your temper against you," he added. "I know how natural a lack of moderation is for those your age. I myself was immoderate too often in the past to condemn the failing harshly now."

When I reached the foot of the hill and crossed the inner palisade, which by the grace of God had been untouched by the enemy attack, I saw the dead lined up in the courtyard: on one side, our own men, covered with foliage; on the other, the bloodstained Frisians, their faces gray, stripped of their armor, ready for burning. Though preoccupied with what I would say to the peasants to convince them to share our supper, I was stopped by the smell of death, at once sickly sweet and sulfurous, the odor of dried blood and wounds gone cold. It seized me by the throat and choked me. I quickened my pace, to escape that menacing breath from the grave, and my haste brought me to the peasant hut before I had decided what to say.

The smoke from the fire that burned on the hard-packed earthen floor prevented me from seeing the people to whom I wished to speak. Slowly, my eyes stinging, I managed to make out a number of peasants seated on beds of straw. Among hens and several pigs lying on their sides, I saw women making baskets for harvests to come, when the war ended. Finally, beyond a group of children busy reenacting our battle, I saw some villagers gathered around Thorer. They sat in a circle, as if holding a council to decide whether or not to remain in our camp. I walked toward them, taking care not to step on any of the serfs and servant girls who lay on the floor in those cramped quarters. Recognizing me, the villagers broke off their discussion, and I joined them in an awkward silence.

Believing it futile to wait for someone to speak first, I told them, with great caution, of my master's invitation.

When I finished, Ivar announced that he would not set foot in our tower, and that if his future wife was not returned to him forthwith, he would go and fetch her himself. Fortunately, before he could go any further, his father took his arm and urged him to be quiet. "My son is right to be angry," he said to me with a sigh, "for in truth Liébaut de Malbray has brought us only misfortune. Yet you may rejoice, squire, for now that the damage is done, no one among us desires to leave this place. Even if the bridge is lowered, no man of Arques would be mad enough to cross it and walk to certain

131

death. For us there is now no refuge outside this castle. We are prisoners between these palisades. Your lord knows very well that he holds us in his hands, and he must indeed be laughing at us."

He was silent for a moment, and I saw that many around him nodded in agreement. "What, then, are we to do when Liébaut de Malbray orders us to his table?" he went on, looking me full in the face. "What choice do we have? Since we are forced to recognize him as our lord, how is it possible for us to flout his will? Answer me, you whom he sends to us as earlier he sent his men-at-arms to take Mathilde."

I stood mute, disturbed by his words. In the depths of the old man's sunken eyes I saw hatred glitter. "If you reject his invitation," I said clumsily, "my lord will take offense."

"And was I not offended," roared Ivar, "when he had his warriors carry off my future wife?"

"He needed her medicine for our wounded," I replied.

"We know that," Thorer said gravely. "But why did he not come himself to tell us? Or does he hold us in too much contempt?"

Silence fell over the smoky hut as men, women, and children, servant girls, serfs, and tenants of Arques awaited my answer. Fifty pairs of eyes were fixed upon me.

"On the contrary," I said. "He holds you in great friendship. He will not rest until he has vanquished the Frisians, restored peace, and rebuilt your village. He is the greatest, the most valiant, the most generous knight of Normandy. He won his first battle when he was no older than I am now, and our duke, the Magnificent, has full confidence in him."

The crackling of the fire behind me and the sound of a child whimpering were the only response to my words.

"Did he not bring your two children back?" I exclaimed, losing patience. "Did he not defeat the Frisians this morning? Are you not still alive thanks only to his valor? Instead of bemoaning your fate, consider how fortunate you are to have as your lord the man who gloriously conquered Auxerre and has since won so many other battles!"

There was a heavier silence, and then Thorer, clearly resenting my fervent words, asked me to leave. "We will consider our decision," he said, tight-lipped.

Thinking—at last with a little wisdom—that my continued presence would do no good, I left without any further effort to convince him and returned to Liébaut in anguish, cursing my own clumsiness and certain that none of the peasants would come to our tower.

When I returned, my lord, busy discussing the reinforcement of our defenses with Bernon and Vilgard de Chambois, asked me what the people of Arques had said. Though I wanted to confess my lack of skill, instead I deceitfully said that Thorer and his people would come, but that they had insisted on discussing the matter among themselves before announcing their decision. Liébaut nodded, blinded by his confidence in me. Believing that I had in fact convinced them, he ordered that pigs and hens be slaughtered for the supper and that white bread and honey cakes be baked. My heart filled with shame, but I said nothing, I did not have the courage.

Before evenfall, as Bernon burned the bodies of the enemy dead on a large pyre, Liébaut led me outside our camp to find a place to bury our own dead the next morning. Throughout our search, my mind was gravely troubled by the lie I had told, for I knew how important my lord considered the supper he hoped to share with Thorer and Ivar. Words of truth burned on my lips every time we paused, but I could not speak them.

My master finally decided to put our cemetery near a spring

halfway up the slope of a small hill on the other side of the Varenne, in an uncultivated field that the Frisians, coming from Deep, would have no reason to cross, even in making an attack. "We will dig the graves here at dawn," he said, turning back toward the castle. "This is far enough from our camp that none of the people of Arques will fear our dead. Were it up to me," he added, "I would bury our dead at the foot of the hill within our walls, for I believe that the worlds of the dead and of the living are one and should commingle, that passage to the hereafter is an act of hope, and that dread of the other world ought to be abolished. But alas, Odilon, many weak minds fear the dead, imagining nameless powers. I pity them, for their minds are afflicted with superstition, and at the moment of their passing they will tremble at the darkness instead of calmly and joyously awaiting the ascent to eternal light."

Upon our return, Liébaut took me up to the great hall to oversee the preparations for supper. Under the gaze of Mathilde, who sat by herself in a shadowy corner, he ordered that a table twice the length of the one on which we usually ate be set up on eight trestles, and that it be covered by a fringed tablecloth strewn with grass, as was the custom in the court of Falaise. He inquired into the baking of the bread and the honey cakes, and into the roasting of the hens and the pork. He asked that the kitchen servants prepare a milk soup and draw several quarts of wine. To compound my shame in my deception, he also tried to soothe Mathilde's fears, assuring her that in due course he would overcome Ivar's and Thórer's resentment. Then he asked me, in full view of the peasant woman, to help him don his tunic with the fur-trimmed buckles. When the food was ready, he lit several candelabra, which filled the room with bright light, as if this was the evening of a feast. Satisfied, he sent for the two of our warriors who knew the art of music, that they might play the monochord and the flute during the meal in honor of his guests.

Liébaut, as lord, sat in the middle, with Bernon on his left and Vilgard de Chambois, the monk Granger, Séguin and Suzanne de Brécy, now fortunately calmer, on his right. I sat on the other side of the table, next to Mathilde, whom Liébaut wanted opposite him. "With Odilon beside you," he told the girl, "you will not be alone among your people." Having taken our places, we began to wait. Time passed, but the guests did not arrive. Twenty times, the truth was on the tip of my tongue. After some aimless discussion, the talk finally turned to what we should do with the nine Frisians taken prisoner. Séguin de Brécy said they were a source of danger and we ought to hang them, but Vilgard de Chambois argued that hostages might be useful as the war continued. The debate became heated, and despite my troubled mind, I took some pleasure in seeing the men of Falaise quarrel among themselves.

Looking more noble than ever in his fur-trimmed tunic, as magnificent as Robert in his court, Liébaut remained aloof from the discussion, possibly out of artifice, though I was not sure of that. Erect in his seat, he seemed more concerned about Mathilde, who sat silently beside me. As time passed and he continued to observe her, I told myself that the harm I was doing by not telling him that Ivar and Thorer were not coming was unforgivable; he would become a ridiculous figure, a man deceived, in front of Séguin de Brécy and Vilgard de Chambois, and this would undermine his power. Why am I like this? I asked myself, my eyes fixed on the man I loved so much. Is it treachery alone that abides in my heart?

Just when I was finally about to confess my shame and say that I had been unable to persuade the people of Arques to come, Draco burst into the hall like a demon driven by the breath of hell. As he passed behind me, he let out a snort that chilled me and went to join his mistress, his mouth twisted in its usual hideousness. Suzanne de Brécy, stroking his bristly hair as one would the sweaty coat of a bloodhound, helped him hoist himself to the bench beside her. With that vile and revolting gaze upon me, those black eyes burning with wickedness, it was now impossible for me to speak. Horrified by my own cowardice, imagining Mathilde's fears as she sat so silently beside me—she would have to spend the rest of the war in this tower because of me—I resolved simply to await the inevitable exposure of my lie.

As I wondered what punishment I would inflict on myself to atone for this transgression, God wrought a true miracle: a kitchen servant came in and announced that the people of Arques were coming up the stairway to join our supper in the great hall.

Thorer was the first to enter, and my lord addressed him: "Welcome, you and your people, to my table." The old man said nothing, but in response to his host's request sat beside Mathilde. Seven tenants followed him, but Ivar was not among them, and I realized that I was the beneficiary of only half a miracle. Thorer's presence, however, was sufficient to conceal my misdeed. No one seemed to want to speak, so my master, bowing his head, invited all those gathered in the great hall to thank God Almighty for the morning's victory and the evening's meal.

When the prayer was over, Liébaut asked the musicians to play and ordered the kitchen servants to serve the soup and pour the wine. Though the people of Arques seemed anything but friendly, he expressed the hope that harmony would now take hold in the village, for our common salvation and for Normandy's glory. Despite these words of peace, a sullen silence continued to hang over our table, and somehow it was made worse by the music and by Draco's perfidious whispering in Suzanne de Brécy's ear.

Then, to my surprise, Thorer spoke. "Why did you invite us to share this supper with you?" he asked Liébaut.

"For the reasons I have just given you: because we must stand together in friendship if we are to vanquish the enemy, because I am your lord and therefore one of you, a man of Arques. My bread and wine are yours as well."

Thorer nodded his gray head as though he understood perfectly. "Many of our people," he said, "among them my son Ivar, whose future wife you hold here by force, refuse to enter your tower. To them you are a foreigner." He paused. "What measures do you intend to take against them?"

"You, Thorer, and you seven others have taken your seats at my table this evening, and for the moment that suffices to cheer me."

"Could we have rejected your invitation?" the old man asked in a grim voice.

"Did I send armed warriors to compel you?" Liébaut countered, looking at them evenly, one by one. "Did I not instead dispatch this squire, whose words I know well are always genial and never spoken in a tone of command?" At this Draco let out a shrill bark of laughter, but my lord ignored him. "I am sure," he continued, "that sooner or later, whether tonight or in days soon to come, we will reach an understanding. As for your son Ivar's wrath, I well understand it, and when this supper is done, Mathilde will freely return to him with you."

My lord then spoke of our wounded men and of Mathilde's aid in caring for them. At great length he praised the merits of the girl, without whom, he said, the lives of several of our men would have ended tragically in the course of the night. Though I felt weary from the morning's battle, and my mind was growing sluggish, I noticed that several of the men of Arques, softened by Liébaut's words, had decided to eat their soup and drink their wine. "Mathilde may rejoin you," Liébaut said, "because now I know how to prepare and administer her medicine myself. I will therefore have no further need to send my warriors or anyone else to fetch her from under your roof. But when she is again among you, as she soon will be," he added, looking at her, "do not forget that everything she did in this tower was done at my command and that in spite of my desire for your friendship, I had no choice but to send for her, in the interests of preserving the strength of my army."

No one answered. Mathilde lowered her eyes, distressed. Draco, drinking steadily, began to whisper in Suzanne de Brécy's ear again, and Thorer, his face impassive, still did not touch the fresh white bread he had been given. For a moment I thought that my master's words had gone for nothing. Mathilde, sitting next to me, twice looked up at the lord who sat opposite her, and twice she averted her eyes to escape his penetrating gaze.

At last, hesitating, Thorer told the girl that he now understood why she had acted as she had. "When Ivar learns all this," he said with the beginning of a smile, "he will receive you with open arms."

From that moment, the meal took a better turn, though it was hardly cordial. Thorer accepted the roast pork and chicken he was served, and because of the wine, which they now consumed in considerable quantities, the peasants exchanged a few words in that difficult language of theirs, Norse mixed with Vulgar Latin and Germanic. The monk Granger, a wise man of great holiness and knowledge, began to talk to them quite skillfully, and soon they were asking him, among other things, whether the wine they were drinking, so similar to that used in the ritual of the mass, was a gift of God to His creatures in His infinite goodness or, on the contrary, a device of the Evil One, who sought to entice men into drunkenness and damnation. Liébaut, apparently content with the prevailing calm and partial understanding, withdrew from the discussion and spoke only when asked his opinion of this or that issue.

A good part of the meal thus passed without anything of consequence being said about Arques or the prosecution of our war. My weariness increased, and soon I found it difficult to keep my eyes open or to stop from falling asleep over my plate. It was Séguin de Brécy who finally roused me from my haze of slumber. This lord—and the reader of my testimony will surely have gathered by now that I did not like him (and in this, unfortunately, I showed good sense, as the further course of our adventure was to prove)—took it into his head to persuade the peasants to fight alongside us, or at least, as he put it, to take the places of those of our warriors who had been killed in the battle.

Lively discussion, made more heated by the wine, arose over this issue. Thorer would not hear of it. The people of Arques, who fortunately had mellowed too much to lose their tempers, said in their increasingly confused language that the war, rekindled against their will, was of no concern to them and that they wanted to stay out of it. Liébaut did not participate in the debate; he intervened on only two occasions, to calm Séguin de Brécy, who became too excited. I looked at my lord carefully and realized that, quite indifferent to the agitation and noise at our table, he was staring at Mathilde.

The affection in his eyes surprised me. It seemed to be very like the feeling he had expressed for me alone. I tried to believe that my view of him was blurred by the flames of the candles that stood between us, and I shifted on the bench to get a better look, my heart full of hope. With nothing impeding my view, and fully awake to my sudden discovery, I saw that I had made no mistake. Although Liébaut de Malbray was not smiling, his handsome face showed tenderness toward this wretched peasant girl. I glanced at Mathilde, and far from finding her eyes lowered before her lord, as would have been normal, I caught her looking straight into his face.

No longer hearing the talk around me, I remembered the time when, sitting at the far end of the table in the court of Falaise, I sought in vain to capture the attention of my future master, and I began to hope now that if I looked hard at my lord, he would finally take note of me. They served the cakes that had been baked for the people of Arques with the little honey we had in our storeroom, but, despite my mute stare, nothing changed. It was as if I no longer existed for Liébaut. In my effort to distract him, to compel him to say something, I joined the argument at the table, and though I was only a squire, I contradicted Séguin de Brécy. My lord said nothing. He let me commit this new misdeed. All I earned was an indifferent glance, devoid of anger, devoid of friendship.

Now in torment, I desired only the end of this meal, and was relieved indeed when Liébaut, finally turning away from Mathilde, rose to announce that the time had come to part and to retire. The people of Arques, slightly drunk, took their leave of my lord, thanking him for the generous meal he had just shared with them, and Thorer assured Liébaut of the goodwill, albeit passive, of the peasants of Arques. "Expect nothing more, Liébaut de Malbray," he added. "Understand that none of us will fight beside you. Be satisfied with our prayers to Almighty God that He grant you the strength and valor to win this war and that He allow us all to survive it. If you conquer, and then rebuild Arques, as you have promised, I will swear allegiance to you, and we will recognize you as our lord."

"I ask for nothing more," Liébaut replied.

To my great satisfaction, my master let Mathilde depart with Thorer without saying a word to her. But as she was leaving the great hall, she turned and her eyes met Liébaut's once more.

"The wretched peasant girl loves your handsome lord too much," Draco whispered mockingly in my ear. "And believe me, squire, your lord returns the favor."

Shocked by the temerity of his words, I felt a terrible hatred rise in my heart, and suddenly I knew that someday I would kill that cursed jester with my bare hands. I turned to spit out an insult, but before I could say a word, the evil creature ran and hid behind Suzanne de Brécy, who, seeing my wrath, tossed her head and offered me a taunting smile.

The kitchen servants cleared the table of scraps, and when Bernon left—he was the last to remain with us, discussing the defenses we should erect around the hut in which we kept the horses—I fulfilled my tasks as squire by the dim light of the last candle burning in the middle of the now-empty great hall. Liébaut made no move to help me as I took off his tunic, breeches, and shirt. He had decided to sleep here, for our own room was occupied by the wounded. It was bitter cold in the tower that night, winter being no more than a few days off, and I noticed that my lord shivered when he was naked. "Shall I rub you with our blanket?" I asked, hoping to please him, to remind him of the affection I felt for him.

"No," he answered absentmindedly, "don't bother."

I did not insist. I too undressed, extinguished the candle, and went to lie beside him on the bed of grass and straw that was laid for us after the people of Arques left. I wrapped myself in the blanket with my lord just as I had done every night since Rouen.

Although he usually spoke to me before going to sleep, Liébaut did not say a word that night, and the silence in the great hall, broken only by the whistling of the wind outside, became intolerable. I wanted to confess my deception to him, but feared that he would send me away in anger, so I said nothing.

Feeling shame and jealousy, no longer master of myself, I moved closer to him and put my arms around his shoulders, embracing him with all the warmth my heart could muster. He drew back slightly, in surprise, but when I did not release him, he ceased to pull away, took me in his arms, and we lay there clasping each other. "What is it, Odilon, my squire?" he asked me softly as I listened to the warm beating of his life, my head against his chest. "Is it the battle that troubles your mind, though you showed valor in it?"

"No. The cold makes me tremble tonight," I lied.

Night was thick around me when I opened my eyes. I felt as though I had been walled up alive, or that I was at the bottom of a well. The morning's battle came to my mind, and for a moment I did not know who had won it, we or the Frisians. I let out a cry, certain that I would suffer an ignoble death, and sat up, eyes wide in the darkness, heart thudding. Gradually, I recovered my wits and remembered that this was the darkness of the great hall, where we were sleeping because of the wounded men in our room. My first thought was that Liébaut must have been awakened by my cry. I listened, but did not hear the familiar, slow breathing of his sleep. Surprised, I reached out—and found only emptiness in our woolen blanket. He was not there.

His absence awoke a new fear in me, different from the unreasoning terror I had just felt. It was not the fear that some misfortune had befallen him in the night. Rather, it was the sudden, violent realization—such as I had experienced on the coast, when he disappeared in the waves behind the cliff—of how helpless was the solitude into which this separation from him plunged me. Gone was the strength that had entered me during recent days, passing slowly from his heart to mine by virtue of my nearness to him. Again I saw his blue gaze resting on Mathilde. Alone in our blanket, deprived of the reassurance of his legs tangled with mine, of the peacefulness of his breath on my face, of the warmth of his chest, again I felt like a child, incapable of defending myself, lacking pride, nobility, honor.

Tonight, a lifetime later, still bitterly mourning the man I loved, I cannot forget that night when I felt, for the first time, the weight of solitude that I have so long endured.

I rose, chilled to the bone, and dressed hurriedly in the dark. Then, touching the walls to guide my steps, I went out in search of my lord. Wind-driven rain lashed my face on the tower walkway. Of the surrounding countryside—of Arques, the Varenne, the hills, the forest, and the coast—I could see only vague expanses dotted with bushy masses of black. Of our camp at the foot of the hill I could recognize only our drawbridge, lit by two resin torches sheltered from the wind, and near it the huddled forms of three guards wrapped in blankets. Having no idea where to find my lord in the menacing night that merged things and people, I questioned the guards on the walkway, but they could tell me nothing. Driven by a desperate desire to find Liébaut, I started down the stairway, prepared to search the entire camp if necessary. But I did not have to look long, for I spied a glimmer of light coming from the floor below, and was delighted to find my master in our room.

Wearing only his linen shirt, he was kneeling beside a candelabrum on the floor, silently tending Arnoul. In his kindness he had returned alone to our wounded warriors in the middle of the night, to care for them. For a moment I remained at a distance, lest I disturb him, but then I went to him, noiselessly, so as not to awaken any of the men, hoping he would need me. As I got near, I saw that Séguin de Brécy's knight, far from improving, was much worse. The poor man lay senseless, his head thrown back and his face as gray as a corpse's. As Liébaut wiped his sweating brow, the unfortunate knight barely breathed through his open mouth, as if there was a great weight on his chest. Kneeling beside the bed, I smelled an unpleasant odor. "It is good you have come, Odilon," Liébaut said, his voice hushed. "I need help in removing the bandage."

Overjoyed by this reception, I lifted the wounded man, but had to fight to hold him up, he was so heavy. The badly stained cloth stuck to the wound, and Liébaut had to tear it away. Blood and fluid flowed, and the raw wound appeared, filled with black clots and bits of quivering flesh awash in that thick white liquid that is a sure sign of corruption. A veil fell over my eyes, and my stomach turned, just as it had on the Norman ship the Frisians had attacked near the Bridge of Arches. I turned away. Biting my lip, fighting to conquer the repugnance that had come over me, I looked at my lord. Even on his hardened face there was a grimace. "Mathilde's remedy has not healed him," he whispered, shaking his head. After a moment of hesitation, he sent me for some wet cloths, urging me not to wake anyone, for he did not want Séguin de Brécy to know.

When I returned, he began to clean away the pus that oozed from that horrible wound, which I now forced myself to look upon in order to harden my heart. When at last Liébaut was finished, I helped him replace the dressing, though my hands and back were bathed in cold sweat. This time, at least, I was able to master my weakness.

"We will return, with Granger, at sext," Liébaut said as we walked back to the great hall.

"Will the other wounded men recover?" I asked.

"Yes," he said. "None of the others has such great fever or such a serious injury. They should be on their feet again in a few days."

When we reached the floor above, I took off his shirt, though the night was still black and the whistling of the wind outside was growing steadily louder. I lay down beside him under our woolen blanket.

Because of Arnoul's wound, I did not dare draw as close to my lord as my heart desired. But since he remained silent and the urge to sleep had left me, in the end I spoke to him, saying that perhaps we should have burned Arnoul's wound immediately after the battle. "No," he replied with a harshness that he had never before revealed to me. "The wound was too deep. Burning would only have made him suffer needlessly. If, God willing, the corruption has ceased to spread through his belly by the hour of sext, I will do the only thing I can do: administer Mathilde's medicine a second time."

Liébaut did not wish to leave our dead in the middle of the camp in full view of everyone, so we gathered in the courtyard at tierce to carry the bodies to their graves. Despite my hope that yesterday's supper had established harmony between ourselves and the people of Arques, only a few peasants joined us on that day of grief, though Tharkall and Sigur, the two churls so cruelly butchered after the battle, were also to be buried. Only Thorer, five other tenants, three serfs, and two weeping women walked with us, and I felt that neither our hospitality nor the return of Mathilde had caused Ivar's anger to abate.

Without further ado, all our dead warriors—fully armored, in greaves, thick breeches, chausses with leather straps, laced hooded hauberks, and helmets—were placed in the coffins the carpenters of Falaise had hastily constructed at my master's orders. We lay their swords, lances, hatchets, and shields at their sides. Thorer and his people, however, lay alongside the bodies of Tharkall and Sigur not only tools, stones, and chipped flints, but also a veritable arsenal of magic: talismans and boar tusks to keep the dead underground in their graves; special stones to ward off demons; coins to assure their journey to the beyond; teeth of wild animals, so that they might retain their vigor in the invisible world in which they would now reside. The peasants added other strange objects as well, whose meaning Liébaut explained to me that evening. Among them I recall linen bags containing pieces of hair and fingernails, which were considered the bearers of vital force because they continued to grow after death; sticks of hazel, a symbol of virility; and earthenware jars filled with meat, nuts, and porridge.

Like many peasants even today, the people of Arques clung to the primitive beliefs of their ancestors. They thought that the dead, like the living, continued to work, fight, love, and eat. That a dead man had a material existence no different from that of a man alive. In their fear of diabolical spirits the peasants did everything they could to ensure that the departed would be at peace in their underground domain. May the Holy Word of God and the teachings of the priests banish forever such confusion from the land of Normandy!

The monk Granger, holding aloft as high as he could a

Cross made of two pieces of wood tied together, led our procession toward the hill where the graves had been dug. On that sad December morning, under a gray sky swept clean of clouds by a sharp sea wind, we crossed the lowered drawbridge and carried ten men to their final resting place. As the army chanted prayers and slowly marched across the land of Arques, many of the warriors of Falaise and of Malbray sighed and wept for their companions who lay lifeless in their coffins. But my eyes remained dry, because I had had no close friend but Liébaut since the beginning of our adventure.

My thoughts turned to Liébaut, who walked two paces ahead of me, in his full armor. I recalled the way his eyes rested on Mathilde as she sat beside me in the great hall, and I heard the sudden harshness in his voice when he told me that it would have been useless to burn Arnoul's wound after the battle instead of using the peasant woman's medicine. At that moment of grief, as we marched out to bury our dead, it became painfully clear to me that my jealousy was childish, mad, sinful, and that what I should fear was not that my lord would show interest in someone else for the brief period of a meal—but myself, my temper, my own passion.

When we reached the hillside cemetery, the bearers of the ten coffins placed them on the ground by the graves dug in the slope near the spring. There was a great silence, and all of us, the people of Falaise, of Arques, and of Malbray, prayed together, asking God Almighty to receive these souls into the repose and light of the life hereafter. Then came the magnificent moment when my lord spoke.

"These men," he said, "like our ancestors of the North, whose exploits the Valkyries sang at Valhalla's gates, met their end with their weapons in their hands, in valiant combat against the cruel barbarians of Frisia, who burn churches, steal holy relics, and slaughter men of the faith. Lord Jesus, Thou who deigned on our behalf to descend to earth from the throne of Thy majesty to save mankind and who rose again to heaven, I beseech Thee in Thine infinite goodness to permit Ogier of Malbray, and Helgaud, Leutard, Eude, Gervin, Arlebaut, Hugues, and Geuzlin of Falaise, and Tharkall and Sigur of the village of Arques, whose souls have left their bodies, to join Thee joyously in fair Paradise.

"Be mindful that we are in a state of war, Lord Christ, and forgive us for not burying them in hallowed ground. We humbly beg Thee—Thou who were poor to make us rich, Thou who were weak to make us strong, Thou who were betrayed to redeem us with Thy blood, Thou who were stripped to cloak us in the mantle of immortality, immaculate lamb who wiped away the sins of the world through Thy Holy Cross laden with all Thy suffering and through the drama of Thy Passion—lead these valiant warriors and these two poor peasants into the land of endless joy."

After a long silence filled with tears for those whose frozen gray faces now expressed neither pain nor fear but only eternal repose, the carpenters nailed the ten wooden covers shut. Sadness filled me at that moment, yet I was relieved not to have to look upon them any longer, for I too dreaded death. The coffins were lowered into the graves, and as we began to cast fistfuls of dirt upon them, I looked at Liébaut and realized that death could well strike us too, him and me, that very day.

Above each warrior we placed a Cross and let the people of Arques, in accordance with their custom, plant evergreen bushes on the graves of the two churls. Then we returned to our camp in sadness, no one speaking.

Though it was not yet sext, Liébaut led me to the tower to visit Arnoul and the other wounded men, even before seeing to the repair and reinforcement of our defenses. We were delighted to find that many of those treated with Mathilde's remedy were now awake and free of fever, just as my lord had hoped. But alas, when we went to Séguin de Brécy's second in command, Arnoul, whom my master wished to treat again, his stiff face and body and the strange emptiness of his eyes told us that he was dead.

Many gloomy hours followed for me in the days after the burial of our men and the death of Arnoul. The mood in the camp now bore no resemblance to the shared fervor of the early days of our adventure, when we believed ourselves invincible. Grief took from us the joy of our victory. Serious faces and somber looks were the rule in our castle, as though the presentiment of death had fallen upon us. Even Bernon Hildetand's usual good humor vanished, and his powerful laugh was heard no longer in the great hall or on the walkways. Though the men of Falaise and Malbray had fought side by side in the Frisian attack, distrust now grew among them. They kept apart, they muttered words of hatred. The cold grew sharper, the first snowflakes fell, and water froze so deeply that we were unable to break up the ice at the bottom of our well. A terrible silence fell over the camp.

Liébaut himself, supervising the strengthening of our defenses as we worked from dawn to vespers, when the icy winter numbed our hands and feet, grew more and more pensive. At first I thought he was troubled by Arnoul's death, but he told me, unexpectedly, as we were carrying that unfortunate man to his resting place, that he had not known him well and had indeed felt no special friendship for this knight of de Brécy's. But I saw that my lord's manner was altered, as if he nursed some private pain, and he led his army with a severity new to him. He made us raise the outer rampart higher, made us double its width, made us deepen the moat and sow it with a veritable forest of sharpened stakes. A great palisade now encircled the hut in which we kept our precious horses, and our drawbridge was reinforced with iron. We were out of bed at lauds every day, frozen to the bone. We opened a clearing in the forest of Arques, felling trees by the hundred, endlessly cutting through trunks, sinking them into ground as hard as stone. Every night, we forged iron, twisted and nailed it, making swords and shields of greater size and strength.

The monk Granger, Vilgard de Chambois, and Séguin de Brécy were spared this labor, as were the peasants, of course, who remained in their huts and pretended not to notice the service we were rendering them. But I, squire of the lord of Arques, had to chop wood, wade into icy water, and burn my face near the flames of the forge. It was not long before I heard murmurs against my master from more than one of the men of Falaise. Though I had no wish to defend the complainers, and though I was warmed with pride to see my lord lead his army as the duke himself would have done, there were times when I thought him too severe—not so much toward me, for I was pleased when he treated me mercilessly, but toward some of his own men, such as his loyal friend Bernon.

Liébaut was at prayer too often, his face dark; he spoke only to issue orders or to discuss defense plans with Vilgard de Chambois; and he invited no one but Bernon, Granger, and me to share his table. Why he withdrew from those around him, I did not know. Now he rarely spoke to me at night in the great hall, where we continued to sleep despite the cold, the wounded being still quartered in our room. This caused me grief, as if it were a sign of his displeasure with me.

As the days wore on, he became more impatient, more irritable. From his brusque gestures and clipped words, I could tell there was anger within him, an anger he fought to keep in check. He lost his temper in the courtyard one Wednesday morning, and part of the army was witness to it. My sole consolation for that painful moment was that the target of his wrath was Séguin de Brécy. This imprudent lord, incapable of holding his tongue, took it into his head to chide Liébaut for the death of Arnoul. "His wound should have been burned," he said, "but you treated him with a witch's medicine."

"The wound was so serious," Liébaut said, "that no remedy would have saved Arnoul's life. But you, instead of spending your time complaining and watching others work, would do better to help with the rebuilding of our castle. Does your arm lack the strength ever to lift a tool?"

Séguin de Brécy, gritting his teeth, was wise enough not to respond to this criticism delivered in front of his own men, but I saw then that the humiliation endured by this ignoble knight would henceforth make him as dangerous to my lord as Ubbo the Frisian or Thorer's angry son Ivar.

The gloom of these days deepened on Thursday night, when, after three applications of Mathilde's medicine, Fulbert, one of the most manly warriors of Malbray, also died. And, though the wounds of Gerbert, Herluin, and William healed, those of Richard, Gerbin (who had lost a hand and part of his arm), and Foulques did not close despite Liébaut's nightly application of the medicine with my aid, but in turn became infested with corruption. Twice my lord considered sending me for Mathilde, who, like most of the people of Arques, no longer ventured from her hut, but after much hesitation decided not to, since he had promised he would not have her brought to the tower again.

One week after the barbarian attack, our castle again seemed impregnable, except at a single place fifteen paces to the left of the drawbridge, a weak point my lord had deliberately allowed to remain, hoping that the enemy would rush to it recklessly. On Friday we erected another line of sharpened stakes and gnarled and tangled branches tied together with rope beyond the moat, and we covered the tower walls with ox skins to prevent fire, even though they were out of range of enemy arrows. On Saturday morning the red-and-gold standards of Normandy once again fluttered proudly from our tower. But our new enclosures, whose width and height had doubled, our iron-reinforced drawbridge, our new shields, loaded catapults, polished armor, and newly honed weapons all failed to restore our confidence. It was in bitter cold and awkward silence that we awaited the enemy, whose cruelty made us tremble.

My lord, despite his own trouble, perceived the division that spread a little further every day in the enclosed space of our castle, and in one of the rare moments when he continued to share his thoughts with me, he confessed that he feared that unless the Frisians attacked soon, our army would not hold together. On Sunday morning before the monk Granger said Mass, I heard him talking to Vilgard de Chambois about the possibility of attacking Ubbo on open ground. "The knights of Normandy fight best on horseback," he said. "That is how they have defeated their enemies for two centuries now, rather than by defending perilous sieges. Would that we were more numerous, so we could engage in open battle with confidence." I understood: he was no longer sure of victory.

We spent two more days waiting. The men of Falaise and of Malbray argued about what to do with the prisoners, whose death many now demanded. It began to snow again, and time seemed to stand still as we wrapped ourselves in blankets and gathered around the large fires that burned throughout our camp. Only Draco continued to laugh and sing, to call out his insults, to juggle idiotically, standing in the snow in front of the huts of the peasants, whom he loved to taunt. And he plotted against me, whispering in his mistress's ear whenever he saw me.

Then, on Tuesday morning, the twelfth of December, a great misfortune occurred.

We never found out exactly how the quarrel began, or which of the two, Harold or Jéboin, dealt the first blow.

At dawn, a lookout alerted Liébaut and me that a Norman vessel was sailing into the port of Deep. We went to the tower walkway and saw, beyond the coast, which was covered with snow though Christmastime had not yet come, a merchant ship entering the mouth of the Varenne, its sail unfurled. Though we scoured the gray expanse of sea behind it, we could see no Frisian craft in pursuit of it. Nevertheless, my lord turned to Bernon and Vilgard de Chambois and declared that he wished to take twenty warriors to meet the ship, to make sure that it passed safely. "Robert expects us to secure Normandy's trade," he said, "and although this ship seems in no danger, it is our duty to protect it. The enemy is full of guile. There is no sign of him now, but he might suddenly appear." He stared vacantly out to the empty sea. "It would be good," he added, "if the battle were joined in this manner, on this day."

"We risk much, dividing our army in two," Vilgard de Chambois said, frowning.

"We will not go far from camp," Liébaut replied. "Once the merchants pass Haguetot, they will be deep enough into Normandy to be out of danger, and we will leave them there. In the event of an attack, our horses will be able to carry us back in time."

Without further ado, Bernon assembled eighteen of our men: sixteen from Falaise and two from Malbray, chosen from among the best knights. Fully armed, commanded by Liébaut and Vilgard de Chambois, we galloped down the road to the Varenne. With my lord's lance and silver, azure, and sable shield attached to my saddle, I spurred my mount to keep up with Normandy's standard at the head of our army. As I rode beside my lord amid the clinking of hauberks and the clattering of armor and swords, I let out a cry of joy. The pride, the excitement of great adventure, and my forgotten dreams of honor and glory returned to me. But as soon as we reached the Varenne and dropped back to a walk in the bitter cold of dawn, the rush of happiness vanished. It was not the fear of death and battle that extinguished my hope and quelled the pounding of my heart in this way; it was, instead, a strange and dark emotion, though I stood on the brink of what might be a magnificent exploit. Gazing at my lord, who sat tall in the saddle, handsome and fearsome in his iron helmet, I told myself that he loved me and that I was foolish to spoil thus the richest hours of my life.

At the riverbank, Liébaut called out to the merchants standing on the deck. They had seen no other ship near Deep, they said. Even so, we accompanied them as far as Haguetot. It took us a long time to get there, for a strong headwind prevented the boat from moving rapidly. When finally we reached the end of our route, we stopped, and the sailors, those proud men so important to Normandy, called out words of friendship, and we in turn wished them good luck before we rode off. We hurried back to our camp, which had already been left too long under the command of Séguin de Brécy. As I gazed at the tranquil countryside around us, I suddenly hoped—inconsistent though this was with my dreams of glory, with my thirst for battle—that the Frisians, defeated in the first encounter, had abandoned our coast and were returning to their northern lands beyond the sea. I shared this new thought with Liébaut, shouting above the noise of our galloping.

"You are mistaken, Odilon," my lord said. "We did not see them today, but they are here and watching us. It is winter, trade has practically ceased anyway, and they can afford to wait, to take the time to construct machines of war. They know now that we are tough adversaries, and they are surely preparing a perilous assault against us. I had hoped that a sortie by a small number of us might lure an attack here, in the open. But after today's silence, I am sure they will never engage us front against front, since they have no horses. Like it or not, my squire, we must gird ourselves for a long siege."

"But why should we wait?" I cried. "Can't we launch an attack against them ourselves?"

"They are three times as numerous as we are," Liébaut answered, "and their hiding place in the hollow of the cliff is impregnable. The only way would be to ride out to meet them on the day of their attack. But when that day comes, they will make sure that no one sees them approach."

I could not recover the excitement of the morning. The brightness of the snow under the sun at sext hurt my eyes, and my head throbbed. I found it difficult to keep my horse close to Liébaut's. After a long ride we reached the frozen fields and meadows of Arques. Entering the burned village, where the blackened trunks of trees stood out against the white ground, we finally reined our horses in, two hundred paces from the camp, and heard shouts, howls of rage, the clash of arms behind our wall. "Something terrible must have happened!" Bernon exclaimed. Spurring our horses anew, we galloped over the drawbridge.

In the courtyard, under the anxious eyes of the peasants who had been drawn out of their huts by the noise, we found twenty warriors of Falaise, swords drawn, facing four men of Malbray. On the ground between them lay Harold, blood still oozing from his chest. Liébaut ran to him, dropped to one knee, and raised his faithful vassal's head. The opposing sides fell silent. Then my lord, in sorrow, announced that the knight, whom he had known for more than ten years, was dead. Shouts rose again, and the hatred of both sides reached such a pitch that Vilgard de Chambois, now standing between them, was barely able to stop them from throwing themselves at each other, in a battle of Norman against Norman. "Come to your senses!" he cried. "The enemy is out there, at the gates of Arques. It is against him that you must fight, him alone!" And the lord of Chambois drove back those few of his own knights of Falaise who continued to advance despite his order.

Liébaut, stunned, held Harold in his arms, and I saw Bernon restraining his friend Odon, who, screaming at the top of his lungs, was trying to get at Jéboin, whose sword was still red with Harold's blood. For a moment I feared the worst, and began to pray to Almighty God that He impel my lord to intervene, but Liébaut, tears in his eyes, did nothing but hold his dead friend. Finally, after a long moment of doubt, several of the men who had gone with us to the banks of the Varenne that morning stepped forward to stop the two halves of our army from joining in battle. Since no warrior of Falaise or Malbray wanted to strike his own comrades, calm returned to the courtyard, and Liébaut, whose grief moved me deeply, gently set Harold down on the blood-stained snow. His first words were to ask that the peasants return to their huts, for this was none of their affair. Then he turned slowly to Granger and Séguin de Brécy and asked for their account of this tragedy.

The monk was the first to speak, lamenting that he had been unable to prevent it. "Alas," he said, "I was at prayer in the great hall when the fight began at the foot of the hill. Angry shouts roused me from my meditation. I ran down, but by then it was too late. When I reached the courtyard, I saw Harold, knight of Malbray, fallen, his hauberk cut open by Jéboin's stroke."

"Jéboin is my nephew," Vilgard de Chambois said. "To accuse him is no light matter. Have you proof of what you claim?"

"Look at his sword," Granger answered humbly. "You will find no blood on any other weapon."

"Is this the truth?" the lord of Chambois asked his nephew.

"Harold insulted me so grievously," Jéboin answered, "that vengeance was required."

"And you who stand silent, Séguin de Brécy," Liébaut said, "were you not present at the beginning of this dispute? Can you tell us why and how it began?"

"The quarrel began over the fate of the prisoners—whom it would have been wise to have hanged before now. While I have no wish to offend you, in this instance it was the men of Malbray alone who were at fault."

"And could you do nothing to prevent it?" exclaimed Vilgard de Chambois, whose judgment and valor impressed me more and more as our adventure wore on, even though he was not one of my lord's men.

Brécy, refusing to argue with a baron of Falaise who was

his equal, merely shrugged helplessly and lowered his eyes. Indeed, far from believing that this perfidious knight, with his ever evasive look, had tried to avert the dispute, I thought that he had probably done his best to inflame it, in order that some misfortune might occur. Today, with the passage of time, I am no longer sure of that, for to act thus would have been stupid, and Séguin de Brécy was not stupid. (I must grant him at least that.)

Vilgard de Chambois, his face painful to look upon, went to his nephew. "Why did you commit this madness?" he asked, looking deep into the young knight's eyes. "Would that you possessed the wisdom and temperance of your father, my older brother, who died at the Magnificent's side fighting the Bretons!" Hearing these words, Liébaut placed his hand on his second in command's shoulder in friendship. Then, his voice breaking, he ordered that Jéboin be divested of his weapons and led to the storeroom, his hands tied with rope, and that he be kept there by two guards until vespers, to await his sentence.

Liébaut and Vilgard de Chambois withdrew to the tower together to hear testimony. Kept outside with the rest of the army, I never learned what they said to each other. When they summoned us after none, however, even before either of them spoke, I could tell from my master's impassive face, from his furrowed brow and the darkness in his eyes, that Jéboin's fate had been decided and that the verdict was unfavorable.

When the knights of Falaise and Malbray had gathered in the great hall, my master, severe in his wide-backed chair, with Granger seated to his right and Vilgard de Chambois to his left, ordered that the accused be brought before him.

I watched him closely, and saw no gentleness now in his gaze, but—for the first time—the cold glint of cruelty. He had become the very image of the warrior I had dreamed of following at the beginning of our adventure. But this new, hard demeanor displeased me, and I was forced to admit that though I had not clearly realized it until now, since our departure from Falaise I had come to love his kindness, his forbearance, and his tenderness, virtues I had once held in contempt.

Jéboin, his hands tied, was led in by two guards. His face was red with indignation, and before Liébaut could say a word, he demanded to be set free. "All I did was defend my life! Had I not killed Harold, he would have killed me!"

"We know, however, that he had not drawn his sword when you struck him," Liébaut said. "But that is not the point. We have heard contradictory testimony and therefore cannot say which of you was the first to insult, then threaten, the other. The important thing is that Norman has slain Norman. Know, Jéboin de Chambois, that had he fatally wounded you, Harold would be here in your place this evening, his hands tied, awaiting our judgment as you now await it, even though he was our vassal."

"Had you hanged the barbarian prisoners, already held in our camp too long, the quarrel would never have taken place!" shouted Jéboin in anger at my lord.

"You will be pleased to hear," Liébaut replied, "that I intend to grant you that satisfaction: all nine of the Frisians held hostage in our castle will be hanged in the courtyard this very evening before compline. Not a single one will be spared, and thus no further dispute will arise on their account."

A murmur swept through the great hall at this announcement, and Jéboin, surprised, fell silent. Knowing that my master was strongly opposed to such a measure, I realized that this was the price he was paying to placate the men of Falaise.

When Liébaut spoke again, it was to pronounce sentence. "Jéboin de Chambois," he said evenly, "in a moment of rage that robs the mind of judgment and measure, you did, with a stroke of your sword, inflict death upon Harold, valiant warrior of our army and, like you, a knight of Normandy. Given the peril that now faces us, I cannot forgive such a transgression. That all the people of Arques may understand that any discord in our ranks will be punished without mercy, I hereby sentence you to be hanged as well, tomorrow at lauds."

A deep silence fell over the great hall at these words. The knights looked at one another, their lips tight. Jéboin, struck dumb, seemed to shrink into himself as he stared at the lord of Arques, whose face was as cold as stone.

The hanging of the prisoners and especially of Jéboin, the nephew of a baron of Falaise who was also the second in command of our army, spread fear through the camp. The Normans ceased quarreling, and the peasants more than ever stayed inside their huts. Everyone now dreaded Liébaut de Malbray. Our warriors kept their distance from him, lowering their eyes when he addressed them. They spoke to him only when spoken to, and, talking among themselves, fell silent at his approach. Even the monk Granger avoided him. Only Bernon and I continued to stand at his side, which grieved me. I knew, of course, that a lord had to inspire fear if he was to command an army and wage war, but in my great innocence I wanted everyone in Arques to love Liébaut as much as I did.

During these long hours of waiting for the barbarians, my master grew increasingly aloof toward me. Despite the cold in the great hall, where we continued to sleep because in our room three of the wounded men were still gripped by fever, he began to turn his back to me under the blanket. Then he began to sleep in his shirt, and no longer could I feel the warmth of his flesh. Unable to fall asleep, from evening to lauds I wanted—but did not dare—to curl up against him, to entangle my legs with his as I had at the beginning of our adventure, to embrace him, to brush my lips against his shoulder, his soft beard, even his mouth. For hours I listened to his deep slumbering breath and tried to feel its light, sweet touch on my brow. Tears rolled down my cheeks as I lay there alone in the darkness, separated from the man I loved by what seemed an impassable wall. The more distant Liébaut de Malbray became, the stronger the flame of desire burned within me and the greater was my suffering. In my mind I begged him, over and over, not to abandon me, for now more than ever I needed his strength, his beauty!

Finally, on the Sunday evening after Jéboin was hanged, unable to keep silent any longer, I asked him whether I had somehow displeased him. Surprised, he said: "On the contrary, I am most satisfied with your service. You are valiant, you stand always at my side, and, though young, you have the rare virtue of silence. In more than twenty years I have had no better squire than you. Why do you think you have displeased me?"

"You scarcely speak to me any more," I answered. "You turn your back on me at night, and no longer reveal your thoughts to me."

He sighed. "This war is difficult," he said, speaking in his gentle voice again, "and it weighs so heavily upon me that I may well seem hard and distant. There is no doubt,

Odilon," he continued after a brief silence, "that this is my final battle. A weariness I never felt before assails my mind and limbs. Before many more seasons have passed, I will be an old man for whom the days of war are over. But that is no cause for sorrow, for every age has its pleasures." He took my hand. "If I seem distant, Odilon, it is because I now fight another battle, a battle against my most fearsome enemy— myself. And I fear I no longer have the self-control I once had, and that in this battle I will be defeated."

At the time I did not understand his words, I thought that my lord meant the barbarian attack we were awaiting—as if the conqueror of Auxerre could fear the Frisians!

Four days before Christmas, when both the sea and the countryside were quieter than usual, Thorer emerged from his hut and approached my lord to ask that the people of Arques be allowed to celebrate the ancient festival of Yule in our castle. "From time immemorial," said the old man, "we have held this festival to honor our departed relatives and to give thanks to the protector gods of our Viking ancestors."

My master, surprised by this request, frowned. "We are at war," he said after much thought, "and may be attacked at any moment. The festival of which you speak—and I am familiar with it—would bring disorder to our camp and interfere with its defense." Thorer started to protest, but my lord silenced him with a motion of his hand. "Let me finish," he said, "and I will show my generosity. I know what this rite means to you and therefore, despite the danger, permit you to hold it in our courtyard—provided that it is not too close to our palisades."

For the first time since our arrival in Arques, I saw joy in the old man's face as he bowed before my master. "Tomorrow night," he said, "we conclude the festival of Yule by eating the animals sacrificed at dawn, in accordance with the ritual. Will you come to our hut as our guest and share it with us, you and your monk and your squire?"

"We will come," Liébaut wisely replied.

I could see, however, that for some reason he was not pleased by the invitation.

The peasants began the celebration at nightfall, lighting a fire in the middle of the courtyard and letting it burn until morning, so that, according to their beliefs, sailors who had died at sea could come in the night to dry their wet clothes before the flames.

At dawn, like any barbarian tribe, they sacrificed five pigs to the remote divinities of the North. Thorer himself cut the throats of the beasts as several men held them on their backs with their legs apart, and bright blood flowed in our court-yard in two narrow streams. Bells and tambourines then sounded. Liébaut, Granger, and I, standing on the walkway above, watched as strange creatures emerged from the huts. Dressed in animal skins, their faces hidden behind masks of woven grass, the men danced, and bracelets of bells on their legs and wrists tinkled. In four processions winding through our courtyard they headed for the foot of the hill, merged at the well, separated at the oven, and wove in and out around the huts. Fortunately, our master had ordered Draco confined to the great hall, and he was therefore unable to join them. We were thus spared the unpleasantness the dwarf would have caused by his loud mockery.

Despite Granger's disapproval of these pagan practices tinged with witchcraft, and despite their noise and disorder, Liébaut was anxious for there to be no resentment and so allowed the festival to continue. For hours, until after vespers, the people of Arques danced. Thus for an entire day our camp was ruled by peasants whose untutored minds confused Odin with the Almighty, Thor with Christ Our Lord, and Fria with the Holy Spirit, and who called Satan Loki and believed that the angels of light were elves that led God's creatures down paths strewn with pitfalls.

At dusk, Liébaut, Granger, and I repaired to Thorer's hut as promised. There, we found ourselves cramped with some fifty villagers huddling against one another for warmth. My generous lord had brought wine, and we sat on the ground beside the village chief, in front of a fire where roasted one of the pigs sacrificed that morning. The smoke in this confined place was so thick that at first I could not see the faces around us. The unpleasant smell of burnt meat choked me and filled my eyes with stinging tears. But finally, across the fire's shimmering heat, I saw Mathilde. She was seated, to my great satisfaction, at Ivar's side, her eyes lowered.

From the beginning of the meal, Liébaut, who had been silent throughout this day of wild idolatry, made an effort to converse with Thorer and the peasants gathered on the straw around us. He spoke of their Viking ancestors, the first to celebrate the festival of Yule. With skill and in great detail he recounted the story of Eric the Red, who began as a murderer forced to leave Iceland. So wonderful were Liébaut's words that the wanderings of that valiant conqueror, condemned to sail the seas for long months without sight of land, came alive for us. He told how Eric discovered a land beyond a narrow strait, a peaceful, fresh land covered with bright flowers in spring, and how he named it Greenland. Then, as Thorer and the peasants listened in rapt silence, Liébaut related the glorious adventure of Rurik the Peaceable, who, in the year 860 after the birth of Christ Our Lord, went with his two brothers, Sinéous the Victorious and Trouvar the Faithful, to defend the inhabitants of far-off Novgorod against Finnish warriors. He told how Rurik, with his powerful army, first camped on the banks of Lake Ilmen and then moved on to Novgorod, where he assumed the title of grand prince and founded the Norman principality of Russia. Everyone in the wretched smoke-filled hut, even Ivar, seemed to forget the misfortune of our war and the cruel enemy that we awaited. My admiration for Liébaut, for his skill, his great knowledge, and the beauty of his words, became so great, it rivaled my admiration for the saints of our Church or even—may God forgive me!—for Our Christ, whose Word, too, has such great power. He spoke at length, that former kindness suddenly returning to his face, to his voice. And, to make my happiness complete, not once during his tale did he look at Mathilde, who sat opposite him, listening with her eyes lowered.

Time seemed to stop during that meal, just as the land of Normandy sometimes grows still under a threatening sky—just before the violent sundering of the first thunderbolt.

When the story-telling was done, and we had eaten the pork and drunk my master's wine, Thorer rose and thanked Liébaut de Malbray for having come and for his marvelous tales. Then he said, with pride, that he had glad tidings to announce in the presence of the lord of Arques. "The day after Christmas, we will celebrate another festival and share another feast." Slowly he looked at the peasants gathered around him, at Granger, my master, and me, as if taking full advantage of the moment. "Six days from now," he continued, "we will rejoice again, for my son Ivar will take Mathilde in marriage. May we hope," he added, turning to our monk, "that the priest of Arques will bless the bride and groom?"

"There can be no marriage except in the sight of God,"

Granger replied. "It is through me alone that Ivar and Mathilde can be joined."

Liébaut looked at the girl for the first time that evening, stared at her as he had in the great hall. But she sat motionless at her future husband's side and did not raise her eyes to him. Then, suddenly impatient, he said to Thorer, "I must go now, for I have orders to give. The enemy may take advantage of the dark to attack us, and I must see to our defenses." When he left the hut, however, he issued no orders. He walked quickly back past the inner enceinte, climbed the hill, and entered the tower without even checking, as he did each night, to see that the lookouts had mounted guard on the palisade bristling with pikes and that the torches had all been lit.

I had to run to catch up to him.

In our room I found him seated on our bed of grass and leaves. He was holding his head in his hands and seemed to be in pain. Though he said not a word, I suddenly understood why he had changed so much since the day of his wound, and what he had meant the night before when he said that he would now have to face his most fearsome enemy: himself.

That night, I could not sleep, and Liébaut, too, tossed and turned under our blanket. I could not forget the way he had looked at Mathilde after the announcement of her wedding, and began, in my anxiety, to hope that the Frisians would soon attack. Then there would be no time to worry about the woman; all that would matter would be our lives, the siege. I even saw death as a deliverance; no longer fearing it, I almost desired it, and felt myself capable of blind valor. I pictured my death and Liébaut de Malbray's occurring to-

166

gether, I saw us falling side by side, our bubbling blood mixing through our gaping wounds.

All night, my master sighed. I pitied him in his struggle against his own desire, I shared his pain, even though I considered the cause of it unworthy of him. I accepted the fact that he could feel such passion for this peasant girl devoid of charm or beauty, who was no older than I. Had not Robert the Magnificent himself, standing on the ramparts of Falaise, blazed with desire for Arlette, a mere tenant's daughter? But, alas, I recalled Draco's taunt as he left the great hall after the supper my master had given for the people of Arques, I heard again that creature of evil whispering spitefully in my ear: "The wretched peasant girl loves your handsome lord too much, and believe me, squire, your lord returns the favor." What if Liébaut committed some irreparable error on Mathilde's account? What if, in his great agitation and discontent, his wisdom failed him? What if he thereby aroused the wrath of the people of Arques, the contempt of his own warriors?

As I waited for lauds, I wondered what evil spell had fallen upon him. What possible interest could a baron of Normandy, lord of Arques and Malbray, conqueror of Auxerre, and close friend of our duke Robert have in a red-haired peasant woman, who was plain of face and half a sorceress? But I did not ask him this, fearing that he might defend Mathilde against me. Toward morning I was unable to bear my silence any longer, and finally I spoke to him. "Why do you torture yourself this way, my lord? I can see that love causes you despair. Why have you let such passion take your heart hostage? Is not Mathilde unworthy of you?"

"You have guessed my innermost thoughts, my squire," he answered, without anger, after a brief silence. "You speak the truth." He sighed. "I overestimated my strength," he murmured. "Time assails it relentlessly, sapping it day by day."

He turned toward me then and brought his face so close to mine that his breath caressed my brow and lips. "I knew passion once before in my life, Odilon," he said in a whisper. "Almost thirty years ago. It was shortly after the Auxerre victory. I was still a young man then, you know. Her name was Drusiana, and she was about my age. Sunlight shone in her face. Her manner was sweet, her beauty the most perfect image of the purity God bestows upon some of his creatures. But she too, alas, was only a peasant girl, and since I had just been dubbed a knight, I silenced my heart out of pride, bade her farewell, and never saw her again. Despite my pain and my desire, I would not let myself search for her and instead devoted myself entirely to the art of war. I lived without her, from battle to battle. For years, in secret grief and loneliness, I mourned Drusiana's fading memory. And then the image of her slender body and sweet face mingled with other images, other faces, other smiles less tender, and was lost. My heart has remained empty all this time, but when Mathilde appeared, its emptiness suddenly frightened me."

He sighed again. I put my head on his shoulder and my arm across his chest.

"I would have liked to have had a son like you," he said.

We were both silent. We knew that the sound of the horn would soon awaken Arques.

"Someday soon," he said, "I will leave this place, lay down my arms, and retire to my castle in Malbray. What will remain in the depths of my memory then? Only the bloody confusion of war."

After the prayers of lauds had been said, Liébaut, looking

gloomier than ever, summoned Bernon. They went into the great hall without me and remained there a long time talking. I wandered aimlessly on the ramparts, hoping that the giant Viking's moderation and friendship would ease my master's passion. Shivering a little from both the cold and my anxiety, I looked out at the countryside: the gray ruins of the village; the forest of Arques, a gloomy mass of black trunks and bare branches; the Varenne River gleaming under the cold sun; the coast, stark above the sea; the port of Deep, distressingly empty and useless, lashed by white waves. How I wished that the enemy would attack us then, and prevent the calamity that deep in my heart I knew was coming.

Just as on that already distant day in Falaise when the duke, so badly deceived about me, first told me of this adventure, so now, once again, under the icy winter light, the world seemed to change. Every hill, every tree, every stream arranged itself in a new order, an order that was perfect yet without warmth, without soul. On the threshold of an ordeal that I dreaded far more than any battle, the landscape became indifferent, colorless, false. On that morning so near the celebration of the Nativity of Christ Our Lord, I felt that the world had ceased to be the reflection of the love the Almighty had bestowed upon us in His perfect creation.

I told myself then that God no longer watched over Arques.

When Bernon left, just after tierce, Liébaut in turn summoned Granger to the great hall, and once again I waited. I stood atop the outer rampart, to the right of the drawbridge, wondering what the priest was saying to my lord. I took a long look at our defenses: the high palisades, the moat bristling with sharpened points, the line of stakes and entangled gnarled branches, and, farther away, the sorrowful ruins of Arques, a heap of ashes, charred trees, black stones, and crumbling walls.

Toward the hour of sext, Liébaut finally came out of the tower. Quickly descending the hill and crossing the inner palisade, he walked alone and unarmed to Thorer's hut and knocked loudly on the door. He spoke with the village chief for a long time. From the ramparts where I stood, I then saw the old man quarrel with his son Ivar, and though I could hear nothing of what either man said, I knew what my lord had come for. Then Mathilde appeared, excessively humble as usual. I do not know what my lord said or what promises he made, but Thorer and Ivar—showing little opposition, to my surprise—let Liébaut take the girl unceremoniously by the wrist and lead her back to the tower.

Naïvely, trying to reassure myself, I told myself that Liébaut was merely taking Mathilde to visit the two wounded men who were still suffering from fever. I waited, a heavy weight on my chest. What were Liébaut and Mathilde doing, what were they saying to each other, in the tower together? By what witchcraft had the peasant woman stolen Liébaut's heart? Had she resorted to the infernal practices of our ancestors, mixing some of her menstrual blood into the medicine when she treated my lord's wound, thereby binding him to her?

There was a commotion in the courtyard below. I saw Ivar, Tyrker, and several others gathering. Gripped by sudden fury, as though they now regretted having allowed Mathilde to follow the lord of Arques, they advanced toward the inner palisade. Several of our warriors, armed, quickly interceded, stopping them. Bernon himself came forward to calm the discord, and I heard him say: "As your lord promised, the girl will be returned to you this evening." No one, of course, dared oppose the giant Viking. Sullenly the peasants went back into Thorer's hut and peace seemed to be restored.

I resolved to do the only thing I could do for my lord: pray.

Ignoring the cold and the glare of the sun, which made my head pound, I stood atop the rampart until the hour of none at least. With all my soul I prayed to Our Savior that my lord keep his promise and send Mathilde back to her hut at nightfall, thus preserving the friendship, so important to us in this war, of the people of Arques.

I was roused from my reverie by the unusual sound of a horse being led out of our castle. Looking down into the courtyard, I saw Liébaut mounted, with Mathilde. He was waiting for the drawbridge to be lowered, ready to leave our camp with her, wearing no armor and with only his sword at his side. The peasant girl sat behind him, her arms around his waist.

I could not believe my eyes. What an insult my lord was hurling at Ivar, what a terrible affront! This woman promised to another, where was he taking her? And what perils would he face in the countryside, or perhaps on the coast or in the port of Deep, without his army and at the mercy of enemy arrows? I rushed down, cried out to make him stop, but, as always, he was faster than I, and he galloped out with the red-haired girl before I could reach him.

No longer understanding my master's actions, I went silently to the great hall and wrapped myself in our blanket, as I would have done had he been at my side. And there I remained, still wearing my tunic, breeches, and chausses, until evening. Despite my great misery and loneliness then, what I felt most of all was fear, fear for Liébaut.

———

They returned at dusk. When he saw me, my lord, surprised, asked me why I was in bed. Through the gathering darkness, I saw a strange glitter in his eyes.

"I had a terrible pain in my head," I lied, "and needed rest."

He did not answer. As I got up, I saw Mathilde. So he had not yet sent her back to Ivar! She disappeared behind Liébaut, like a shadow.

"Where were you, my lord?" I could not stop myself from asking.

"We went for a ride through the countryside," was all he answered.

"What if the enemy had caught you?"

"It is the death of all of us they seek," he said, "not of a single knight."

"If you only knew how I trembled for you!" I murmured bitterly, lowering my eyes.

At that he took me by the shoulder, drew me to him, and gently put his hand on my hair. "You must never worry about me, Odilon," he sighed, "never." He caressed my brow with an affection more tender than that he usually showed me. How I wish I had not seen Mathilde's motionless form behind him at that moment! "Many things will change in this camp, my squire," he said. "I have decided, finally, to torture myself no longer, I have made my choice, as one does in the sunset of one's life. I am weary of the struggle, and never-yielding virtue weighs heavy upon me."

Refusing to understand his words, though they were clear, I closed my eyes, as if darkness could protect me from the misfortune that was coming.

"Odilon," he said calmly, "you will have to sleep in our room with the wounded tonight, for I wish to be alone with Mathilde until morning."

BOOK FOUR

The sun has disappeared behind the lantern tower, but my clouded eyes can still see a bit of daylight. Night spreads over Jumièges, rising from the earth, descending from the sky, and the battle is lost: darkness will vanquish the last glimmer of day just as surely as death will soon extinguish me. I gather my tools: my reed pen, my ink, my thick parchment. When night falls, I light four candles. My time of labor begins.

I would like to reread all the pages I have been writing, night after night, in the gloom and silence of my cell for more than a year now, but courage fails me. I look around, see my straw mattress, my pillow, my single blanket, my stone wall with the unadorned Cross hanging in the center. Farther off I can make out the lectern, which I no longer use, for I cannot stand erect; my back is bowed, my kidneys are caught in the jaws of an iron vise, my legs have been covered with deep black sores since winter's end. Farther still, through the bars of my window, I can see the blurry shadows of the chapter house, the pigsties, the stables, and the forge, and in the distance the black shape of the forest. Here behind my closed door, I can imagine the abbey's dim corridors, the darkened dormitories, the kitchen and storeroom, the deserted refectory, its bare walls and empty tables. I am weary. A choking cough tears at the inside of my chest. I would love to rest, to lie down and close my eyes. My hand trembles. I am alone, shut in upon myself, like a mole in his tunnel, and everything sinks with me earthward.

Despite my increasing pain, rare are the nights that I do not dip my reed pen in the ink and write laboriously from the hour of vespers. Night after night, I relive the distant past: my impatient wait in Falaise, my deplorable hunt for the boar, Robert the Devil's too confident words, my first supper in Liébaut de Malbray's presence, the departure of our army, the unforgettable night in Rouen, our arrival in Arques, the war and the tending of the wounded. I see once more the handsome or baleful faces of Vilgard de Chambois, baron of Normandy; Bernon Hildetand, the one-eyed Viking; the monk Granger, holy by the Almighty's grace; Jéboin, the hotheaded nephew; Thorer, the sullen village chief; and, of course, Séguin de Brécy, Suzanne, and their insane and wicked dwarf, Draco. I see the threatening figures of Ivar, Tyrker, Ubbo the barbarian enemy of God, and Talvos the thief; I see Arlette the tenant's daughter, with fair shoulders and pale gaze, and Mathilde the red-haired peasant girl with her wondrous medicine. Hour by hour my adventure is reborn before my eyes, and its players too, those who lived it with me, both the loved and the hated.

But for more than a month now, writing has become increasingly difficult for me. My vision is poor, and despite my constant struggle against myself, I am sometimes forced to stop in the middle of a sentence, lie down on my straw mattress, and yield to the sleep that wipes away all torments.

I am weak. The reed pen slips from my fingers, ruins the beautiful shape of my letters, spreads ink across the parchment and forces me to begin the page again. When I first began my labor, I wrote with fair speed, but now I advance with infinite slowness. Night plunges me into a haze that obscures words and confuses sentences despite my four candles. Ever since the celebration of Good Friday last, I am no longer able, after compline, to draw neat vertical lines or set out my margins.

This testimony, a source of pride last winter, at last becomes an act of expiation. But was expiation really what I sought?

The physical pain is only part of my ordeal. Indeed, though by the grace of God my precious memories remain intact though I have passed my sixtieth year of existence, I now begin to doubt the words with which I bring them back to life beyond the bounds of time. Confident at first, I now find myself despairing of producing a work of beauty, the final desire of a sorrowful, presumptuous old man. Though I have now brought my testimony to the brink of its most dramatic pages, I am no longer certain that this book will be a thing of value, deserving to be illuminated, ornamented, richly bound, and decorated, on its cover, with stones and pieces of copper. I am no longer certain that it will be worthy of being preserved, for the edification and admonition of others, in the library of our abbey alongside the most esteemed, respected, and sacred of writings.

Yes, my laudable desire to expiate and testify is once again tainted with pride, with contemptible self-contentment. For though it may be necessary for a work to attain beauty if it is to be preserved, read, and understood, its goal should never be to glorify its author. Rather, a book possesses a value of

177

its own, and will be praised only for what lies within its pages. Now, I hereby confess that though my testimony is intended to bring Liébaut back from beyond the grave and honor him, it is also intended, in my secret mind, to lead me beyond my own death and win for me some degree of immortal glory. Let those who read these pages condemn me for the sin I will soon confess when I continue my account; that is only just. But let them neither disdain my book nor forget it. Their condemnation cannot trouble me, for I know that I will never be saved, that my soul will never be purified.

But then a terrible thought occurs to me: that my true punishment will be to fail to create a work of sufficient beauty to be preserved.

Two days and two nights now have I spent bent over my parchment, rising only to pray. I form my letters one by one, put the words carefully together, but alas, this patience is not rewarded. What I have written recently is worthless. Can it be that, having arrived at the place in my tale where nothing remains but to reveal my crime, I am no longer capable of breathing life into the words that memory brings to me? Is it God's intention now that I fall silent? Does He punish me thus for my pride, so that I will be buried beneath the earth forever, the memory of my existence erased along with that of Liébaut de Malbray?

I am now in such pain that it is difficult even to remain seated at my table, reed pen in trembling hand. A drumming mounts in my chest as if to shatter it, and my right arm, the arm with which I write, stiffens in terror. The moment I stop praying, I feel the icy breath of death on my neck, and when I turn my gaze from the simple Cross on the wall, I smell the unspeakable stench of hell.

Grant me more time, I beseech Thee, Thou who giveth and

taketh life, for I must complete this task that I have set myself.

A clear spring sun shines during the day now, and the nights are growing mild. The ink no longer freezes on the table, the cold has stopped numbing this old man's twisted thoughts and limbs. If I fall silent now, I will have no excuse. When I think of the grief Our Christ Jesus endured, his hands and feet pierced by the nails of crucifixion, I am ashamed of the plaints and hesitation that besiege my mind. Can it be that as I near the end of my testimony, I am finally succumbing to the fear of imperfection?

The call of nocturn will soon sound in Jumièges, and I will throw my hood over my shaven skull and join the somber procession through the abbey's endless corridors to the chancel of the ancient church, as I have done each night for nearly forty-five years. Chanting the fifteen psalms composed in olden days by Saint Ambrose, I will call upon Our Crucified Savior and upon Liébaut, lord of Malbray, to illuminate together the dark tunnel in which I am striving with all my might not to forget the words and images that will bring him back to life.

On this day, the octave of Pentecost, when custom tells us to rejoice in honor of the Resurrection and Ascension and the coming of the Holy Spirit, a deluge has been pouring down on Jumièges. At prime, the sky was covered with great leaden clouds. The first warm, soft drops began to fall on our procession, and there was silent, yellow lightning as we repaired to the chapter house to read and discuss the day's Gospel, having already chanted the three psalms and recited the Bible verse and the Kyrie eleison. Rain fell on the Norman countryside until after vespers. I watched through my window as it soaked the earth, and again I asked myself many questions and found no answers.

Tonight, I approached our abbot, as our rules permit, intending to speak to him about the impotence against which I now struggle, but I fell silent when I saw the holy man at prayer. As I have been doing for months now to punish myself for my pride, I refrained from sharing with my brother monks the bread of *cena*, the fruits, and the thin griddlecakes pressed warm between iron plates. I returned to my cell. Night fell before I had the strength to pray. The world outside, shimmering with rain, darkened. The odor of moist earth reminded me of my mother's freshly dug grave—behind our tower in Bernay one autumn morning, in the seventh year of my life. I saw again her pallid body in the open coffin. Her eyes were closed and sunken, her lips were tight. Her long shiny hair was spread to her shoulders. A wooden Crucifix lay in her translucent hands. I cast a dried flower, browned by the pale October sun, upon her, and tonight, in my mind, I placed my mouth—for the thousandth time—on her stone-cold brow. Then another vision of death came to me, one crueler still. I lit my four candles in an effort to drive it away. Golden light danced hazily around me. I stared at the Cross on the wall; it wavered, surrounded by shifting shadows.

When the lantern tower went dark and the earth merged with the mud-colored sky, I sat down at my table. Despite myself—for after four days without writing, I felt I no longer had the strength to testify—I dipped my reed pen into the scribe's ink.

With the words that came to me I tried again to summon that sad night I spent alone among the wounded in our room in Arques, sundered from my master by an ordinary peasant girl. I was able to form several sentences, and found, to my surprise, that if I did not try to draw personal joy from the writing, the images in my memory came to the parchment with less difficulty. I took up my testimony again, and wrote for a long time.

With nocturn approaching, I have ceased my work after this surge of confidence and find, alas, that my weariness has returned. My mind is suddenly so empty, my back in such pain, that I feel truly forsaken by God. Why is it that the Almighty, after restoring some hope to me on this night, now rejects me so cruelly?

A strange and terrible thought comes to me on this new night of torment: that what I am in truth attempting to do through my writing is to bring the dead back to life.

But that is something that God, unique Creator and sole source of life, will not tolerate.

What He has undone cannot be redone. Moreover, the sole medium of our Creation is the clay that He Himself shaped at the beginning, when He fashioned man in His image. And here I challenge this divine order with my words, themselves now also the bearers of life.

This is why God rejects me.

Suddenly I see that although memory, ink, and parchment are my only weapons, I am indeed pitting myself—an unbelievable sin—against the Master of the universe.

If my testimony is preserved, men whom God has created will die before those whom I have resurrected.

It is therefore inevitable that there be war between the Creator and me, His wretched creature, a man mad with pride, who seeks to be His equal and even to surpass Him.

My weakness will nevermore be strength; my doubts will not be answered; my infernal pain will not be eased, for of the flame of my youth only ashes remain. My fear, that the thread of my testimony will be severed by the blade of death, grows as my hand trembles, as my sight clouds. And it will worsen night by night, for I am old and I challenge God.

I still love Liébaut de Malbray with a passion beyond measure, but here at the end of my road I feel no more joy as I restore him to life, as the point of my pen, dipped in ink, brings him before me in the dazzling nobility of his beauty. I feel only sadness now, as my sentences join and he speaks to me in his gentle voice.

Yet, though God rejects me so cruelly, I persist, with the stubbornness of an old man, in writing the story of our adventure. Close to tears, just as I was more than forty years ago, I relive my first night of solitude in our room in Arques.

Let God freeze my fingers with the chill of death if He wishes to halt my sacrilegious challenge. It does not matter. I am already damned—with complete justice.

My work ceases to be a source of pride. I am plagued, instead, with the fear of its imperfection, that it will be found unworthy of preservation, that no one will read it.

Tomorrow I will break the fast through which I have mortified and weakened my body these past months. I cannot tame my arrogance, it is pointless to try. And no longer will I flog myself with questions day and night, bemoaning my fate, hoping against hope to recover the vigor of my youth.

Through the Eucharist, instrument of Salvation, I will once again take into my soul the most Holy Body of Christ Our Lord, filling myself with the light of God, who in His infinite goodness judged and condemned me more than forty years ago.

I will render Him praise to my dying breath, my soul humble before Him.

May my last remaining strength be preserved from this night onward as I sit, night after night, hour after hour, before this parchment.

Until the night when, my testimony done, the gates of hell open before me.

Alone in our room, indifferent to the distress of our last two wounded men—Foulques, who had been in a haze of fever for several days, his entire leg now gripped by corruption, and Gerbin, who had lost a hand and part of his arm and showed no sign of healing—I undressed by the faint light of a single candle.

With tears in my eyes, I lay down on what had been Arnoul's bed and stared at the ceiling that separated me from the man I loved. I could not get his words out of my mind: that he was weary of the struggle against himself. I whispered, "Will we ever again sleep together, lord of Arques and Malbray?" I told myself that the peasant girl would leave his side at dawn. That tomorrow he and I would lie together under our blanket again, and I would forget the pain I felt now.

So hard did I stare at the ceiling that my thoughts pierced it, and, as in a nightmare, I saw the lord of Arques draw close to that wretched girl. I saw her small hand timid on his naked warrior's chest as he took her by the shoulder and pulled her to him. I saw her lower her forehead, saw it brush Liébaut's parted smiling lips. I saw his fingers caress her neck. Then they moved together, and suddenly I had a vision of my own legs mingling with Liébaut's, in this room in which I now slept alone. No! I could not bear it. Not wanting to see any more, I pulled the blanket over my head and covered my eyes with my hands.

The groans of Foulques, who lay, probably dying, only ten steps away, were suddenly intolerable to me. Despite the cold, I got out of bed and went to make him stop. But when I reached him, I saw, in the candle's faint light, the sweat that covered his face, the grimace of pain that twisted his parched lips. What was happening to me? I asked myself. Was I going mad?

I paced for a long time. As God Almighty is my witness, I did everything I could to cast off this passion that so sorely troubled my mind. At last I lay down again and wrapped myself in the blanket. But then other words of Liébaut's came back to me. Many things would change in our camp, he had said before sending me away. Repeating these words to myself, I understood their meaning better. It was not merely for one night that Liébaut had taken Mathilde.

There would be no peace in our castle until the uncertain end of this war. What had happened to the judgment of the noblest of Normandy's knights? I asked myself. How would he restore tranquillity to our camp after this abduction? How would he turn his mind, now blinded by love, to war? What magic had caused him to endanger our lives in this way, to endanger the Norman army whose command the Magnificent had entrusted to him? Draco's horrible voice reverberated within me again. "The wretched peasant girl loves your handsome lord too much," he had hissed viperlike in my ear, "and believe me, squire, your lord returns the favor."

What would Vilgard de Chambois and Séguin de Brécy think? Would they return to Falaise and there accuse my master of being too naturally inclined to evil, too weak, to lead an army? I recalled Arlette's pale gaze resting upon me in our duke's bedroom three months before. The beautiful lady with the wide brow had stared at me as she lay on her bed, beneath its cloth canopy held aloft by four golden posts. Why had she stared at me like that? A mere tenant's daughter, dressed in a delicate chemise, she held in her arms her son William, a bastard child barely a year old (who in time would be called the Conqueror). She too, like many of the simplest peasant girls, had been taken by her lord. How could Robert condemn a sin of which he himself was guilty, a sin which the majority of his barons joyfully committed in their fiefdoms every year?

The sighs of Gerbin, who was also at death's door, even with Liébaut's daily morning application of the medicine to his hideously severed arm, brought me out of my reverie. I looked around the room—"our room"—which since the battle had become a sad place of pain and death. Yet it was here that I had spent the most wonderful hours of my life, here that I had warmed myself by mingling my legs with Liébaut de Malbray's and held myself against his powerful chest, that my heart might absorb the strength of the most beautiful of all the lords of war.

Then Ivar's burning look came to my mind. Any other peasant would fear his lord too much to dare to seek revenge. . . . Liébaut could never send Mathilde back to Ivar. Now impure, she would be worthless to him. She would not be able to assure him the honor of her children, that he was their father. All Liébaut could do now—such was the practice— was pay Ivar a sum of money. But that would never happen, Ivar was too proud to accept money for the woman he had chosen to marry.

And not only Thorer's son, but also a number of other men of Arques might rebel against an unjust master. Who would then remember Liébaut de Malbray's solemn promise to rebuild the village? Normandy had already seen the lamentable spectacle of peasants rebelling. Until the inevitable punishment fell upon them.

Tormented by these black thoughts, I felt grief more than jealousy on that cursed night. After matins, however, one hope did come to me: that Liébaut, disappointed and angered by Mathilde's shyness, by her excessive humility and passivity, would send her away in the morning as pure as she had been when he abducted her.

I began to pray with all my soul that that might happen.

The Almighty did not heed me.

For the first time since our arrival in Arques, Liébaut did not rise at lauds, and Bernon asked Granger to say the matin prayers without him. Anxiously I watched Vilgard de Chambois and Séguin de Brécy as they knelt beside me on the floor to render thanks to God, as we did every morning, for the new day. Neither of them showed any sign of surprise, or the least displeasure. It was as if they had foreseen Liébaut's absence and accepted it as natural.

Immediately after the prayers, my master still in the great hall with the peasant girl, I walked alone through the courtyard and climbed to the ramparts to check for indications of unrest. To my disappointment, I found none. Our camp was as tranquil as it had been on other mornings. The lookouts stood on the walkway and the archers were posted at the palisades as if nothing had happened. The kitchen servants were already firing the oven to bake bread and griddlecakes, and Thorer's hut was closed, silent. Draco, who had seen me near the drawbridge and now had good reason to taunt me and to ridicule my master, hurled none of his usual invective. Soon Bernon began to sharpen his sword on the millstone near the well, and three of Vilgard de Chambois's men began training with their bows, shooting arrows into the straw dummies. The blacksmith's hammer rang out as it struck red-hot iron on the anvil, and two peasant women in front of their huts began to pluck chickens whose heads they had just cut off. Finally, at tierce, with the door of the great hall still closed, I saw Thorer emerge from his hut. He passed Bernon without apparent anger and went to the fire that burned in the middle of our courtyard every day in this season of great cold. There he joined Witton, one of the tenants of Arques, and began to talk to him.

Nothing in our camp seemed to have changed.

I wished, even more strongly than on the previous day, that the Frisians would attack. But this time I prayed to the Almighty that Thorer, Ivar, Draco, and especially the woman who held my master in shameful thrall might die together in the battle. I asked God to inflict the most horrible death upon her, who was so perilously distracting the lord of Arques from the struggle against the enemies of the Faith.

Liébaut did not appear until sext. I saw him then on the walkway at the top of the tower. He had donned his fur-trimmed tunic and his breeches without waiting for me, his squire, who had served him faithfully since our departure from Falaise. He gazed out at the landscape as if unmindful of the enemy that would attack us. Soon Mathilde appeared, in her miserable peasant dress, her red hair falling to her shoulders, at the door to the great hall. She went to my master. He turned slightly toward her and spoke to her, pointing in the direction of Deep. Thinking herself unobserved, she took the arm of the lord of Arques and huddled against him.

That afternoon Liébaut rode out into the countryside alone with Mathilde, just as he had the day before. For several hours I stood waiting for him to come back, my mind full of fear that he might be ambushed, my heart full of jealousy. I was unable to do anything, neither practice the bow nor train with Bernon in the use of the mace and the hatchet, weapons in which I lacked skill.

Liébaut did not return until after vespers, as dusk was already darkening the winter sky and the kitchen servants were preparing supper. From the rampart on which I had stood for most of the day, I watched him drop to the ground in the courtyard, hold out his hand to the peasant girl, and take her in his arms to help her dismount.

My eyes were fixed on them as they crossed the inner palisade, went up the hill, and entered the tower, walking much too close to each other.

I waited for evening to fall and, estimating that the table would be set up by then, went to the great hall. There I found, ready to share our meal, not only the monk and Bernon, but also Vilgard de Chambois and Séguin and Suzanne de Brécy, whom my master had invited to his table only on Sundays ever since deep distrust had settled over our camp with Arnoul's death. I sat opposite the place Liébaut usually took. On the tablecloth I noticed, side by side, the two platters and two goblets that had been set out for the lord of Arques and "his lady." As we waited in silence for the two lovers, I recalled the long suppers at Robert's court in Falaise, the Magnificent seated on his golden chair, wearing his crown studded with precious stones, and dressed in his tunic of dazzling white linen. In my mind, Robert's serious face merged with the face of Arlette, young, proud, and wise. The duke of Normandy too lived only for a girl with the look of a princess of old; in his castle he did not appear during the day, and neglected to dispense his justice, just as my master was neglecting our war; he allowed poachers to empty his realm of game, and spent long hours on his bed with that tenant's daughter and their bastard son, William. He too was melancholy. Because of his unlawful lady, the days of his glory and exploits were over, and those of the conqueror of Auxerre soon would be over as well.

When Liébaut finally appeared with Mathilde, who still wore the same coarse dress cinched at the waist by a length of rope, but now had her hair pulled back to reveal her forehead, he did not so much as look in my direction. Smiling, he took his place, seating the peasant girl beside him. Then, with a very contemplative Granger, he thanked God for granting us this meal.

Raising his head and speaking even before the supper had begun, he announced his desire that we gather at his table, all of us, every night from now on.

He served us himself, carving the pork and holding out to each of us, in turn, a slice with a piece of bread, just as the Magnificent had done for the mendicants sheltered in his castle. Granger, then Vilgard de Chambois, Séguin and Suzanne de Brécy took their portions and thanked him. Mathilde, astonishingly erect beside him, watched his every move, and I thought I saw the shadow of a smile on her pale face. When he held out my portion, I did not move, I did not take it, not to refuse his meat and bread, but to remind him, if only for a moment, of my existence. He looked at me in surprise. What did he read in my face? Did he understand my wordless reproach? His hand hung in the air, for a lord cannot reach out too far to his squire. Did I detect, despite this impudence toward him, sweetness and friendship in his eyes? Unable, alas, to prolong the moment, I took the meat and bread due me and thanked him.

As had been his custom before love had set his heart ablaze, he began to speak to us again as we shared his meal. First he talked at length with Vilgard de Chambois and Bernon about how we would have to defend ourselves soon, and that in the event our outer defenses were breached, we would have to find a way to save at least eight of the horses, because the enemy, to prevent our escape, would seek to slaughter them the moment they entered our camp. To my astonishment, Liébaut then suggested to Séguin and Suzanne de Brécy that they take ten of our warriors and organize a hunt in the forest of Arques at sext the next day, so that this table might be lavish, as he put it, for Christmas dinner.

I watched him closely. His face, so gloomy just the day before, was now serene. There seemed fewer wrinkles on his brow. Once again he made those languid gestures that had so surprised and displeased me when he first arrived at the court of Normandy. His genial smile lit up his face again, and that glimmer of kindness, the reflection of the greatness of his heart, shone from deep within him. Though now I would have preferred to see him look old, I had to admit that despite his gray hair and beard he still had a young man's bearing. But too often did he look at Mathilde with blazing eyes, even in the presence of his guests.

To heighten my anger, this peasant girl—unlike Arlette, who never dared so much as raise her eyes to the duke during those suppers in Falaise—did not hesitate to look directly at my lord, though fortunately she kept silent. Sometimes she seemed sad, perhaps troubled by the change in her life, but often I saw affection in her eyes, great affection, as she gazed at Liébaut. So she too had chosen the road that she would follow. I recalled the admiration I had seen in her face when the lord of Arques treated Arnoul's terrible wound, and I realized now what a fool I had been to think that she would remain humble and passive at his side during the night.

It seemed that nothing would interrupt the course of my grief. In our camp, life went on tranquilly. Jéboin's shadow still hovered around the gallows, which on Liébaut's orders remained standing in the courtyard. The men of Falaise did not quarrel with those of Malbray, but beneath that calm, many of our warriors harbored rancor. Out of fear, Thorer, Tyrker, and the other people of Arques kept their feelings in check. They avoided us, merely casting unfriendly glances in our direction. Only Ivar remained shut up in his hut. Except for him, everyone in our castle went about and did his work in silence.

No one spoke of Mathilde.

Even on Christmas morning, as our army prepared to celebrate the Nativity of Christ, Liébaut did not emerge until after tierce, though day had long since dawned. During the hours of prayer and celebration, he spoke to me only to ask me to keep his weapons and equipment ready at all times. But though he still told everyone that an attack was imminent, he continued to take rides through the countryside alone with the peasant woman, ignoring the war.

Finally, weary of waiting for his return and unable to control my jealousy, I approached Bernon. "Why does the lord of Arques abandon his post in this way?" I asked.

"A squire must not concern himself with his master's affairs," was all he answered, his tone curt.

At supper, on that Christmas evening, Mathilde discarded her peasant dress for the first time and, as if to sharpen my suffering even more, appeared in the great hall dressed like a lady of the court. She wore a long, brightly colored wool tunic with wide sleeves, decorated by an embroidered band at the knees and cinched at the waist by a red girdle. This dress, I learned later, had been given to her by Suzanne de Brécy, at Liébaut's request. I was enraged. She sat almost directly opposite me. Unable to stand the sight of her long red hair attractively braided and adorned with colored ribbons, I turned away from her, did not look at her during the lavish supper supplied by Séguin de Brécy's hunt.

Liébaut, whose keen mind sparkled admirably during that holiday feast, took care to talk and laugh with everyone. But I did not listen to his words when he spoke to me. Unlike previous evenings, he looked suddenly old beside this girl barely out of childhood. Compared with Mathilde's perfectly smooth white skin, his face was much marked by the years. In his eyes I saw lassitude instead of kindness, the same lassitude that had quelled my father's gaze for the past two winters. I counted more than thirty lines on his brow. I looked at his gray hair and told myself that soon he would begin to bald.

I told myself that I was seeing him finally as he really was, and that I could no longer love him.

And then, at dawn the next day, once again my wait began: I stood on the ramparts in the rain, staring at the closed door to the great hall on the walkway at the top of the tower.

Four days passed. Mathilde continued to dress like a lady of the court. At the end of each supper, my master sent us away so that he could retire with her to the great hall. My nights were terrible. I shivered with cold in our room, alone with the two wounded, dying men.

I claim no excuse for what I did, but even today I believe

that what I endured there in the darkness was close to the torments of hell.

My first misdeed was committed in the morning of the Sunday after Christmas. My first step on the road of mortal sin.

After Granger said Mass in our room and Liébaut retired to the great hall with the peasant girl, I went to join Séguin de Brécy as he stood alone by the inner palisade. "My lord," I said, though from the beginning of our adventure I had always distrusted him, "my master neglects his army, his castle, and his war. By some witchcraft unknown to me, Mathilde holds his heart and mind hostage. Without his leadership, we will suffer a most cruel defeat, a most bloody slaughter. Would it not be possible for you, whom our duke holds in such high esteem, to take some action to send this evil girl away? Can you not do something, as second in command of our army, to restore Liébaut de Malbray's judgment and vigor, to make him come to his senses?"

Séguin de Brécy looked at me in great surprise, that I had thus revealed to him my innermost thoughts. "The second in command of this army is Vilgard de Chambois, not I," he said. "Why do you not address yourself to him?"

"He himself has been troubled since the harsh sentence passed against his nephew," I said in an attempt to conceal my dread of speaking to the baron of Chambois. "He would not listen to me."

Séguin de Brécy nodded, then turned and looked out at the forest of Arques, where he so loved to hunt.

"You alone can ward off this new peril that threatens us now," I went on, relieved that he had neither laughed at me nor repulsed me, as I had feared he would.

"What would you have me do, squire?" he sighed. "Do you really believe that your master has so lost his wits that someone must bring him to reason?"

"You could assemble your warriors, you could lead half our army to Liébaut de Malbray, to make him see the road the lord of Arques must follow."

"I see," Brécy replied without looking at me. "It is quite a task that you would have me undertake. Have you spoken to any other knight about this?"

"No," I said. "No one here has as many men as you do. No one commands as much strength as you do, to compel my master."

"Compel him!" he exclaimed, his elusive eyes resting on me for an instant. "Compel the conqueror of Auxerre! That is a task indeed!"

He turned away again, and I watched him in silence, watched that slight smile on his face, which twisted his mouth to one side and made him look deceitful. Doubt assailed me. Had it been a mistake to approach him?

"I must think about it," he finally said, with a seriousness that did not seem feigned. "I cannot give you an answer now. Come to my hut at vespers, before supper. Then we will speak of Liébaut de Malbray and Mathilde again, and I will tell you what I intend to do."

That evening, afraid that I had said too much, but hoping that Brécy would act, I went to the hut his men had built for him behind the hill at the foot of the inner enceinte. Entering this hut for the first time, I saw that it was heated by a wood fire. Brécy I found lying beside Suzanne on a wide bed that his men had built from trees cut down in the forest of Arques. To my astonishment, I saw above the couple a fabric canopy supported by four posts, a canopy like the one in the bedroom of the Magnificent. There were other surprises as I looked around me: all his effects—his linen shirts, breeches, and shoes, his richly adorned tunics and reddish-brown mantle, as well as his wife's coifs, veils, guimpes, belts and silk girdles, and embroidered dresses—were laid out on top of the carved coffers that had been brought with such labor from Falaise. Close by him, on a long trestle table draped with a fringed cloth, I saw crockery, the pieces and cloth grid of a chess set, a silver vase, a copy of the Gospels studded with precious stones, several heavy candelabra, two silver plates, valuable glassware, magnificent brooches, jewels, metal clasps, goblets filled with wine, the remnants and sucked bones of a half-eaten chicken, a loaf of bread cut in half, and three large griddlecakes made that morning. Even with the little sense that remained to me, I thought such jumbled wealth grotesque in the midst of the war that we were waging.

Séguin de Brécy stared at me, saying nothing. Suzanne's gaze was unfriendly, and I noticed Draco snickering on the floor near her, in the shadows at the foot of the bed.

Feeling as though I had fallen into an enemy trap, I was about to leave, but Brécy held me there with an astonishing question. "What do you want, squire?" As though he had completely forgotten our morning talk.

"You asked me to come!" I said.

"Why, in Christ's name?"

"Why? To talk about Liébaut de Malbray and Mathilde again, to tell me what you intend to do," I answered idiotically, thus playing, to his great pleasure, the game by which he meant to humiliate me.

"What I intend to do!" he exclaimed. "You must tell me that, for in truth I am wholly ignorant of my intentions, and that grieves me greatly."

"Should you not assemble your warriors?" I continued stubbornly.

"For what purpose?"

"To lead them to Liébaut de Malbray, so that, hearing them, he will see reason and understand the road the lord of Arques must follow."

"He would slam the door in our faces, he would turn us out," the baron said with mock seriousness.

"Then you must show your anger," I cried, "and threaten to depart this ill-defended camp."

"And what makes you think that we are angry?" Séguin asked in the tone one uses to question children.

"No, this young man gives good advice," Draco suddenly burst out, clapping his hands. "In this way everyone, warriors of Falaise and Brécy alike, will swing from the gallows at dawn tomorrow, like Jéboin, their tongues hanging out."

Ignoring this, I stepped toward the bed, to be closer to the man I sought to convince, but the dwarf thought I was coming to strike him. He opened his big mouth, baring his teeth, and screamed, curling up against his mistress's knee and clinging to the hem of her dress.

"You know, Odilon de Bernay," said Suzanne de Brécy, who had disliked me ever since I smote her jester, "it is not right for a squire to claim that his master has lost his mind."

"I have said not a word against Liébaut!" I exclaimed. "On the contrary, I seek to save him from the woman who holds him prisoner. I love my master more than anything, I love him as I do the saints of our Church."

"Blasphemy! The boy blasphemes!" snorted Draco.

I looked to Séguin de Brécy, hoping for some word of reassurance, but all I could see on his face was a deceitful, taunting, evil smile.

"Couldn't you at least send a messenger to Robert?" I asked. "Surely he would bring Liébaut to his senses."

Suzanne laughed.

"What sort of advice is that, Odilon de Bernay, urging me

to disturb the duke of Normandy?" Séguin said sharply. "Go instead and serve your lord. Close your eyes, stop your ears, and try to control your tongue."

"But don't you see the danger that threatens us?" I insisted, like a madman.

"If this young man does not shut up," Draco whispered to his mistress, but loud enough for me to hear, "then this very evening I, the wisest of jesters—dancer, tumbler, and sole minstrel of this glorious army—will be forced to warn the lord of Arques, the noble Liébaut de Malbray, conqueror of Auxerre, against his evil squire."

I struggled not to show my fury against this castoff from hell, and not to reveal how frightened I was by his threat.

"You should know, Odilon de Bernay, that your master's passion for the peasant girl Mathilde, which is none of my affair in any case, is merely the equal of what I feel for my own sweet wife, and that I too know lust and the fire of desire," said Séguin, brazenly baring Suzanne's breasts and fondling them as I looked on.

Shocked and shamed by such insolence, I realized then what a great mistake I had made in coming to this hut.

"I warned him, but he refused to listen," the dwarf said. "And now no one can douse the fire that consumes Liébaut de Malbray. The baron of Arques will never be parted from the red-haired Mathilde, sister of a thief though she is. Unless," he added hoarsely, "some clever warrior with no fear for his life manages, through cunning, to kill the peasant girl while the lord of Malbray is away."

Though at supper they smiled tauntingly at me, Suzanne and Séguin de Brécy said nothing to Liébaut about my visit. I was relieved, but also aware of the new danger that now threatened me: that my master might learn of my brazen rebellion against the life he was leading in the midst of a war. Draco had been banished from our table, yet the dwarf might murmur evil words in Liébaut's ear at any moment, and then I would be lost. I felt that I had no choice but to act quickly.

Much of the night I spent wondering what to do. Brécy's reluctance to act convinced me that my master's safety—and the return of my happiness—depended on me alone. Worried and angered by the temerity of the peasant girl, who that evening, for the first time, had dared to speak during supper, I tossed and turned under my blanket. I forced myself to lie still and stared at the ceiling. I remembered Suzanne de Brécy's bare breasts, swollen under her husband's shameful caresses, then imagined Mathilde's white breasts in my lord's hand, and that painful vision would not leave me.

Draco's words echoed in my mind, that a cunning warrior might be able to extinguish the fire consuming Liébaut de Malbray by killing the girl—and I began to think of murder. I swear on this parchment that in my madness this thought did not cause me to tremble, and that after much hesitation I rejected the idea only because I feared that once the crime was done, I would be betrayed by Suzanne and Séguin de Brécy, before whom I had revealed too much.

But in the course of that long night, I became convinced that only the peasant girl's death would release Liébaut from his passion, and that, of all of us gathered here behind the palisades in Arques, there was only one man who was desperate enough—and had the desire—to kill her. I decided that I would approach that man.

I had to wait until the hour of none, when Thorer, Tyrker, and the others finally came out into the courtyard, as they did each day, to talk among themselves around the great fire that burned near the inner enceinte. Only then did I risk entering their hut. Inside, among scrabbling chickens, I found women busy weaving wool, mothers with young children, and two old men silently carving wooden bowls. In the rear, sitting alone in the shadows on a bed of straw, next to an enormous dog, was the one to whom I wished to speak.

As I expected, Ivar shot me a look of hatred when he saw me. Concealing my fear, I went and sat beside him. Amazed at my audacity, he glared at me. "I come not as an enemy," I said gently, almost in a whisper, so that no one else in the hut could hear, "but as a friend. Yes, I am troubled by your grief. In fact," I went on, not giving him time to speak, "I know and share your pain, for I love Liébaut de Malbray as much as you love Mathilde. It is not in the name of the master of this place, therefore, that I come to you now, but in my own, and I risk punishment by doing so. The shame that you have suffered is great. Though you are a peasant and I a squire, we are the same age, and we feel a like grief in this ordeal. Forget who it is I serve, and regard me only as a companion."

"If it was not your master who sent you here," said Ivar, despondent, "then perhaps it was Mathilde, whose friend you may have become. Did she ask you to placate me?"

"In all the time that she has shared Liébaut de Malbray's bed, Mathilde, now full of pride, has not spoken a single word to me. Though I sit facing her at every supper, the new mistress of Arques completely ignores me."

"Yet you were a good squire," the peasant said bitterly, maliciously.

"Since the woman you were to have wed arrived in our tower, Liébaut de Malbray has had no further need of a squire," I sighed.

I did not know whether Ivar believed me. He continued

200

to stare at me, perhaps hoping that I would reveal something more. Afraid to avert my eyes, lest he guess that I had come to deceive him, I looked directly at him. I was astonished by his appearance. His grief had aged him. His face was drawn, his strong jaw covered by a beard much thicker than mine. There were gray circles under his eyes. His sorrow and rage, which I intended to make use of, horrified me, and I hesitated, as though the lie I had prepared would bring about some terrible misfortune, a misfortune far beyond what I planned. At that moment—I well remember—it seemed to me that my lie would cast me into a bottomless pit of evil. I fear this peasant more than Draco, I said to myself.

"Ivar," I went on, "I must tell you just how shameless Mathilde has become, for that truth will quell your regret. Not content with having robbed the lord of Malbray of his judgment through some evil spell, she now forgets her past humility. In full view of everyone she covers my master with kisses, drawing him into depravity, she binds him to their bed for hours night and day, and with adulterous delights and defilements has driven him mad. In her impurity she abandons herself to nocturnal forces, to the cycle of the moon, mingles her body with the lord of Malbray's, wearied by war and combat as he is, and now reduces him—he who was once so noble and so proud—to little more than a living corpse. Such is the life Mathilde leads in our tower! Do not pine for her, she is an evil woman and will never return to you!"

Ivar was silent now, his eyes downcast. I knew that my words were consuming his heart and mind, that in the hours and days to come they would fuel his hatred. "And that is not all," I added, wanting to fuel his hatred more. "Yesterday, at supper in the great hall, she drank much wine and laughed at you in front of everyone, in front of our monk, the baron of Chambois, the lord of Brécy and his wife, and

As I draw near to the most distressing hours of this adventure, as our misfortune and my sin come to life again on this parchment that I can barely see, my lord Liébaut de Malbray has visited me in my sleep.

Last night he appeared in a white robe and walked toward me slowly, his countenance grave. He regarded me not in anger but with great gentleness. Under my cover, my head on my hard pillow, I did not move. He loomed tall over this wretched body of mine undone by the years, but I looked back at him without fear, filling my mind with his noble face, his hair, his gray beard, the deep creases on his brow, his blue eyes, the curl of his lip that suggested cruelty, his square jaw that showed firmness of character, determination. He turned slightly, and I saw that my old man's memory had not deceived me: his hooked nose, as I have written here, gave him the profile of a bird of prey. In sudden joy I reached out to him, but my trembling fingers felt only empty air. All my young man's love returned to me, and I called out to this vision, begged him to join me again as in bygone days when we slept together in the tower in Arques wrapped in our woolen blanket. But there was no answer, Liébaut de Malbray was an apparition only, immaterial. I fell back upon my mattress, breathless, a terrible pain in my chest, and I believed the moment of my death had come. "Not yet," I cried, "not now. I must finish my testimony, so that in years to come the world will know how much I loved you, my master, my lord, despite my sin." When I opened my eyes again, I saw that, though serious, Liébaut was looking at me with the old tenderness. "I know that your presence heralds my death," I murmured. "But have mercy, grant me a little more time, lend me your strength, for life ebbs from me day by day."

Liébaut then slowly receded. "Stay!" I cried. But in vain, for he grew hazier, more distant. Soon I could no longer see his warrior's face. "It is not I, Odilon, who decides how much time you have left," he said as he vanished.

The Frisian attack was sudden and unexpected. On the eve
of the second Sunday after Christmas, as a cloudy, moonless
winter's night covered the land, our army's deep repose was
shattered by the horn from the top of the tower. I rushed
out of our room and ran up to the walkway, where Liébaut
stood half-naked, having just been torn from the peasant
woman's arms. Below, I saw Ubbo's two hundred warriors
amid the dark ruins of Arques. Advancing slowly and silently
in a line, lances to the fore, they had taken us by surprise.
The thought that this long-awaited battle would change
everything in Arques filled me with joy, my first joy in many
weeks.

"Go, fetch my gear," my master ordered, giving me no
time to observe the enemy. Quickly obeying, I brought him
his shield, his weapons, his helmet. "Help me," he said, as
in the time when I served him faithfully. I threw his shirt
over his chest and laced it, happy to be near him again, both
of us perhaps on the threshold of death. I pulled on his hauberk, buckled his belt, tied the straps of his chausses. "You

get ready too," he said, when I handed him his mace and his sword. "And this time stay with me during the battle. I will have great need of protection against blows from the rear."

Hastily donning my own gear, I joined him in the court-yard with Bernon Hildetand and the baron of Chambois, who were also helmeted and covered with mail. Liébaut ordered that six of our horses be moved to the more secure protection of the storeroom, then led us to the outer palisade just above the drawbridge. The archers were in position, ready to loose their arrows.

As we looked out at the enemy, now only a hundred paces from our rampart, we saw that more than twenty of the barbarians were pushing before them a device made of four beams of extraordinary length and breadth, tied together in five places by thick rope and ending in a carved goat's head, its horns forward. Mounted on wooden wheels as big as a man, it slowed the enemy's advance so much that the men seemed almost stationary despite the shifting of their bodies in the night and their footfalls. I did not see how they would be able to cross our moat with such a heavy war machine.

Liébaut, as if reading my thoughts, announced that we had to defend the drawbridge at all costs, for once that battering ram penetrated the courtyard, our adversaries would easily breach the inner palisade with it. Their pointed helmets with horns and their iron pikes and swords gleamed in the light of the torches set up along our rampart. The barbarians, consumed by hatred, thirsting for blood, did not look human. It was as if a horde of beasts was about to attack us, to tear our flesh with claws and fangs. Yet I did not tremble. Our warriors were as motionless and silent as statues, watching this army that, after so many days of waiting, was finally advancing to annihilate us.

When the barbarians were sixty paces away, Liébaut gave

the order to release the catapults. Two enormous stones flew into the air, but alas, they were badly aimed; one fell behind the barbarians, the other in front of the ram, doing it no damage. Only the barrier of sharpened stakes and gnarled and tangled branches, which had been set up around our camp after the first battle, stopped the enemy. Some of the attackers fell, their bodies pierced by arrows, but that first line of our defense soon yielded to hatchets. More than thirty of the enemy entered the moat and began to hew the forest of stakes we had planted there. The battering ram, pushed by forty arms, again advanced toward the drawbridge, and savage war cries began to fill the night.

Though we hurled many stones into the black water, which now roiled and spouted everywhere, we were unable to prevent the Frisians from cutting openings in the wall of stakes. Crossing that obstacle, several barbarians charged the outer palisade under a hail of arrows. Our army, gathered on the rampart, was troubled at the ease with which the enemy had crossed our initial defenses. I saw many anxious faces around me, but still I felt no fear. As I gripped my father's sword and stood behind my shield to face this peril, it seemed to me that somehow the valor of the conqueror of Auxerre had finally entered me, that he had never forsaken me. I turned to him. "Tonight I have no fear, Liébaut de Malbray," I said proudly. He looked at me. Despite the helmet that covered half his face, I thought I read tenderness, the old tenderness, in his eyes. My heart joyful, I forgot my misfortunes and told myself that my master loved me again on the brink of this fierce battle.

The barbarian assault broke against our reinforced, iron-tipped palisade, and, as Liébaut had predicted, most of the enemy army, falling into our trap, rushed to the weakest point in the rampart, fifteen paces to the left of the drawbridge. Before long it began to give way. My master led us into the courtyard and positioned us just behind the narrow passage the Frisians were opening with their mace and hatchet blows.

The first barbarian to come through the breach, which was too narrow to allow two men to pass abreast, fell immediately, his chest pierced by the sword of the lord of Arques. Eight Frisians, one after another, fell in their gushing blood. Aware at last of the ambush, they halted their assault, and for a moment an astonishing silence fell over the two armies.

The silence was soon shattered by shouts. Fifteen barbarians had scaled ladders and now stood on our rampart. We saw them brandishing their swords and maces above our warriors. Most were repulsed, but three of them, swinging their weapons and howling like demons, slew four of our men. More barbarians climbed onto the rampart overlooking the courtyard, and the fight became truly bloody. The palisade was quickly overrun. The moment one enemy fell, another took his place, and the Normans, despite their valor in this hand-to-hand encounter, had to give way. "They are going to get in," Liébaut said, beside me. "There are not enough of us to drive them back. Take the peasants into the tower storeroom," he ordered Bernon, "and give swords to those who wish to fight with us, if any there are, to save their own lives." Then he turned to Vilgard de Chambois and told him to assemble his warriors in battle formation in the courtyard, for we would have to face the enemy now in the very heart of the castle.

For a long time Liébaut defended the drawbridge, with me and two knights of Malbray at his side. He cast off his shield and swung his mace with both hands, and I stood near him and protected him, as he had asked. Despite our archers, more of the enemy scaled the rampart, and we were soon surrounded by an army of savages.

Caring only about my lord, and anxious for him to see how valiantly I served him, I became reckless, and a violent blow tore my sword from my hand. Standing back to back with Liébaut, I withstood incredible strokes with my shield, which fortunately had been reinforced with iron. Lances and pikes broke against it, and an ax sank into it. Yet an amazing anger gave me strength.

Liébaut fought like ten men, striking tirelessly, sowing death around him. With his mace he splintered bones, stove in heads. Hands slick with blood clawed at the mail of his hauberk, slid down his belly, clung to his legs in a last, mad hope of surviving. Years had passed, it seemed, since the horn at the top of the tower wrenched him from the peasant woman's arms. I was intoxicated, I saw a golden light shine from his face. He had become, to my great joy, the conqueror of Auxerre again.

The barbarians near us retreated, stumbling over the bodies of their own men, and now I could see many wounded warriors farther off, amid the fighting that raged in the courtyard between Vilgard de Chambois's men and the enemy. Both Normans and Frisians crawled on the ground, groaning with pain. In the darkness I could not tell who was winning. Then we were attacked again, and the helmet of one of the knights of Malbray was split by a hatchet blow. The poor man fell at my feet and with a last effort handed me his sword.

Though many Frisians lay dead around us, it seemed to me that we would never subdue these barbarians. Their whole army was now overrunning our camp. Liébaut, struck on the arm, lowered his weapon for an instant. Looking at him, I did not see the flail, bristling with nails, that was falling upon me, and my shield was torn away in a great clatter. Defenseless now beside my master, who I feared was wounded, I threw myself in front of him. The hour of our death had come, and his blood and mine would now mingle. I offered my chest to the iron-tipped lances, but Liébaut, recovering, swung his mace and crushed the skull of the Frisian who was about to run me through. "Pick up a sword and shield!" he cried. "Everyone, to the tower!" When they saw us retreating, the barbarians rushed to lower the bridge. Certain that victory was theirs, they sounded their shrill dragon-headed horns.

We ran through threatening shadows, through the darkness behind the warriors of Vilgard de Chambois, who also fled. Our archers, commanded by Bernon, meanwhile gathered atop the inner palisade, whose gate, defended by several Normans, was closing again.

When we reached the foot of the hill, we heard a clamor behind us. I turned and saw the battering ram. Drawn by thirty barbarians, its wheels creaking, its carved horns thrusting forward, it was crossing our moat.

When he reached the tower, Liébaut hurried to speak to the people of Arques, who were assembled in the storeroom along with six of our horses. Squeezed into a space too small for them, the frightened peasants—with their old men, women, and children—huddled together among our provisions and weapons. Some prayed, appealing to both Thor and Christ Our Lord, and some wept. I saw Ivar sitting apart with his father, withdrawn into himself as usual. Liébaut, covered with enemy blood and raising his voice above the cries of the children and the noise of the battle, audible even here, spoke to them.

"We are in great peril," he said. "Though we have slain more than sixty Frisians, many of our men have also lost their lives. The barbarians, massed at the foot of the hill, are preparing to attack the inner palisade. They are too numerous to be repulsed. Soon they will be here, in this tower, in this storeroom. Unless you come now and fight beside us, many of you will be slaughtered within the hour. I have no time to try to convince you, since for our common protection I must rejoin the army of Arques. So take up these axes and swords that we have forged since our arrival here, and for your own salvation, and for that of your fathers, your wives, and your children, hurry valiantly to our rampart."

Liébaut fell silent and looked at the people, who were made even more wretched by their fear of death. Most of the men of arms-bearing age lowered their eyes in shame. "I await you," he added before returning to the battle, "with hope in my heart."

Outside, the sky was red. Columns of flame and black smoke as high as the tower rose with a dull crackling. Four of our huts, the ox skins torn off by the enemy, were burning.

Arrows, spears, and stones rained down upon the barbarian army below our palisade. Dozens of pierced and broken bodies were strewn on the ground. Yet nothing stopped Ubbo's warriors, and the carved goat's head smashed into our rampart. We found the baron of Chambois, his chest torn by a pike, lying on the rampart next to Granger, who stood praying, Crucifix in hand. "Take him to our room," my master cried, his voice breaking.

The smell of fire and blood was everywhere. We heard

211

groans all around us. I sensed that Liébaut was weakening, that he believed the end, our death, was near.

Sparks carried by the wind were falling into the courtyard. The roof of the hut Mathilde had lived in collapsed with a great crash, and the fire spread to the hut in which our other horses were quartered. Now we could not escape.

When the battering ram hit the palisade for the sixth time, the wall gave way in spite of its iron reinforcement. Two Frisians rushed through the breach. Felling them with his ax, Liébaut ordered our warriors and the five peasants who had finally joined us to retreat to the tower. He called to our archers to get ready to shoot from the tower walkway and told Séguin de Brécy's men to stay in the storeroom with the peasants.

One of our horses bolted from the blazing hut. Panic-stricken, the beast, rearing in every direction, ringed by flames and dragging a trail of sparks behind him, swept through the enemy, and this enabled our men to retreat unnoticed.

Terrifying visions assailed my eyes. The countryside looked like the second circle of hell, where heretics, murderers, lapsed clerics, sodomites, and usurers stewed in boiling blood for all eternity. I stood alone with my master at the palisade and tried to protect him from blows, as I had done since the beginning of the battle. But weariness was overcoming me, the sword and shield I carried grew too heavy. We began to fall back, facing ten barbarians, and withdrew up the path cut into the hillside.

Liébaut's ax slew three of the enemy but broke on the fourth. He tossed it aside and drew his sword. Swinging it back and forth, cutting and thrusting, he slew five more men.

Taking courage from such great valor, I felt that the Frisians were now weakening too, that they were pressing in fewer numbers, that their blows were losing force. Certainly more than a hundred barbarians—half Ubbo's army—were out of the battle, either dead or fatally wounded. Still, my strength was leaving me. Smoke stung my eyes and choked my breath. My legs shook, my hand trembled. What if I alone died, leaving Liébaut to languish in the peasant girl's evil embrace? I looked at him, my indefatigable lord of war, so glorious at my side, and hatred filled my heart. Would that I had strangled Mathilde with my own hands!

Suddenly an enemy wearing no helmet stood before the lord of Arques. He raised his mace. I saw yellow hair, a callow face that looked as young as my own, and then I saw terror in his eyes, and he fell at our feet, slain by my lord, his throat slashed.

An incredible thing happened then.

The Frisian immediately behind this reckless young warrior let out a heartrending scream, and all the Frisians around him stopped fighting. Though he himself had suffered no blow, this barbarian, wearing a helmet that gleamed like gold, fell to his knees on the pathway. Imploring the heavens in words I could not understand, he stripped to the waist, tearing off the collar of stones, the chain mail, and the animal skin that covered and protected his chest.

Arques was saved only because the Frisian attack ceased at the very moment they reached the tower.

Four enemy warriors lay down their arms and picked up the bleeding body of the young, fair-haired barbarian. Silently they carried it out of our camp as everyone stood and watched. To our great amazement, the entire enemy army, with almost certain victory in their grasp, turned and followed them. Only the warrior with the gold helmet, wringing his hands, wailing, and lamenting, remained. Kneeling on the ground before us, he covered his chest and face with earth. Then at last he rose, picked up his heavy sword, and pointed it angrily at Liébaut. Fearsome in his hatred, like a dead man returned from the beyond to curse the living, he stood in the flickering red light of the fire devouring our camp below and hurled words of grief and violence at my master in his strange tongue. Then he turned his back, suddenly looking like a wretched old man despite his great stature, and walked away, following the barbarian horde down the path strewn with the bodies of his men. He passed the broken inner palisade and continued across the courtyard amid sparks that flew in the night like wandering lights, like tiny stars driven by the wind. Soon he was only a shadow, and he disappeared into the wreaths of black smoke without looking back.

Bernon, who understood the language of the Frisians, told us that the old warrior who had just sworn terrible vengeance against Liébaut was none other than Ubbo, and that my lord, with a single stroke of his sword, had cut the throat of Ubbo's only son.

Smoking ash was all that remained of Thorer's hut. Half of the courtyard was now an inferno, and the flying sparks threatened to spread the fire to the tower. So the surviving warriors of Arques, instead of resting and rejoicing in the barbarian withdrawal, had to rush to fetch buckets, pots, basins, and fill them at the well. "Water, more water!" Bernon shouted through the roar of the blaze. As we ran in all directions, I lost sight of my lord. The faces I saw, in that red furnace, were twisted by horror. I passed Séguin de

Brécy, whose wealth-filled hut was being consumed by flame. His eyes vacant, his brow blackened with smoke, he looked like a man gone mad. Seeing him so helpless, I could not help pitying him and went to join the fight against the fire, but in my haste I ran into one of our warriors, and the earthenware jar I was carrying fell and broke.

Perhaps, I thought, I should instead look for Liébaut, who might still require my aid. As I strained to find him among the shadows and the flames, I heard a violent crackling and turned to see what it was. Séguin de Brécy's hut collapsed in a crash of broken beams, spewing a thousand flakes of fire. I heard the desperate cry of Suzanne de Brécy, who, having tried in vain to get inside the hut to rescue her riches, was now being restrained by her husband, held to the ground. Coughing, her face black with soot, her eyes red, she wept, as fluttering scraps of her precious clothes and parchments, carried by the wind, blazed above her, rising.

Leaving the lady of Brécy to her misfortune, I looked for my master in the stifling heat, going from hut to hut, stumbling over bodies. Finally I found him by our inner rampart. He was trying to douse the fire in the hut where our horses had been. An awful stench of scorched flesh rose from the rubble as I looked upon the dreadful sight of the charred carcasses of our beasts, their limbs stiff, their skin split, their manes gone, their skulls and bellies burst. The necks were still tethered. "We tied them too tightly, afraid the enemy might steal them," Liébaut said. "Only three horses were able to escape."

At the side of the lord of Arques again, I tried to help him extinguish the flames that threatened the tower. Our throats scorched by the smoke, our eyes filled with stinging tears, we beat at the blaze with knotted blankets. My weariness and agitation, alas, made me clumsy, and at first all I did was scatter new sparks around me. But I persisted, remaining with Liébaut de Malbray until matins.

Gradually we put the fire out. Deciding to wait until dawn to collect our dead—black with soot and dried blood, they were impossible to find in the darkness—we returned to the storeroom exhausted, staggering, our minds confused.

There, finally breaking his heavy silence, Liébaut spoke to me before all the people of Arques, who still sat huddled together. "I owe it to you, my squire, that I am still alive." Affectionately he placed his hand on my shoulder. "You fought valiantly, and I am proud of you. Robert will hear of your loyalty and courage, and you may be sure that upon our return to Falaise he will be told that you merit being dubbed a knight of Normandy."

At these words, so sweet to my ears, I threw myself into his arms. "All I want is to serve you and remain always at your side," I said, making no effort to hold back my tears. He stroked my hair as he used to do, and pulled me close with unbounded friendship.

But then the peasant girl appeared and, abandoning all restraint, ran wildly to Liébaut in full view of the assembled villagers. The instant he saw her, my master released me and took her in his arms, rested her head against his chest, her head instead of mine. "I was so afraid for the lord of Arques," she murmured, no more than six steps from Ivar, who sat in the shadows next to Thorer.

Because our wounded were taken to our room, where they lay under Granger's care, I stayed in the storeroom with our warriors and the people of Arques, crammed in among weapons, provisions, tools, plows, and harnesses. Lying between one of our archers and a peasant, overwhelmed with weariness, my mind numb and empty—incapable even of thinking about how my lord had just abandoned me for the peasant girl in front of everyone—I sank into a deep sleep.

The sound of the horn at dawn roused me from a dreamless night. At first, when I opened my eyes and looked around at the peasants, at the women and children piled almost on top of each other, at the warriors, still dressed in their armor and lying on the ground so tightly packed that their legs and arms intermingled, I did not know where I was. Then I saw Ivar, sitting with his back against a pile of wood, and the pain in my limbs reminded me of the terrible battle. I remembered the dead, the blood, the fire, and how the lord of Arques had sent me away so that he could embrace Mathilde.

Crushed, regretting that I had not fallen under Frisian blows, I pretended that I was feverish and still too weak to help our men gather the dead and begin rebuilding the inner palisade. When he heard my excuse, Liébaut de Malbray repeated his declaration of friendship and said that I should rest. He held out his hand to me and brushed my cheek in a gesture of affection. But I told myself that his kind words and tender gesture no longer meant anything to me.

I lay three days in the storeroom, not seeing the sun, and my only desire was to find an opportunity to speak to Ivar again, to feed his anger. Feigning such weariness that everyone thought I really was in the grip of a fever, I waited until he was alone.

Twice, during those interminable hours when our men buried the dead and dug out the moat again beyond the reinforced outer palisade, Mathilde, arm in arm with Liébaut, passed by us without so much as glancing at the man who had been her betrothed. Ivar stared at me then, eyes burning, as if to make sure that I was not laughing at him. Seeing that he, too, chose to remain in the storeroom, I had no doubt of the depth of his despair, and I waited patiently for Thorer and the others to leave us. Finally, at vespers on the evening of the first Sunday after the battle, we found ourselves in the storeroom with only four old men.

"Ivar," I whispered, leaning close to him, "we cannot remain here, you and I, prisoners of our grief. Mathilde passes you and looks the other way, and it was on her account that my lord Liébaut de Malbray abandoned me after the battle. Your pain and mine are alike, for we are both rejected, and in my heart I have as much love for my master as you have for Mathilde. True, it is not the same desire, but there are friendships as deep as the need a man has for a woman, if not deeper. To our misfortune, Mathilde has poisoned the lord of Malbray's mind. Forget her, Ivar, as I now strive to forget my love for my master! Do not remain in the darkness like this, but return to life. Your suffering gives too much joy to this evil woman who, driven by her thirst for power, has ensnared the most noble of the barons of Normandy. She despises you as much as she despises me. Drive her from your thoughts, from your heart!"

Ivar turned and looked at me. I saw no hatred in his eyes this time, only a feverish apathy.

"Join your family, hunt some game for supper," I suggested, uneasy at seeing him so calm. "Leave this closed place where the sun does not shine. You have lost Mathilde. Why sit here like a dead man on her account? Why let your life be ruined by grief? It only amuses her to know that you are broken. Wake up, Ivar," I insisted. "Free your heart, as I would like to free mine!"

Two more days passed. Still in the storeroom, I learned that the baron of Chambois's wound had worsened and that one of our men-at-arms had set out on horseback for Falaise to ask that twenty archers be speedily dispatched to reinforce us.

Refusing to sit opposite the peasant girl at the table of the lord of Arques, I continued to feign fever and fatigue, lying in the darkness near Ivar. I felt that our adventure was drawing to a close one way or another, and that there was little time left for me to rid myself forever of Mathilde. I watched Ivar constantly, carefully, listened to his sighs, to the few words he exchanged with his father. For hours on end I waited for some sign of anger, but all I saw was a wretched peasant. I despaired.

On Monday evening it began to snow, and the icy wind howled all night. The cold, already bitter, became terrible in the storeroom, which could not be heated because of the risk of fire. We huddled together in our blankets, peasants and warriors alike, with pieces of cloth wrapped around our hands and feet, and around our faces to protect our ears and necks. With the noise of the storm and the coughs that racked the old people and some of the women, I could not sleep. My own chest became inflamed, and I developed a real fever, which made me shiver. At dawn, when I saw that Ivar was still silent, still passive, I realized that I would have to kill the peasant girl myself, that Ivar, no matter what lies I told, would not lift his hand in revenge against Mathilde. But how was I to do the deed, without being seen? The fever, however, prevented me from thinking of a plan. Drenched with sweat, short of breath, my chest on fire, I spent some of the darkest hours of my life.

Then, after vespers, something unexpected happened. Draco, who had not been seen since the battle—perhaps he had been hiding—walked into the storeroom behind his mistress. Looking around at the people of Arques, he spotted Ivar and me wrapped in our blankets. The jester pointed at us and guffawed. "Behold these two unfortunates, both enduring the torments of hell because of a woman! Behold them and laugh! And when you have laughed long and well, consider the lesson of their stupidity, for once love grips men, they become simple of mind, fools for the sake of a bright pair of eyes or a pair of shapely breasts. Warriors and people of Arques, heed the words of Draco the Wise, for he is here to tell you that the beauty of women is but skin deep, that inside their pretty heads there is only treachery, that beneath the delicious wrapper of the body lie ill temper, bile, bloody discharge, snot, and excrement. Except, of course, for this lady here, the baroness of Brécy," he added, his tone venomous, "who is sweet and beautiful within and without alike. As for the alleged beauty of men, knights of Normandy and others—for it also may happen, for example, that a foolish squire falls in love with his master—I will say nothing, out of deference to our noble and magnificent lord."

Ignoring the shame that the dwarf had just heaped upon me, I immediately understood the favor he had done me, for Ivar, too, had been humiliated in front of the assembled people of Arques, and I had to force myself not to burst out laughing with the peasants, amused as they were by Draco's speech.

At tierce the next day I approached Ivar, taking advantage of the absence of Thorer and the others. "Even the baron of Brécy's dwarf taunts us," I whispered to him, my voice hoarse with the malady that stung my throat. "We must not tolerate this any longer, for everyone now makes sport of our grief. At the hour of none I will go to the courtyard to train with the sword. Come with me if you want, and I will teach you how to cut through an enemy's mail. It will help you forget how much pain the girl you loved has caused you."

Ivar did not come out into the thick snow to train with the sword, but when I returned to the storeroom, the blackness of his glance told me that hatred once more burned within him.

At prime on Saturday, the seventh day after the battle, as we awaited the arrival of the archers from Falaise, a horn sounded from the tower again. Warriors and peasants rushed outside together, and from the top of the hill we saw with dread that the remaining half of the enemy army was passing through the ruins of Arques, now mere mounds of white, and marching toward us under a yellow sky in which a few snowflakes fluttered.

My head still feverish, I put on my hauberk and helmet and took my father's sword and shield. With this evil eating at me, I wondered, how would I find the strength to defend Liébaut and preserve my own life? I was about to rush to the great hall to do my duty as squire, when my master appeared in the storeroom with Bernon. Already in his armor, he led me immediately to the outer rampart.

When we looked out at the Frisians, we were surprised to see that they were dragging no war machine with them, and that they carried no ladders. Perhaps they were attacking without preparation, driven by rage alone. For a moment, hope returned to our hearts. "Knights of Falaise and of Malbray, defenders of Arques," Liébaut called out loudly, "this will be the deciding battle. It will be difficult, but victory can be ours, for the enemy has been weakened. For the glory of Our Almighty Savior, who preserved us from death seven days ago, and for the glory of the Magnificent, who waits in Falaise to bestow honors upon us, let each of us fight to the limit of his strength, to the last drop of blood if need be! Brave knights, faithful and generous warriors, let us kill without mercy: for Christ, for Robert, for Normandy!"

The enemy army, to our surprise, stopped outside the shattered and burned outer palisade, now shapeless beneath a thick layer of snow. Only Ubbo—wearing his golden helmet, dressed in furs, and protected by his mail—advanced to the middle of the devastated courtyard. He stood fifteen paces from the hill, legs apart, clenched fists resting on his hips, and spoke to us angrily in the Frisian tongue. At the end of his brief speech, he stood motionless, waiting. "He wants to end this war with a fight to the death between himself and the Norman who cut his son's throat," Bernon told us. "He promises the immediate withdrawal of his army and their return to distant Frisia if he is slain. On the other hand, if he slays the one he has just challenged, we must surrender to him, and he will decide our fate."

"In other words," my lord sighed, "he will slaughter the lot of you, warriors and peasants alike. No one will be spared, and nothing will remain of Arques."

Liébaut de Malbray fell silent, his face grave. The only sound was the cawing of crows flying low overhead. He regarded the barbarian, whose sword, much larger than his own, hung from his belt. Fear gripped me as I looked at that massive warrior and his powerful shoulders. "His hatred is so great that it will double his strength," I said to my lord. "Reject this combat, in which you may lose your life, and let us endure the assault army against army. You said yourself that the barbarians have been weakened and that we can defeat them. God will come to our aid once more, and I will stand beside you and protect you from blows from the rear."

222

"And many a Norman, perhaps everyone here, will die within the hour, for the outcome of the battle is far from certain," he replied. "I know that you will protect me, Odilon, but what value would my life have then, if others perish? Soon, my squire, when your time comes to take command of an army like this one, you will learn that a knight of Normandy must not avoid the enemy's blows, but must expose himself to them, in order to save his men, no matter how great the peril."

Turning to Granger, he bowed his head and asked for the monk's blessing, then told Bernon to announce that he would accept the challenge. I watched helplessly as he walked out onto the lowered drawbridge, crossed the moat, and advanced alone toward Ubbo.

"Spare his life, Lord Christ," I murmured. "And grant him victory!" I saw a very pale Mathilde, accompanied by Suzanne de Brécy and Draco, coming up the path to join us on the hill and watch the combat.

The two warriors stood face to face in the courtyard between the well and the ruins of the hut in which Ivar had lived. Suddenly the Frisian let out a cry and drew his sword, and Liébaut drew his. The adversaries began to circle, stepping in ankle-deep snow, their eyes locked. A new fear hammered in my breast. Never before in this adventure had it occurred to me that Liébaut might die without me; I had not thought of his death, his fate, separate from my own. How I hated the peasant girl who now stood five steps from me, anguish in her face, undoubtedly also praying for the safety of her lord!

The barbarian was the first to raise his sword, and the two blades met in a loud crash.

Twenty times the slashing swords whirled and fell against shield or helmet. At first the combatants kept a cautious distance between them, and it seemed to me that they were slow to strike, stiff in their heavy armor. But then the Frisian suddenly charged Liébaut headfirst. My master quickly jumped aside, but the barbarian had been even quicker, had reached past the shield and wounded him in the side. Blood flowed, the snow was tinged with red, and Ubbo uttered a hoarse cry, raising his sword aloft. My lord turned sideways to protect his stomach and drove the Frisian back with a sharp blow. I could see the torn mail just below the wound from Auxerre.

Then, as the enemy army watched, ready to cross our outer enceinte and slaughter us, the two warriors, knees slightly bent, stood and stared at each other again. I turned for an instant and saw that several peasants had joined us. Everyone, even Draco, held his breath. Again the clash of blades rang out in the deathly silence that hung over our camp. "Christ Jesus," I prayed, "have pity and spare my lord, who now bears the burden of combat for the sake of those who believe in Thy Church."

The combatants, circling, came to a tree. There it was Liébaut's turn to charge his adversary, but the Frisian, on guard, eluded his sword point. The two exchanged countless blows, each one delivered with force and skill. There were thrusts, feints, parries, and soon they began to groan as they fought and could barely lift their arms. But Ubbo, driven by hatred, continued to strike at Liébaut's shield and forced him back, toward the outer enceinte, where the enemy army waited impatiently.

Suddenly my master staggered, nearly fell. He leaped to the side again, eluding the Frisian's sharp blade, but then a blow of incredible force cracked his shield before he could defend himself. I closed my eyes, but Mathilde, standing beside me, let out a cry, and despite my desire not to see, not to follow the struggle to the death, I looked again and saw, through my tears, that my master was now protecting himself only with his sword. The barbarian, with another blow, managed to wrench his helmet off. Bareheaded, exhausted, Liébaut swayed, made an ill-considered movement, and was wounded in the arm. Blood spattered him as he staggered again, caught his heel on some charred wood, and fell backward into the snow.

Ubbo threw his shield aside, let out a cry of victory, and raised his enormous sword in both hands as he stood over the lord of Arques, hiding him from view. But then the barbarian froze, his sword in the air, froze just as he was about to strike. He stood erect, motionless, as if to savor his victory a moment longer. Then, with astonishing slowness, he lowered his sword. Curling into himself, as he had done after his son's death, he dropped his weapon and collapsed to the ground. His face sank into the snow, and his golden helmet rolled at Liébaut's feet.

My master, half lying on his back, was holding his sword straight out in front of him, and its blade was red with blood, to the hilt.

Liébaut de Malbray, once again victorious, got to his feet. Mathilde rushed to him, joined him in the courtyard, ran into his arms, while I, robbed of joy by her action, stood with our warriors fifteen paces from the Frisians.

Bernon ordered our archers to prepare for an attack, and he and Hugues, swords in hand, went to their lord while the peasant girl, unable to contain herself, showered him with shameless kisses in front of everyone. The barbarians, stunned by the death of their chief, who lay in the bloodred snow, stood facing us but did not move. I feared they might avenge themselves on Liébaut and his unworthy peasant consort, ablaze with love even on the field of battle, only a few steps from the fallen Ubbo, but they kept their word, and the wounded lord of Arques, supported by Bernon and Mathilde, was able to cross the drawbridge and retire behind the inner palisade without incident.

He looked at me as he passed. "You see, my squire," he said, his voice faint, "because of my decision, no Norman will perish on this day. Remember that, when the time of your own wars comes." I lowered my eyes so that he would not see the anger that burned within me. He stared at me with needless tenderness, then asked me to follow him to the great hall to help him remove his armor. As we climbed the path up the hill, there was a noise behind us. I turned and saw that the Frisians were departing, carrying Ubbo's body as they had carried his son's seven days before.

Many of the peasants now came out of the tower—tenants, serfs, women, children. Joined by our warriors, they rushed to their lord to touch him, to kneel at his feet as one would kneel before a saint, to kiss his hands. Mathilde, who once again had taken my place as squire, continued to support him, though buffeted on all sides. Holding him firmly, preventing her people from coming too close to him, she showed everyone that the lord of Arques truly belonged to her, body and soul. My only comfort, in that moment of victory and jubilation, was to see Ivar brooding in the shadows of the storeroom, to see him glare fiercely at Mathilde as she passed. She completely ignored Ivar's presence, her arm around Liébaut de Malbray and her head resting fondly against his chest. I remained behind them, and before mounting the first steps of the stairway I turned to Ivar, looked him in the eye, and sighed, affecting my most grieved and compassionate air.

Because of the apathy of these times, in which all men have withdrawn into sterile silence, the events of the past four or five hundred years in the Church of God and the kingdoms of Christendom are virtually unknown to us. Yet through this writing, Liébaut de Malbray's adventure, when he became the lord of Arques, will be known. Though we are better acquainted with events that occurred a thousand years ago than with what has transpired in our own day, I hope that no aspect of my treachery will remain concealed.

In four times seven days I will complete what I have undertaken. My grief reaches its end, and my entire life, down to this very night, becomes clear through the magic of writing. Soon I will drift off to the depths, but before the final sleep, let me experience the ultimate lucidity, let that be granted to me before my punishment.

My pride, happily, has faded. This testimony, now nearly finished, has gone beyond me, assuming a life of its own. It no longer seems to have been born of my memory, nor fashioned of the words that I laid end to end. It is not I who speak; it is, rather, the words that speak, that lead me on. This manuscript, so patiently written, ceases to belong to me, and as my existence ends, its own begins, outside me. May it live long and be of profit to those who come after!

May God Almighty be praised for having preserved the feeble breath in me despite His anger, for having left enough strength in my trembling hand and twisted fingers to hold the reed pen, for not having extinguished completely the light of my eyes! Because of His infinite goodness, my work will soon be done. The life I took through my treachery I now humbly restore, for the memory of times to come.

It is clear in Jumièges tonight, as I can see through my cell window. It is a night of anxiety and grief, but through the power of the written word it is a night, also, of accomplishment, beyond all suffering, all shame, and all penance.

Liébaut, injured by the Frisian's blows, spent an entire day resting in the great hall. Mathilde applied her medicine to his two wounds, and against my will I had to help her tie pieces of cloth around his arm and his side. When that was done, Liébaut, to my surprise, asked me to stay with him and the peasant girl, and he began to tell me his plans for the reconstruction of the village. "The first of our tasks," he said, "will be to rebuild the church, so that Granger can say Mass there to thank the Almighty for the victory He has accorded us." Weary and feverish, he finally sank into sleep, thus leaving me alone with Mathilde.

Aware of the enmity I bore her, the peasant girl had the wisdom not to try to talk to me. She simply sat there on a coffer across from me, near Liébaut, silent, her eyes lowered as she twisted and coiled thread around her spindle. I watched her for a long while. Still dressed like a lady of the court, in a long dyed woolen tunic, her red hair drawn into a braid adorned with colored ribbons, she looked older than on the day my master first kept her with him. She had lost her child's cheeks, and small creases sometimes appeared in the middle of her high forehead. She now seemed older than me; she had become like any lady of Falaise. As we both sat there with Liébaut, she raised her green eyes to me, without anger, with a gentleness, even, as if asking me to break the silence that divided us, as if to tell me that she was ready to be my friend. And the more she looked at me, the more I had to admit that, dressed and combed as she was, she was not without nobility, not without beauty. But I could see myself plunging a dagger into her breast, into her long neck, as Liébaut slept. I placed my hope in the hatred that my treachery had kindled in Ivar's heart, and we remained there, she and I, staring at each other from none to vespers.

Then the lord of Arques woke, and since suppertime was near, I withdrew to the storeroom, where the warriors and peasants huddled together for warmth, and again I took a place not far from Ivar, and cast meaningful glances at him before our torches were extinguished. In the dark of night I prayed that God would finally move him to rescue Liébaut from Mathilde.

At dawn, impatient, I spoke to Ivar once more. "Liébaut de Malbray has decided to rebuild Arques," I whispered. "You should join our warriors in the work. Mathilde, knowing of your passion, causes everyone to laugh at you, and soon they will jeer at you as Draco did. Your only way to avoid this great shame is to work. That will show them that you have forgotten this contemptible woman. I beseech you, Ivar, do not remain withdrawn and solitary! Do not give

Mathilde the victory! You alone can make her hold her tongue."

"Go away!" the peasant groaned, his face red. "Leave me! You are the first to laugh at me."

"It is true that you are laughable," I said. "But we are so close in our grief that, laughing at you, I only laugh at myself."

"Leave me!" he said through clenched teeth.

Satisfied that he was enraged, I moved away, little knowing that this had been my last chance to avert the catastrophe that was to fall upon Arques that day.

At tierce the lord of Arques summoned me to the great hall to help him don his armor, and despite his two open wounds he led me through the countryside to the coast, to the hollow in the cliff where we had discovered the Frisian ships at the beginning of our adventure. One behind the other, and holding back our mounts, we rode down the narrow pathway carved into the cliff side. When we reached the bottom, sixty feet below, I followed my master across the narrow pebble-strewn beach between the roiling sea and the enormous white wall that towered over us. The waves hurled spray in our faces as we reached the rock that jutted out into the foam like the prow of a ship. There, dismounting, Liébaut de Malbray took off his hauberk and greaves and waded bare-chested into the angry sea.

Once again I waited for him on that strip of beach, and suddenly I could not tell which moment of our adventure this was, its beginning or its end, as if time were running backward through the weeks and months instead of following its natural order. In my mind's eye I saw him sink, carried off by the hate-filled waves, just as I had on the fourth morning after our arrival in Arques. To still my fear, I told myself that soon I would sleep beside him again under the same woolen blanket, the warmth of his chest on mine, his breath on my face, our legs entangled.

When he reappeared, clinging to the rock and streaming with water, I felt a great happiness, as if he were returning to me, only to me. He stepped onto the flat rocks and called out above the crashing of the waves that the barbarians were gone and that we had restored peace to Arques, for the glory of Normandy. I ran to him when I heard this news—my eyes blur with tears at the memory—and with the thick cloth I had brought along I rubbed his back, his hard belly, his chest, just as in the happy times.

The catastrophe occurred at the hour of none. Liébaut decided to speak to the people of Arques, to tell them that, as he had promised, he and our warriors, and the twenty archers who had arrived from Falaise the evening before, would rebuild their church, rebuild their village, and protect the new homes with an enclosure, and that he would draw the plow through their fields with his own hands. Removing his armor, he left the great hall with Bernon, Mathilde, and me to tell Thorer and the peasants of his plans. As I descended the stairway, two steps behind Mathilde, who clung to his arm, my mind was filled only with the hope that Ivar would finally take his revenge. So it was that we passed through the storeroom.

Just as we reached the door that opened onto the pathway that led down the hill, a shadow fell across the lord of Arques, and he doubled over as if in great pain. Before Bernon or anyone else had time to seize the man who continued to strike, his knife poised to fall for a third time, red with my master's blood, I drew my own dagger and, roaring like a beast, stabbed Ivar in the back as he half crouched over my master, and then I cut his throat.

Amid the shouts and the confusion, Arlebaut, Bernon, and I picked up the lord of Arques from where he lay, pushed back the peasants, who were terrified by what they had just witnessed, and hastily carried him back up to the great hall. There we laid him on his bed, removed his fur-trimmed tunic, and opened his linen shirt. We saw the two wounds immediately. The first stab had torn through the pieces of cloth wrapped around his chest to cover the wound Ubbo had inflicted under his arm. The second, more horrible, had parted the flesh of his lower belly. As in a dream, I tore off the cloth I had wrapped around my neck against the cold, rolled it up, and pressed it to the deeper wound to stop the bleeding. My master, his eyes wide, raised his head slightly and looked at me with the most tender friendship. Then, as if his body was growing too heavy to move, he turned with infinite slowness to Mathilde, who knelt and wept beside him. "My time has come," he murmured. "Weep no tears for me. Death, which will take me to God Almighty, causes me no fear."

"Stay with us!" I cried. "Who will rebuild Arques without you?"

He smiled faintly and let his head fall back. Fever already drenched his brow. His lips were white. He began to tremble. His eyes clouded.

"Mathilde," he said, taking the peasant girl's hand, "you who have been my life's last happiness, leave this place without delay, for Thorer and the people of Arques may now seek vengeance against you. Go far from here, to the court of Normandy, and there forget me and live the years of your youth to the full." He was silent for a moment, his mouth open as though he was short of breath. Without releasing Mathilde, he sought my hand too. I held it out to him, and he joined it to the peasant girl's above his bloody chest. "And you, Odilon," he said even more softly, "you who have served faithfully, you who will become the most valiant knight of Normandy, you whom I would have loved to have had as a son, protect this woman, take her to the court of Falaise this very night, and entrust her to Robert in the name of your love for me." I lowered my eyes before this blind confidence, and shame swept over me. "Swear to me, Odilon, my squire, that you will do as I ask," my master added breathlessly.

"I swear it before God," I replied, choked by my pain.

Hearing my vow, Liébaut grew calmer. But a moment later he began to tremble again, so we covered him with four woolen blankets. "I am so tired, so cold, yet at the same time I see, so clearly, the warmest of lights," he said then, his lips barely moving.

Soon he closed his eyes.

Mathilde and I, not daring to separate, remained hand in hand above him. Then Granger appeared, and we moved aside to let him recite the prayer for the dying.

Unable to shed tears, my mind numb as I knelt beside Mathilde, I stared at Liébaut de Malbray's face until day's end. In its repose, it was more than ever like the stone-carved saints that watch over our churches.

THE LAST BOOK

As I had vowed, at nightfall I took two of our horses and led Mathilde away from Arques. Bidding farewell to the body of Liébaut de Malbray, I touched it one last time as it lay cold. Not thinking, blind to my surroundings, remote from the world, I rode through the darkness with the woman I hated, leaving our camp forever.

We passed through Bois-Robert and crossed the Varenne. Locked in silence, we urged our mounts down unknown roads. At the first light of dawn, pierced by the cold, we found ourselves in a wide and windswept valley. Not knowing where we were, we stopped for a moment and let our horses rest. Then we set out again on a journey that seemed endless.

Weary, crushed by the armor that bore down on my shoulders, wanting only to sleep and to forget, I could not find the road to Rouen. Passing from valley to valley, riding along narrow glades of green turned white by the frost, crossing snow-covered fields, we reached the Seine at last. We followed the river. When night fell, we trembled with fever, barely able to hold ourselves in the saddle. Then we saw the walls of Rouen before us, ringed by gloomy hills and lit by a few torches.

Just as I had during our march to Arques in an autumn now lost in the mists of the past, I crossed the moat, rode through the fortified gates, then into the deserted city with Mathilde, who was as mute and pale as a woman returned from the dead. I thought I saw my master, proud and tall on his mount, magnificent in his armor, at a narrow corner twenty paces away. He turned toward me, the nose guard of his helmet raised, and motioned for me to follow him. As I rode toward that vision, it disappeared behind the corner of a building. I spurred my horse to catch up to it, but at the corner before me there was only a narrow black street, disquieting and empty.

I led Mathilde to the castle of Richard the Fearless, called out who I was, and had them open the gates. Once in the courtyard, I refused to tell what had happened, saying only that I was a messenger from the lord of Malbray, conqueror of the Frisians in Arques, and that I demanded supper and a bed in which to spend the night. Mathilde and I warmed ourselves at the fire that burned in the stone hearth in the great hall. We were given bread and cheese and shown to a room similar to the one in which Liébaut de Malbray's burning strength had entered me for the first time as I rubbed his back and chest and hard belly. That heat, now extinguished, was alive despite everything, and as I stood near the wide bed, a pain impossible to describe shot through me. Sobbing, the tears finally streaming down my face, I fell onto the bed and buried my head in the blanket. Mathilde, who had not spoken a word to me since our departure from Arques, lay down beside me. "I, too, loved him," she said in my ear. "In memory of what he was, we must not despair. Both of us—you whom he loved as a son and I whom he loved as a wife—must be strong, because he is watching us, he sees us now, and for his sake we must live the days of our youth as fully as we can."

These words, so wise for a peasant girl, finally made me understand why my master, my beloved lord, slain through my treachery, had chosen Mathilde for his wife.

I cried for a long time as she lay beside me on the bed. Then I turned and looked at her, my face wet with tears. Her face, a peasant's and a lady's at the same time, was close to mine and also wet with tears. She looked at me. The two of us, equally young and equally lost, were suddenly like a brother and sister whose father had just died. The enormity of my sin loomed before me, terrifying. Mathilde's look of pain pierced me. Why had I not let her live in peace with her lord, who was my lord too? Could not the three of us have known a kind of happiness? Could not I have continued to fight at the side of Liébaut de Malbray, husband of Mathilde? Why had I not resigned myself, why had I not continued to admire, in silence, the feats of Normandy's most noble knight? Why had I refused to listen to him, to serve him as he was? Why had I cost him his life instead of defending it? I moved my lips to speak, to confess the truth of my treachery to Mathilde, but, alas, I could not say a word, and so continued to conceal the ugliness of my soul, just as I had concealed it ever since the cursed day of the hunt in the forests of Falaise.

We lost our way again and wandered for three days before finally reaching Falaise. There, saying nothing about my crime, I told the duke how death had claimed the conqueror of Auxerre. Robert, deeply pained, long mourned the most courageous and best loved of his barons. He had several High Masses said for him, and he asked me to recount our battles to three minstrels, that they might compose a song in praise of Liébaut de Malbray's feats, enshrining them in memory.

The Magnificent took Mathilde, whose story was so similar to that of his beloved Arlette, under his protection, and though I wished to return to my father's tower in Bernay, there to hide my shame, he insisted that I remain in his court, misled as he was by my deceitful silence.

At Easter some of the knights and guards returned from Arques, now partially rebuilt, and spoke of the loyalty with which I had served Liébaut de Malbray, of the peace I had afforded him by slaying Ivar the criminal before his very eyes. They all told of the valor with which, without regard for my own life, I had protected him from blows from the rear during our battles. Bernon Hildetand, the new lord of Arques, traveled to Falaise to receive his duke's orders and there affirmed that before his death Liébaut de Malbray had expressed the wish that I be dubbed a knight of Neustria without delay, because of my courage in combat and the good judgment I had shown during our war. Only Séguin and Suzanne de Brécy, having returned to the court of Normandy, kept silent in my regard. Wallowing in falsehood, I let myself be praised, and on a bright day in the middle of spring, in the presence of the assembled barons and of my aged father, who was bursting with pride, I stood in the chapel of Falaise, faced God's Altar, and in secret dishonor was dubbed a knight of Normandy by the Magnificent himself.

Robert promised to take me with him to Jerusalem, and though I was not quite seventeen years of age, I was assigned a squire of my own to serve me, to maintain my gear, lace up my hauberk, and carry my weapons, lance, and shield.

In my torment, I began to fast and mortify my flesh, as

though penance could earn me forgiveness for my sin. Consumed by remorse yet incapable of confessing my crime, I grew irritable, violent. When Robert asked me to rid the forests of Falaise of poachers, I sowed terror in the surrounding villages. I began to drink too much wine. I became more and more belligerent, challenging Guilbert de Saint-Céneri to a duel for no other reason than that he had looked at me too insistently. In an unjust rage, I wounded him seriously with my mace. Before long everyone in the court of Falaise feared me despite my youth, and few dared to speak to me.

One night I saw Liébaut de Malbray's blue eyes watching me, judging me, condemning me. I tried to flee, riding long into the night, but I could not escape them. Merciless and reproachful, when they had once been so sweet, they remained fixed upon me until my departure from Falaise.

Whereas I, moody and often violent, inspired only fear and mistrust, Mathilde won everyone's friendship and respect as the widow of a lord of Normandy. She undertook to learn reading, writing, and the art of tapestry. She was seen more and more often in the company of Arlette, and no one remembered that she was in fact only a poor peasant woman. Toward the middle of the summer, I began to visit her: to speak of the man we both had loved. Many times, when there were long silences, I wanted to tell her of my sin, but the words never left my lips.

At the beginning of autumn, the thought of my inevitable damnation began to occupy my mind. I prayed, keeping to my bedroom for hours, begging for the forgiveness of Our Lord Jesus Christ, who was crucified to take our sins upon Himself. Every morning I practiced self-flagellation, and for a time decided—as I often did in later life—to deprive myself, unworthy as I was, of the Holy Sacrament of the Eucharist. I forced myself to sleep on the hard icy floor of my room. I never entered the great hall, where the duke took his supper with the people of his household. Eager for suffering, I let the wounds of the whip fester on my back untreated, and would not let myself drink more than five swallows of water a day.

Despite all this mortification, my nights were filled with visions of the infernal abyss. Fire rained down upon me, and I saw myself trapped in the icy marsh of Cocytus. Weakened by fasting and penance, I was struck by a strange malady that covered the flesh of my belly and arms with scabs and thin whitish crusts. Even with medicines, enemas of ash, and baths of hot water prepared for me in wooden vats, no man of science was able to cure me. The malady spread to my chest and neck, and the Magnificent had to leave without me for Jerusalem, to which I had dreamed of going to expiate my sin. Because of this scourge sent by God to sully my body and deprive me of forgiveness and glory, I gradually came to realize that only the monastic life, a life based on the virtues of poverty, chastity, obedience, silence, and humility, might enable me to escape eternal damnation.

Upon my father's death, a year after the death of Liébaut de Malbray, I entered the abbey of Jumièges as a novice instead of returning to my castle in Bernay. I signed my lands and property over to this holy community.

Fearing that I might be cast out of a place beloved of God, I kept silent about my sin, even in confession, just as I had in Arques and in Falaise. Yet, despite my new deceit, my malady disappeared in the tranquillity of this retreat, and my skin became smooth and clear again. Liébaut's eyes no longer pursued me.

Only my visions of hell remained.

The master of novices long pondered whether I truly sought God, whether I had the zeal to do His work and to accept the obedience and the humiliations. He tested my spirit, as the apostle had taught him. For two months I devoted myself to spiritual exercises and to meditations on the harsh and bitter things that lead one to the Almighty. At the end of that time, the rule was read to me and I was told: "If you wish to observe it, you may enter. If not, you are free to withdraw." Still determined, I entered the community of the brothers of Jumièges fully.

Sacrificing my hair and my beard, the beard that had begun to grow just a few months earlier, I wrote out and signed my vows, and without regret placed on the Altar the document that is still preserved within these walls. Swearing to remain within this community in the monastic state until my death, I recited the vows of stability, of obedience to the rule and to the abbey, and of the renunciation of all things worldly, the vows of chastity and poverty.

I cast off my tunic of a knight of Neustria and lord of Bernay and abandoned my chausses, my shirt, my breeches, my father's precious collar, and all the other objects I still wore. As my assembled brothers watched, I donned the robe and coarse cowl. And so, taking the vow of silence for the length of my unhappy life, in dread and in the mad hope of salvation, and inspired by the fear of God, Who alone knew my sin, I became a monk.

When God Almighty decided to put together the pieces of the machinery of this world, it took Him six days to complete the task, and when His work was done, before He rested, He created man in His own image, granting him dominion over all inferior creatures and laying the treasures of the earth before him. Unlike the animals, forever mired in ignorance, man was given reason and free will, and the world's innumerable temptations. In the six times a thousand years that have passed since that epoch, God has sent miraculous signs and wonders of revelation, that man might know His power. He became flesh in the person of Our Lord Christ, His only son, and gave the Scriptures, testimony of light and source of all truth. Enlightened thus by the Holy Word, man can no longer ignore the paths that lead to his Creator. He is duty bound to use the divine gift of reason to discipline himself and to love God in perfect humility. Through prayers and offerings, man must ask God to preserve this discernment within him. Those such as I, Odilon de Bernay, who in their stupidity and wickedness fail to triumph over their vices and show only ingratitude for the Almighty's gifts, fall from grace and cause their own everlasting misery. Descending lower than the animals, they will suffer a punishment commensurate with their sins.

I thank God for having kept me alive until this beautiful night despite my sins and lies and presumption. How merciful and good He must be to allow me such a moment! I thank God, the source of all things, for not having stilled my trembling hand, for not having extinguished altogether my fog-shrouded sight, for not having strangled my old man's breath in my throat. For this may He be praised forever!

In this early hour I behold my unhappy existence with such clarity that the peace of mind for which I have waited more than forty-five years sweeps over me at last. Thanks to this final strength that God has breathed into my miserable body during this strange night, I now know that it is not so much Liébaut de Malbray's adventure as my own story that I have recounted, alone in my cell for twelve seasons, reed pen in hand. Thus have I done a thing most difficult to believe, a thing that no one does in these times, for in extoling the magnificence and nobility of a beloved lord, I have most of all spoken of myself. Overturning centuries of tradition, a tradition that holds that the storyteller must withdraw to the background as he presents his hero, I have, through this account, unburdened my heart and written the most sincere, the most accurate, and the most belated confession—a confession not only for those to come, but also for myself, for my soul. Nor do I feel shame, for I have done this without indulgence or mercy, and readers of my testimony will find me so wretched that none will be moved to praise me. On the contrary, they will admire the beauty and valor of the lord of Arques, but me they will judge for what I was and what I am: a traitor, a liar, a presumptuous man who, having committed his crime, thought to do penance while pride and arrogance lurked behind his pose of abnegation.

Thanks be unto Thee, Jesus Christ Our Savior, for having allowed me to discover the power of words, words that when assembled cannot only bring the dead back from their graves, but also bring light to the blackest of souls. Though my eyes fail me, I see more clearly now than when I first arrived in Falaise forty-seven years ago. I humbly thank Thee, O God, for this miracle, which surpasses my understanding.

At last the confession has been made. Tomorrow Uselin, the scribe of Jumièges, at the behest of our abbot—to whom I have spoken of this manuscript in our scriptorium every morning for the past nine days, though without completely divulging its contents—will undertake to copy this story of a mad passion. Then everyone in the abbey will know my mortal sin. To them, my brothers in Christ, I say: Despite the horror that will inevitably fill your hearts and minds, keep this book, preserve it in your library along with the most precious writings, and ensure that it is read, so that Liébaut de Malbray may live, and so that others may learn from my excesses and deceit. You, whom I have wronged, who even offered to make me the grand master of your liturgy and regard me as holy even now, punish me for having deceived you so: deny me a Christian burial. Burn my body on a pyre by night, with no ceremony, burn me with my two tunics, my two cowls, my bowl, and the few objects that belong to me. Let the fire die of its own accord, that nothing might be left of me. When my flesh is consumed, break my blackened bones with a mace and cast my ashes to the wind. Let nothing remain of me but this testimony, this warning, through which the most noble knight of Neustria lives again.

And now that my task is completed in joy beyond my wildest hope, now that the darkness has led me to light, now that all my strength is spent and it remains only to fall silent, I will extinguish the flames of my four candles. Leaving the manuscript open on the lectern beside my ink pot and reed pen, I will lie down on my straw mattress in the dark silence of my cell. I will lay my head on my pillow, my eyes open. I will pull my goatskin blanket over me.

Slowly, delivered of my fear, rocked by gentle waves, as if I were lying in a boat, I will drift toward the great darkness that awaits me.

In this final calm before hell's fury, forgetting all pain, all grief, all the tortures of my body, I will mingle my naked legs with Liébaut de Malbray's under the woolen blanket. Taking advantage of his slumber, I will move closer to him and lay my head on his chest.

I will feel the hardness of his belly against my own.

I will touch the wound he suffered in Auxerre.

His breath will caress my brow. His life will throb beneath my hands. The warmth of his body will set me ablaze.

On the threshold of the final repose, his strength will enter me at last.